The author is a mature, retired police officer who has had a lot of life experience. He is a people-person, and a devoted family man, though sadly divorced. Having experienced or witnessed at first hand the pain and lessons of some of life's worst vicissitudes, he writes in a heart-felt, insightful way about matters which impact people emotionally. He enjoys the simple things in life, such as family and creative hobbies such DIY, gardening, and playing the piano. He has discovered his penchant for writing, and this is now his fifth novel.

Bruno Beaches

CONSEQUENTIAL URGES

AUSTIN MACAULEY PUBLISHERS™

LONDON * CAMBRIDGE * NEW YORK * SHARJAH

A CIP catalogue record for this title is available from the British Library.

ISBN 9781398491403 (Paperback)
ISBN 9781398491410 (ePub e-book)

www.austinmacauley.com

First Published 2023
Austin Macauley Publishers Ltd®
1 Canada Square
Canary Wharf
London
E14 5AA

I wish to express my hearty thanks to CYNTHIA.

She is a practicing humanistic psychologist who very kindly agreed to give me her professional input as to how the counselling sessions in the story between Pablo and a counsellor like her might have gone. She was a pleasure to work with and the only reward she wanted was to know that her wise words might be of some constructive use to some of the readers of this book, and to help provide awareness that there are always skilful capable counsellors out there ready to help people who are only too willing to assist people struggling with any kind of life issues. I am very grateful for being allowed to introduce her voice into parts of the story. Her particular discipline goes beyond the behaviourist and psychodynamic approach of psychology and looks at free will and the individual as a whole and emphasises the importance of the individual striving towards personal growth and fulfilment.

Table of Contents

Chapter 1

Pablo didn't want to cry. For a grown man in his mid-sixties, six feet tall and muscular, crying gives the impression of cracking up, of having lost one's grip on life, and as a proud man, he didn't wish to misrepresent himself in that way. He was very much in control of events in his life. Perhaps more so than ever before. He probably would cry though, but only because he was an emotional person, and he already felt tearful at the thought of revealing his innermost feelings. Standing on the doorstep, he could already feel himself regressing into a boyish, open, vulnerable-person mode, and he knew he would shortly be sharing things that would upset him.

He knocked on her door apprehensively. As he stared expectantly at the solid dark-panelled wood around the misty glass window, he pulled his T shirt nice and straight and sucked on his teeth, hoping the flossing hadn't missed anything. His nostrils soaked up the fresh smell of recent rain. It was such a wonderfully promising smell at that time of the year; the harbinger of new life swelling the emerging buds posited all around him. The door swung open and the vivacious Cynthia stood there seemingly pleased to see him, but that was her way. She loved people. All people, and she evidenced that with an abounding, beaming smile when greeting. He knew her from the days when dancing had been allowed. She had been an excellent dancer. She was a part of that weird dancing set up where they would meet occasionally on the dance floor, and for a few minutes, they would either embrace closely, swaying gently to the beauty of slow music, nestled anonymously amongst the dense throng of musically engaged other couples, or if the music was more energetic, they would playfully and skilfully interact, expertly intertwining their dancing skills to weave a circular journey of creativity and intuitive collaboration. This would last for the length of the track, and then they would indulge in at least one more track, and it would be another three minutes of 'musicality' magic. No more than three tracks though. That was the sole terrain of people who were involved in a relationship.

Then, off the dance floor, they would know nothing about each other. The closeness dancers felt on the dance floor was all to do with the beauty of the music and the magic of dance in that rarefied moment.

Actually, Pablo did know that Cynthia was a counsellor from the posts she shared on social media, but that was all. She knew nothing of him. He wondered how many of her clients were men who just wanted to spend a little time with a pretty, bubbly, vivacious and very attractive woman, but she was clever to boot. She would surely weed out any players. He was genuinely there to explore himself and his motivation. He had become a curiosity to himself.

She led him through the spacious, light hall, past a succession of bright Leonid Afremov prints hanging cheerfully on the cream walls, to her consultation room. She casually indicated the well-worn two-seater, cream, leather sofa for him to sit on. He had been in quite a few counselling rooms over the years, and they all tried to achieve that casual, comfortable, feel-at-home mix of furniture and decor. She sat almost opposite him in her stiff, upright, padded office chair, separated only by a low glass coffee table adorned simply with a pretty small box of tissues, a glass bowl of coloured beads, two glasses of water, and two short, dumpy, pink candles flickering happily, as they dispersed a mild rose bouquet into the warm air.

She was dressed smart casual, as befitted the situation and smart dark trousers with a lighter jacket that still matched. This was his first visit, although in preparation, she had engaged him in a lengthy and detailed phone conversation almost two weeks earlier. Then, she had thoroughly explained her role, giving him all the options available to him via alternative sources. It was important to her that she would be the right fit for him both professionally and financially. She even outlined some of the free counselling resources available in general, although she did warn him that there would be quite a waiting time for those. She gave him details of other professional bodies and counsellors because she wanted him to choose her only if she seemed to be the best fit after he had done his homework, and had considered all the other options. She explained carefully her duty of care to a client, tempered with the need for her to be ethically sound. She would be duty bound to pass on information to the authorities if she was informed of crimes or a threat to someone else's safety. In terms of keeping herself safe, she obtained his full name, address, contact details and doctor's details, and made it clear that at all times, someone else knew where she was and exactly who she was with. All details submitted would be verified before any meetings could occur. She explained that normally she would engage in a course of six sessions with a client and finally ascertained in general terms what issues he wanted help and support with. He answered tersely, "Self-harm." She then ensured that he recorded the phone number of the Samaritans on his phone, just in case he was overcome with desperation at any point, and she made him promise that he would ring it if he felt desperate. He wasn't sure that he wanted to commit to six pre-booked sessions. That seemed a bit heavy. He asked if he could just commit to one at a time, when he felt like it. She was amenable to this, reminding him that she was there to help and would accommodate his agenda as best she could, given other commitments, but that she would prefer to see him regularly in order to establish a working relationship and a mutual understanding…

Her office was in her home. It was a very middle-class house, nicely furnished, with reasonably sized gardens back and front, which appeared to be well-kept. What person would seek help and advice from someone housed in a gritty high-rise council flat, where the ambience spoke of poverty and deprivation, and the lifts stank of urine? Yet was that logical? He wondered silently. For a counsellor to be successfully received, or actually effective, did they need to be surrounded by the trappings of middle-class success?

"Are the glasses of water to put the candles out if they get out of hand, or can I drink one?"

Cynthia tittered at his attempt to be jovial. She indicated for him to have one with an outstretched arm.

"Please, help yourself, and just let me know if you want a tea or coffee."

He thanked her politely and quickly downed half a glass. She continued brightly.

"And how are you today, Pablo?"

He was glad that she happily used his first name. He always felt that when ladies who knew him used his surname, they were being somehow playful. Maybe something to do with it being a reference to him as a married man, which of course, he actually wasn't. He was still very single, twice divorced and alone for the past five years. He carefully repositioned the glass.

"Very well, thank you," he replied positively. He didn't need her to hear about the age-related pain in his knees. He was always positive. He couldn't see the point of being miserable.

"Tell me why you have come to see me today."

A lot of Cynthia's work revolved around intimate relationships, and the difficulties appertaining to them, but Pablo's issues were more complex. He was a syndrome. He had been through the broken relationships stage years previously, and the grief and frustration from those were still making him angry, maybe even more so as time went on. The sense of loss weighed more heavily as time passed by, as if somehow the loss of each year piled on top of the following year, making it ever more heavy. Weren't things meant to feel less of a burden with the healing passage of time? He really wasn't sure if he could be entirely honest with her. He wasn't sure if he'd ever been entirely honest with himself.

A bird started pecking on the outside of the window. That was a strange interruption, as they both briefly allowed their attention to stray to it.

"Have you got a tame sparrow who wants to join us, Cynthia?" Pablo asked, bemused.

She chuckled, surprised, but then turned back to him. Pablo needed more encouragement.

"You said on the phone that you were concerned about self harming. Why?"

"Not all the time. Just sometimes."

He was already defensive, even though he didn't want to be. She remained quiet as he pondered a little. Then he continued.

"Out of anger, a kind of protest to the world that I've tried my best with my life, but it all got fucked up, if you'll excuse my French."

"Have you contemplated suicide?"

"Not seriously I suppose, or I wouldn't be here, would I?"

He gave a little chuckle and she smiled politely, staying silent to coax more out of him.

"But sometimes I do feel like making the ultimate protest."

She took him seriously and asked, "Have you ever thought about how you might kill yourself?"

"I used to be in the police. I've seen them all. People walking in front of trains, jumping off bridges, cutting their wrists in a bath of hot water, overdosing on drugs. Hanging. Hanging was always very popular, but it always seemed a vile way to go to me. I wouldn't want to do any of those."

"So, what would you do?"

"Use a shotgun."

He looked at her guiltily. Had he shocked her? He had been brought up to have the utmost respect for the sanctity of life. All life, including his own. He felt guilty even talking this way. She remained calm and composed.

"Have you got a shotgun?"

"No," he replied quietly.

She didn't look any more relieved. She knew that if someone really wanted to hurt themselves, they would find the wherewithal to do it.

"Can you lay your hands on one?"

"No, although I'm sure it wouldn't be that difficult to get one, but it would take time."

"Why a shotgun?"

"Quick. Certain. Instant. Messy."

She cringed just a tiny little bit. She didn't ask him what part of his body he would blow off, presuming it would be his head.

"You said that this stems out of anger. What are you angry about?"

He didn't relish going over all the crap that had happened over the past ten years, but it was only fair to her that he try to explain things. He spent quite a few minutes going over his story, of which she knew nothing. The thirty-year marriage. The grown-up children. The wonderful family. The empty nest syndrome – yes, it affected men too. The allegations at work when he was working in rehabilitation of criminally active drug addicts. The loss of his job. The loss of his marriage and then his beautiful home.

She questioned him about the nature of his work at the time of the allegations.

"Was it to do with an intimate relationship?"

"No. The complainant was female, but it was an allegation about forcing her to engage with a rehabilitation programme."

"Had your work been transparent and recorded?"

"Yes. Thoroughly. Always. Over a period of two years in her case."

"Were your meetings with clients in a public place?"

"Always, and always by arrangement and mutual agreement. The entire programme was voluntary."

"What happened?"

"I got suspended during the investigation, and eventually, the allegations were judged to be groundless and malicious, but in the meantime, the Internal Affairs department decided to throw their own extra charge at me. They're well known for this sort of thing. It's because overall, they are a paper tiger, and if they can make anything stick, anything at all, they will."

Cynthia didn't show any emotion.

"How could they do that?"

"I'd been moved sideways into the Prolific Offender Unit, which only dealt with the offenders who had been awarded the 'prolific' badge. What they said was that any research I was doing regarding other drug addicts in my area, including all my previous clients, was contrary to the Data Protection Act."

"Was it?"

"You need to know that we were bombarded daily with reams and reams of intel. A tiny fraction of it might be relevant to any one officer. There were absolutely no restrictions in place about what you could research, and anyway, I was focusing only on my specific target group and their associates. It really didn't make any sense at all. Drug addicts had become my specialty."

Then he backtracked to the part about his wife pulling away from him because of the complaint. She didn't trust him anymore. She thought that he must have been up to no good with this female complainant.

"But you weren't, right?" she asked, as if just making sure she was getting her facts straight.

"Absolutely not."

She looked directly at Pablo as she stated,

"For your wife, her reaction would have been the culmination of a lot of other events. Do you know what they were?"

"Yes, I suppose so. She was always concerned that I was over friendly with ladies that I worked with, and I never took her concerns seriously."

"Because?"

"I suppose that I just thought that they were ridiculous. I couldn't understand her perspective."

"With my male clients, they almost always talk about things happening out of the blue, but in reality, they had not been listening to the warning signals over a long period of time."

Pablo took that one on the chin. He didn't argue. This was clearly true.

"Anyway, my wife wanted me to plead guilty to the data protection charges, and for her, I did, because my marriage was far more important to me than my job. So, in due course, after being suspended for over two years, I lost my job. She carried on and divorced me anyway. Eventually I discovered that she had

14

been having an affair for most of the time I had been suspended. I had no idea. That made me really angry. I would have done things differently had I known."

Now he was feeling tearful, but he was doing a great job at fighting the tears back. Cynthia didn't speak. She didn't want to interrupt his flow.

"Then, after a few more years on my own, I met my second wife. We got married very quickly."

He smiled at her momentarily, pleased with this memory, and then quickly moved on.

"But around that time, my first wife made contact with me. She wanted to build bridges for the sake of the family, and I was totally up for that."

That made Cynthia curious.

"Did you want a relationship with her?"

"Just a working one. A re-establishment of communication."

"Was she with someone else?"

"Yes, but not the bloke she was having the affair with. She moved on to another guy. I didn't have an axe to grind with him, as he came on the scene after she had divorced me."

"The affair had been a stepping stone," she added thoughtfully.

"Yes, I suppose so."

"What did your new wife think about this contact with your ex-wife?"

Pablo looked a little embarrassed. "Not a lot."

"But you went ahead anyway?"

Now he was positively sheepish. "Yes."

"Did you include her in your dealings with your ex-wife?"

"No," he replied rather guiltily, looking at her even more sheepishly.

"History repeating itself. Not listening. Then what happened?"

"Over the next few years, she seemed to pull away from me, until eventually, she just left."

She looked at him knowingly, but she was curious how things had panned out with the rest of the family.

"Do you get on with your kids?"

"Thank God we all get on great. They didn't take sides or blame either party. They just wanted to make the best of a bad situation. They're fine with me and their mum too."

He was comfortable talking to her about his thoughts and feelings, but he couldn't mention some of his actions. He didn't want her feeling obliged to report him for anything, and no doubt she wouldn't want to be put in that awkward position. He made sure that they just talked about acceptable thoughts, not unacceptable thoughts, and certainly not unacceptable actions. They continued to talk for quite a while, her fishing for facts and clues as to what made him tick and how he interpreted outcomes. Eventually their time was coming to a close.

"Pablo, our time will be coming to a close shortly. Would you like a hot drink before you go?"

He declined. She checked that he was feeling okay about revealing his innermost thoughts to her and that he had things to occupy him for the rest of the day. She encouraged him to exercise and eat well before arranging another appointment for a week or so hence. She reminded him of their agreement.

"Pablo, your contract with me is that if you do feel like self-harming, you will phone someone. Either a friend, your doctor, the Samaritans or me. Okay?"

"Yes."

"Be careful who you talk to. A counselling session causes people to open up, and they can leave here in opened-up mode, and then carry on opening up to people who might not be very well equipped to deal with their issues, and that can sometimes make matters worse. So, be mindful of that please, okay?"

"Okay."

Pablo had never been a violent man all his life, but a few months earlier, he had been, and it concerned him. He hadn't regretted it. Was he changing? Or was it just changing circumstances? He couldn't talk about it to Cynthia because of her ethical code. He had gone away for a mini break, near to where his daughter lived with her partner, Johnny, but the purpose hadn't been to have a holiday, and it wasn't in order to visit Sarah. During his last visit, she had informed him about how they had been hit financially by a default from one of John's customers. John had done some building work for a man called Bill for four full weeks, but Bill, who lived in a very nice comfortable house and drove a big expensive car, just as his wife did, and apparently earned good money, refused to pay the bill. He had convincingly fobbed John off with clever, plausible excuses for as long as he could, but when push came to shove, he simply refused to pay without reason. Then, he taunted John to sue him. He proved to be just a smooth-talking con man. Of course John didn't think the effort and legal expenses would be worth all the hassle, so he just took the loss, even though he really couldn't afford to absorb it. Pablo was quietly livid. So much of this kind of injustice went on, and the perpetrators usually got clean away with it, but he wasn't going to stand for it. Not when it came to his own daughter. He would do something for what he believed in.

He went down to her locality without her knowledge, having booked a quiet little three-night rental. He'd already unobtrusively gleaned enough information to identify the offender. He then located his home, which was in a salubrious, spacious, suburban street. Very pleasant it was too. Mature maples lined the street periodically, naked and stark, swaying gently in the breeze. A few stubborn brown leaves clung on from autumn and flapped defiantly. He spent two days watching Bill's house, intermittently and surreptitiously from his car, taking care to park in different places and not to draw attention to himself. It was mid-winter, cold and wet, so there were few people out and about to notice him. He learned who lived there and what their movements were. By day three, he had found the perfect opportunity. It was early evening and Bill was home alone. There appeared to be no children in the home, and the wife had just gone out in a taxi. Pablo presumed that she would be out for a while, and he wouldn't need long. It was already quite dark. He was no less livid with this swindler, having been mulling the matter over whilst watching his coming and going. He had no reservations about pressing ahead with his plan. From his time in the police service, he had unintentionally learned the best way to commit crimes.

He parked several streets away in a very quiet location and walked back to Bill's suburban house. He wore dark clothing with black leather gloves, with a dark floppy cap hanging over his head. He also had a black balaclava in his pocket, which he would put on just prior to entry. He had nothing on him which might drop off. No watch. No jewellery. His nails were clipped short. His head was shaved. The dimly lit street was deserted. Not even a single dog-walker. He quickly darted off the street when he got to Bill's house, walking briskly down the side passage where he found the door to the kitchen. It was unlocked. He had been quite ready to smash his way through it if necessary and was very relieved that he wouldn't have to because of the noise that might make. He donned the balaclava and carefully pocketed the cap. Then he sternly marched into the house. He found Bill sitting in the front room masturbating to porn on the huge TV screen. Bill immediately stood up, preoccupied with putting his erect cock away and trying to do up his flies. He seemed simply astonished and bewildered at the sudden intrusion of an unexpected visitor, and one in a balaclava was immensely scary.

Pablo felt a surge of energy as he unleashed his rage upon this indolent, obnoxious, pathetic excuse of a man. A flabby, breathless, struggling, physical wreck, who clearly lacked any physical or mental ability to defend himself. Moments later, after a horrendously powerful flurry of blows, Bill was groaning on the floor, oozing broken teeth, blood and urine, defending his face with both hands. The magnolia carpet was recording the man's trauma colourfully in slow motion. He was trembling, too scared and damaged to be able to speak properly, wondering if his nose and jawbones were actually broken, which they surely were. He was shaking in sheer terror, his mind in a whirl, trying to work out who this avenging psycho was.

Pablo stood over him, powerful, dangerous and supremely menacing.

"You disgusting piece of shit," he growled hatefully.

Without getting down to Bill's level, the only way to deliver more damage and pain would be to kick the poor man, but that was beneath him. He was happy to employ his fists and to headbutt, but he had never kicked a man on the ground. He guessed rightly that Bill had reneged on many debts. Bill would have no idea who Pablo was representing.

"You owe a lot of people. I'll be back in a few weeks if you haven't settled your debts by then, and I'll break every fucking bone in your disgusting fat body. You got that shit face?"

"Yes, yes, okay, I hear you," he spluttered painfully and only partially coherently. He felt a strange feeling of teeth suddenly missing in front of his tongue, the sensation of hot blood seeping out of his mouth and the searing pain of broken facial bones. Pablo could smell the metallic scent of the blood mixed in with the sweet aroma of fresh urine. He felt no need to issue any other warnings. He had succeeded in putting the fear of God into this man, to whom he was merely an unidentifiable angel of death. He turned to go.

"Wait!" Bill spluttered through broken teeth and blood.

"Who are you here for?"

Pablo turned back to him, staring at him in disgust.

"All of them, you dense fucker!"

He really felt like kicking him now, but he maintained his restraint and left the house the same way he had entered, rapidly tearing the balaclava off, taking care to securely pocket it. He deftly replaced it with the cap before hitting the street. He quickly returned to his car, his heart racing. He could feel veins throbbing. His adrenaline levels were so high. This sort of thing could give a man of his age a heart attack. He smiled to himself. "Not today," he whispered to himself reassuringly. He felt good and very alive! He was forensically aware, but of course, he was anxious. Inevitably, he may have left a virtually invisible genetic fingerprint behind. He had done his best to avoid shedding anything, but now it was down to luck, luck that Bill might not report the incident and luck that if he did, the investigators wouldn't find anything with his DNA on.

He drove to a nearby beauty-spot car park. It was very dark. There were just a few cars there, probably illicit lovers, but he parked at the far end away from the others. He took off all his outer clothing, including the old pair of trainers he was wearing. There would undoubtedly be splatters of Bill's blood on all of these, probably his urine too, and he placed them all in a black bin bag and dressed in fresh similar clothes. He then drove near to a supermarket car park where he knew they had big rubbish dumpsters. He walked in and deposited the bag in a bin. He didn't drive in. He didn't want any cameras recording his car registration mark. Then he returned to his accommodation for a very thorough shower. Job done. He still felt good and strangely energised. He had accomplished something important and beneficial. Maybe his life still had some purpose left in it.

Chapter 2

Pablo visited his daughter, Sarah, again, months after their last meeting, and whilst in that locality, it suited him to also visit his best friend, Tim. They hadn't seen each other for so long. They used to live close by each other, but then Pablo moved away to keep out of harm's way following his first divorce. They stayed in touch by phone though, regularly. Real old-fashioned phone calls. They both loved to hear each other's voices. They had a rare and genuine connection.

Tim took him to a rather lovely local country pub. On the journey in Tim's car, they chatted amiably, teasing each other as much as possible as was their way. It was a mild early spring evening and sitting outside under canvas over a traditional pub picnic bench with a couple of pints wasn't particularly unpleasant. So long as they remained sitting, they were allowed to face each other maskless. It wasn't busy. Not everyone wants to sit outside when socialising, if it's not particularly hot, but it enabled Tim to be able to smoke. He spoke affectionately.

"It's great to see you, bro. I'm glad you're okay. How was Sarah?"

"Mate, she's fine. It's nice to see her settled down with a really nice guy. They seem really happy together. To be honest, he's lucky to have her, and he knows it, so he treats her well."

"Oh that's good, bro; yeah, really good. Yeah, she's a really special girl."

"Yeah, really special. Not special like you, you know, special needs, but I know what you mean."

Tim laughed, and then Pablo continued.

"They were a bit chuffed. Since I last saw them they got some money which they weren't expecting."

"Oh, that's nice. And did you see Delilah?"

"Of course I did. I always see her when I come down to see Sarah. We both spent most of the day yesterday at her place. It was really lovely."

Tim was thoughtful.

"You're really lucky that you two get on so well after all the shit you went through. She still loves you, mate."

"I know, bro, but she'll never admit it, will she?"

Pablo laughed. He was happy that they'd made the best of a bad job, then he added.

"It's amazing, but it does make life so easy for everyone else in the family."

"Yes, mate. You are lucky."

He thought quietly, then queried.

"I don't suppose that you've heard from Hellion?"

"No such luck there, mate. She's still wallowing in self-pity or self-loathing or whatever it is that plagues her. She's still down the same hole she went down five years ago. I think she probably still hates me."

That wasn't meant to be funny. He looked really sad.

"And you're leaving her alone."

"I don't have any choice after she got me nicked. I'm not going through all that shite again."

"True. I'm glad you're leaving her alone now, mate. She's not worth getting into trouble for."

"I dunno, mate. I still send her a Valentine's card every year, but only anonymously."

Tim would normally react in animated fashion to such a revelation, chiding Pablo like an old woman, but today he was listless. Pablo was concerned.

"You okay, bud? You look surprisingly thoughtful. Your couple of brain cells overworking at the moment?"

"No, everything's okay, mate, really."

"Tim, I can see that something's bothering you. Do you know something about Sarah that I don't?"

At that, Tim managed a little laugh. He didn't want to alarm his best friend.

"No, it's nothing to do with Sarah, mate; 'course it isn't."

"Come on then, you dozy pillock. Spill the beans, You know you can tell Uncle Pablo. Has Bev finally come to her senses and had enough of you?"

Pablo was trying his best to provoke him, but he wasn't getting much response. Tim seemed rather languid as he sat half-slumped onto the picnic bench, staring vacantly into his pint. Pablo searched his face. Tim was always expressive facially, but his body lacked the energetic, exaggerated movements that were so characteristic of him. He was always so open as a person, and that was a big part of what made him so lovable. He would make a terrible poker player. Pablo felt that he was making a very bad job of hiding something and now he seemed to have sunk into a distracting dazed state. He wondered what was occupying him so.

"Come on, you one-braincell wonder. Talk to me!"

Tim moved his head slowly from side to side. No one was particularly close by. Nevertheless, he lowered his head and leaned into Pablo who was sitting right opposite him, and half whispered.

"It's Sammy, my youngest. She got raped."

Pablo was genuinely and instantly aghast. The statement assaulted his senses. He was truly shocked.

"What? When?"

Tim resumed his low, quiet delivery.

"She had just started going out with some complete turd, and he raped her on their second date. You know what young impressionable girls are like. They are attracted to the bad-boy image, but she didn't expect that."

"Mate, that's terrible. I'm really sorry. How is she?"

"I dunno, mate. I'm worried about her. She's gone back to live with her mum now. She doesn't want to be living alone. Not long ago, she was so proud of renting her own first little flat. She was so chuffed with it, but now, she doesn't want to be alone. She's lost her mojo, and she's not looking after herself properly. It's changed her."

"Tim, I'm so sorry. Obviously that was terrible for her, but it's also terrible for you. I know what us dads are like about our daughters; well, all our kids really, but especially our daughters. We always want only the best for them."

"Tell me about it. I'm so upset by it, Pabs. I'd like to get hold of that little bastard."

With that, he looked suddenly energised as he held his hands firmly in front himself, rigid in a grip stance before slowly folding his fingers into tight, hard fists. His face went taut with aggression, as if he was reinforcing his words. Pablo quietly mulled the matter over, unsure as to how to respond. He wanted to be sensitive and supportive, but of course, he was just plain curious too, which might be annoying for Tim.

"Did the bloke get nicked?"

"Not initially. She went straight back to her mother's and wouldn't talk about it, but after a few days, Susie got it out of her. Obviously she could tell that something really bad had happened. Then she called the police, even though Sammy didn't want her to."

"What a fuck up, if you'll excuse the terminology. So, what happened then?"

"Susie made Sammy talk to the police. They got a statement from her. The turd got nicked and interviewed, but the CPS wouldn't pursue it."

"What? Why not?"

"The waters were too muddy. Too many red-herrings. You know. She'd got off with him at a club a few days earlier. This was their second date. She went back to his place willingly. His word against hers and all that. They can't see the damage he's done. Or they just don't care."

Tim looked so sad. Defeated.

"Now there's a surprise. Not a straightforward case, so they ditch it without even trying. Pathetic, feeble, immoral bastards!"

Tim's surge of energy was quickly spent, and he slipped back into enervation.

"Yeah."

"Mate, when did all of this happen?"

"About three months ago."

"And you haven't told me?"

"Bro, It's not something that I wanted to talk about. It's so depressing."

Pablo felt like chiding him for not talking earlier to his best mate, but this was certainly not the right time.

"Okay, mate, I get that, but what happens about this turd bloke?"

Tim looked sad and defeated, his shoulders slumped forwards as if in surrender.

"Nothing."

"What do you mean, nothing? We can't just let him get away with it."

Pablo sounded and looked very determined. He was outraged. This could just as easily have been his own one and only daughter. He had never met Tim's daughters, but he well knew that they meant the world to him, and now like a true brother, he shared his anger.

Two weeks after his first session with Cynthia, he was back there, smelling the candles. She was as bright and bubbly as always.

"And how are you today, Pablo?"

"Yeah, I'm good, thank you."

He was actually feeling a little nervous, as for him, any counselling session was a form of interrogation. Cynthia spoke easily to help him get grounded and focussed. The important thing for her was to build connection and trust. She wanted him to feel safe and comfortable, able to open up as he saw fit. She was not there to interrogate him or lead him. She wanted him to open up about whatever subject he wanted to open up about. They chatted about a few things in general. The weather, dancing, work. She was gently searching for the issues. She knew that by the time anyone contacted her, they would already be near a crisis point. She knew from their first session together that he had lost his sense of self-worth, his sense of purpose.

"Pablo, I'd like to understand your core values. Can you explain them to me, please?"

He stared at the flickering candles. They were very relaxing to watch. All that energy and prettiness. His mind shifted to the time he had been with Oprah, a life coach friend of Hellion's. She had asked him exactly the same question, years earlier. That made it easier to answer.

"Being reliable. Working hard. Always. Being faithful and honest. Being kind to people."

He looked at her to see if he'd said enough. She encouraged him to expand.

"What's important to you as a man? How do you see yourself as a man?"

That immediately made him think about himself as a husband and a father.

"To be a good provider to my family."

Even as he said that, it felt a little hollow, as his family were all gone now.

"To be a good role model."

He salvaged himself a little. He could still aspire to that one, even if from a distance. He would always carry the mantle of whatever example he had set for his children, and he hoped it had been a good one. He would always be a father, a grandfather and an ex. She waited. There was a pause, as he considered more.

"Not being selfish. Doing things to make my family happy."

Cynthia looked at him purposefully.

"You've said a lot about being a family man and a provider for your kids, but now they're all gone. How do you think that has impacted you?"

He twisted on his seat whilst he mulled that one over.

"I think that empty-nest syndrome is regarded as something that affects mothers mainly, because they're the ones who actually give birth, but I think it affects fathers too."

Cynthia hmmmed.

"I mean, I believe in the notion of giving your kids roots and wings, and that the wings are very important, but that doesn't mean to say that you don't miss their companionship when they're gone. You still love them."

"Okay, but it sounds like you accept that that is a natural progression. The kids get their wings and fly, but let's go back to your core values. You've mentioned about being a good provider. What does that mean and why is that important?"

"I saw it as my role to make sure that all the bills were paid, that there was always food on the table, a car in the drive with petrol in it, etcetera, etcetera. I was responsible to ensure that everyone else was facilitated in their lives."

"You talk of responsibility. What was behind that? What made you feel that those particular responsibilities were important?"

"I suppose that it was what my father demonstrated to me. He was always a good provider, so I wanted to be a good provider too."

Cynthia clearly wanted to expand this notion of responsibility further. As she coaxed his thoughts out of him, he expressed disappointment that he now felt redundant. That all the good work he had done previously had not been good enough. At this point, she quickly fetched a large notepad. She drew a large circle on it and handed it to him.

"I want you to write down words inside the circle related to your core values, and how you have demonstrated them in your life. Words to describe how you were responsible and fulfilled your role."

With a little coaxing he wrote down 'loving', 'honourable', 'capable', 'reliable', 'hard-working', 'competent', 'being the best'.

She pushed him. Why was it important to work so hard and be a good provider?

He reflected for a few moments and then expounded.

"It wasn't so much about buying things. When my kids were young, there weren't all the things that today's kids have to have, like iPads and screen games. It was more about enabling them, giving them things to do, teaching them to swim, to ride bikes, providing holidays and trips out together as a family, visiting relatives, playing outside with cousins, sharing experiences, building memories, in essence, helping them to develop as individuals, not just to have things."

After some reflection, he added proudly.

"I taught them all to snowboard, in the Alps."

She waited to see if he had anything to add. He stayed quiet. She asked him to write more words in the circle, which he did, and then she asked him a question.

"Teaching your kids to swim and ride bikes was about keeping them safe. How was the world around you? Did it feel like a safe place or a dangerous place?"

He was quick to answer that one, with enthusiasm.

"No, the world was a wonderful place, to be explored and enjoyed. I would shove them out the door and say go off and enjoy yourselves. Have fun, play, do things, but stay together and look out for each other. When they were older, I pushed them down a snowy mountain on a board with a cry of 'swing your hips!' I was lucky because my wife and I were on the same page. Mostly, we enjoyed similar things, and our vision for the kids was the same. We never clashed over the kids, ever."

She looked down over his words in the circle.

"Looking at those words in your circle. Are you happy with them?"

He glanced over them again.

"Totally!"

"Do you think they reflect that as a father and a provider you were good enough?"

"Absolutely!"

"Do you think that it was the right path that you took?"

"Definitely."

"Looking at those words, do you have any regrets?"

He looked at them again.

"None at all. Well, looking back, you always wish you'd made more time to be with them, but at that time, you're so busy earning the money to pay for everything. I actually think that we did a great job, and my kids have all turned out into wonderful people!"

"So, you're happy that you taught your children important life skills, and that you helped them make cherished memories?"

"Totally!"

"It sounds like they had the kind of childhood we would all want for our children. They were given opportunities to experience things and grow, and they felt love and cared for. Mum and Dad were singing off the same hymn sheet. So, what kind of a job do you think you did as a father?"

"A great one." He smiled, but then he saddened.

"When they were gone, how did that leave you in relation to the connection you had with your wife?"

She wondered if he still felt a sense of purpose.

"Well, I thought we had it all to look forward to. We would have more time for each other, but also we would have the opportunity with the grandchildren to transfer all the parenting skills we had acquired over thirty years into helping build and enjoy them, together. That's largely why I'm so sad now. I expected so much to happen all over again with the grandchildren in a softer, gentler round two."

She looked at him kindly.

"Pablo, you have evidenced what a great job you did as a father, that you achieved all the goals you set for yourself, and you have every right to be pleased with what you have achieved. Now you are starting to talk about other losses. Losses caused by external circumstances, not because of you. You are talking of the expectations you had for the future not being met now. We call that shattered assumptions."

"Shattered assumptions," he repeated, thinking that it was a very apt description of what he felt. She continued.

"Your core values are still the same, Pablo, and you're happy with them, but your world has been shattered because your wife is no longer on the same page as you. Sometimes, our vision for the future is shattered, and that is really, really painful, and we have to find a new vision. Circumstances often change beyond our control. It might be a tsunami, a volcano or a car crash. Then we have to make new expectations."

She was getting drawn into a new topic, but she felt like that should wait for another session. She took him back to his core values.

"You used the word 'honourable'. That's such a big word. We could use a whole session exploring its meaning for us. How would you define it?"

Pablo composed his thoughts momentarily, then,

"Acting and thinking in a way that complies with your ethics, where your morality is borne out in your actions."

She smiled broadly. "That's a beautiful description of what it means, Pablo, and you think that as a father and a husband you acted honourably."

"Yes."

"Knowing what you know now, would you do everything the same? Would you work as hard, or maybe put more time and effort elsewhere?"

"I'd definitely pay more attention to the relationship with my wife."

"What advice would you give your children about raising their children?"

"Money shouldn't be the priority."

"That's learning lesson number one."

"Harmony. Make sure you understand what your wife is feeling. I must have overlooked things."

They chatted for a while longer, but when the time came for him to leave, he felt quite pleased with himself.

Chapter 3

The raping turd was not hard to identify. Not only did Tim know his name and address, but he was able to send Pablo pictures of him on social media. His name was Sean. He was aged twenty-six, was about five feet nine inches tall and of lean build with a shaved head. He was extensively tattooed, with that art work extending up both sides of his neck, stopping just short of his jawline. Pablo was unsure these days as to whether or not tattoos were intended to appear menacing or were merely permanent artistic accoutrements. As they had become almost ubiquitous over recent decades, he presumed the latter. Sean wore gold earrings in each ear and smiled readily for the camera, appearing to think a lot of himself. He would be strong because he worked as a roofer. He was young and would have good stamina with well-developed muscles.

Tim had been careful about finding out information about him. He hadn't wanted to draw attention to himself, and understandably, it would have been difficult to talk to Sammy about him. She just wanted to forget all about him. When Pablo first mooted the idea of teaching the turd a lesson, Tim was adamantly against it because he really didn't want Pablo getting into trouble, but Pablo reassured him that it was doable and that he really wanted to do something nice for his bestie. Tim had been so kind, supportive and hospitable to him in the past, and now he wanted to repay his kindness by beating someone up. Tim didn't take too long to warm to the idea because he was riddled with pain and resentment, and he hoped that some kind of retribution would make him feel better. After he had acquired all the details Pablo needed, he was sworn to absolute secrecy.

Despite his age, Pablo had great confidence in his fighting skills. In his youth, he had learned to box, and he had been outstanding. He had played a lot of rugby and proved to be as tough as bricks. The only reason that he hadn't pursued a career in boxing in his youth was that he had been in love with his brain. Then, during his career in the police service, he received regular training in self-defence and unarmed combat. He had been an excellent exponent of those skills, and over the years, he always reinforced his confidence during real-life confrontations. He could boast that he had never come off worse in any physical altercations with anyone, ever. And he had always kept himself fit and strong. But he was always circumspect too. He carefully assessed situations. What did he know about his opponent's physical state, fitness, capability? Did that person have any specialist training? Were they impaired by injury or drugs? Were they armed? Were there any potential weapons nearby? Was someone else likely to appear and wade in? He would always try to use the benefit of surprise and unpredictability.

With Sean, he was confident that despite his adversary's youth and strength, he would have the skill set sufficient to overcome him. However, he also admitted to himself that he would be slower these days, and he was not nearly as agile as he had been in his prime. Yes, he was still strong, quick enough and skilled, but an extra advantage of some sort would not go amiss. He learned that Sean was quite a drinker. Therefore, the best time to deal with him was when he was at least partially inebriated. That would give him his advantage.

He found a good time to take a few days off work, and yet again, he was off for a mini holiday. He went towards the end of the week. Another nondescript short-term rental. He would deal with Sean at the end of a day, when he was tired after a hard day's work and preferably after he had been drinking too. Late on a Thursday afternoon, he parked his car in the residents and visitors' car park adjacent to a small tower block. It wasn't huge, at only eight floors tall, and it was one of a pair which mirrored each other fifty yards apart. Both blocks had their large charcoal-coloured car parks on opposite sides to each other, surrounded by a large expanse of plain grass, which eventually bordered 1960s terraced streets of magnolia rendered houses. Pablo looked out of his window, craning his neck to watch the block with interest, looking and listening for any signs of life that would give him a feel for the pulse of the life of the block. At about 5.30 p.m., a small, dirty flat-bed scaffold lorry pulled up noisily in the road adjacent to the front doors. Pablo watched a young man in tattered jeans and a dirty sweatshirt drop out of the passenger side and give a brief dismissive wave before turning away and striding purposefully towards the door. He recognised him immediately as Sean. He noted the way he walked. He looked tired, his shoulders stooping forwards, and yet his gait was still reasonably quick. It is said that each person has a completely individual gait, just as individual as their fingerprint.

As Sean slid through the doorway and out of sight, Pablo's thoughts moved on to the block itself. There were a lot of residents in a tower that large, and most of them probably wouldn't know or recognise a lot of the others. He hoped he would be able to come and go without arousing suspicion. As he observed the location, he wondered about the yawning expanse of grass and carparks lazily surrounding these high towers, as the homes themselves had been cramped into such tight spaces. It seemed such a strange use of land.

Sean stayed in that evening. The next morning, Pablo was up bright and early, and was able to observe Sean leave for work before eight o'clock. Then, having parked further away, he walked back to carry out a recce. The communal front door was coded, and he didn't know the code. He didn't see any CCTV cameras anywhere. That was a big relief. Had there been any they would probably be vandalised on a regular basis. He had always been an avid non-smoker, but he had brought a packet of cigarettes with him, with a lighter, for precisely this event. He loitered just outside the main entrance, leaning back against the dusty wall next to the door, and lit up a fag. He knew how to look like a relaxed, seasoned smoker just taking a casual break. He had watched so many smokers during his lifetime. He inhaled just enough to look like a seasoned smoker, without taking in enough to make himself cough. Again, he was wearing dark nondescript clothing, with a big floppy cap covering his head. In a building this size, with so many occupants, it wouldn't be long before someone entered or exited.

Within minutes, he heard the screeching voice of a young mother on the inside, dishing out orders to two young children, laden with cuddly toys, waddling behind her. She tapped the exit button beside the double doors, which were made of reinforced glass of the old-fashioned type, where you could distinctly see the wire grid embedded in the glass. She negotiated the electronic doorway, trying to keep the toddlers close as she manoeuvred a pushchair containing a baby. As the door steadily creaked open, Pablo kindly lent around it to hold it open for her. That wasn't necessary at all because the door was mechanical, but it was received as a kind gesture.

"Thanks love," she declared in her shrill voice. With the other hand, Pablo held his cigarette low, so as to keep it as far as possible from the children. He only wanted to get in for a look around, and now he could easily pop in, but on the spur of the moment, he chanced his hand.

"Excuse me, love. I'm new here and I still need to have a bit of paper with the code on, and I've accidentally left it inside. It's my age, you know."

He looked at her kindly and smiled. She laughed. He was very plausible.

"Oh, that's okay, love. We all have our moments. It's X6852Y."

She repeated loudly, "X6852Y."

Pablo chuckled. She obviously thought that he really was quite dense or deaf.

"Thank you. I think I've got it now."

She looked at him, smiling.

"What floor are you on?"

He had seen from the sign by the door that each floor had numbers starting with the floor number. The building went up to eight floors. He didn't want to choose her floor and make her suspicious of him, but he also couldn't pretend to be so thick that he'd also forgotten his own flat number too. He made a quick guess that with three small children, she'd been on one of the lower floors so he said,

"Seven."

"Oh," she exclaimed, apparently warmed by his closeness.

"The floor below me. Lovely! Great views, don't you think?"

"Yes. Stunning."

"You must come up and see us sometime. Mine's the one with piles of kids' stuff by the front door. You know what it's like."

She was ignoring the little boy tugging at her ripped jeans, trying to get her to move on. Pablo blushed just a little.

"Yes, of course. That would be lovely. Have a nice afternoon."

With that, he dropped his cigarette and slid inside as she and her troop wandered noisily off. He noted the entry code on his mobile phone before forgetting it. A pair of foreboding stainless-steel doors for two sets of lefts were situated at the centre of the vestibule. They were dull and faded from relentless scrubbing off of painted graffiti over many years. He pressed the button to go up. He was surprised that the light in the button actually worked, because the place had an air of decay about it. As he waited for the lift to come down, he took in all the detail of his surroundings. There was an unusual smell, which he put down to old, musty disinfectant, maybe mixed with paint remover. Apart from all the faded stainless steel around him, the rendered walls were patchy with old paint that might once have been uniformly cream or magnolia. Now they were now deeper and various shades of dull yellow, with long smears of greyish black at chest to shoulder height from years of people scuffing along them.

He waited nervously, hoping that no one would challenge him. As he looked around the empty echoey lobby, he observed that there was still no CCTV. That was good, very good. He listened to the clanking of the lift mechanisms and watched intermittently as the lit number above the doors slowly changed and gradually descended to zero. The doors opened and an old couple, who appeared to be very overdressed for the time of year, shuffled out, arm in arm, paying no attention to him at all. He entered alone and keyed in the fourth floor. He memorised his movements. Come out of the lift. Turn right. Go through a push swing double door and turn right again. Now he was on an outside corridor facing the road. He counted the doors to Sean's. Five. His number was 405. He checked to make sure all the doors had numbers on. They did. He looked to see if there was any communal lighting in the corridor. There was, but that didn't mean to say that it actually worked. He hoped it did. The old-fashioned front doors were wooden ones painted very dark red with large opaque windows at face level. Later on, when it was dark, some of those might be emitting some guiding light. Out in the road were street lights. He should be fine later. He didn't loiter. He walked slowly past Sean's door and carried on to the end of the passageway to see where it led. An open stairway. *Keep to the left to go up. Keep to the right to go down.* He walked down the stairs, going over all the details in his head time and again. He would be returning in the dark, and things would seem different then. The only thing that disturbed him was the sudden flapping of pigeons' wings as he disturbed them as he walked briskly down the deserted stairway and burst out onto the grass outside through a fire door.

That evening, he returned in time to discreetly wait for Sean's return from work. He parked his car where he hoped it wouldn't garner any attention. Whichever way he did this, he was taking a chance. Whether his presence was noted or not depended on how nosey the neighbours were, and of course, that was out of his hands. That was simply a chance he had to take. All he could do was pick a parking spot as discreet as possible whilst still having sight of the front door. The waiting was boring. It reminded him of the days when he used to drive the out-of-hours doctors to home visits, and he would have to sit in the car outside the patient's house for up to an hour. He was in the large communal car park reserved for residents and their visitors. Other residents came and went, but nobody seemed to pay him or his car any attention. Sean returned at about 5.30

p.m. as he had done the previous day. Then Pablo waited to see if he would go out. Sure enough, about an hour and a half later, a taxi turned up and Sean emerged from the building and got into it. Momentarily, Pablo considered following it but decided against it. What would be the point? He already had a plan, and he would stick to it. He left his observation point and found a steakhouse for a meal, and of course, no alcohol, returning to his post at about 10 p.m.

Now it was dark. It was also raining lightly, which made visibility even more of a problem, and there were far fewer parking spaces to pick from. He couldn't find a place in the car park where he could see the front door sufficiently well, so he had to park in the roadway opposite the building. He didn't like that. It felt too prominent. On this side of the street, there were just maisonettes, far more likely to wonder about a man sitting in his car outside. After about half an hour, there was a tap on his window. He only lowered it a little, grateful that the drips of rain sliding down the glass would make it difficult for the enquirer to see him well. But they might still note his registration mark.

"Yes?" Pablo asked tentatively but politely.

A little middle-aged man wearing a wet grey mac and holding a brolly over his head spoke authoritatively.

"I noticed you sitting out here for a while. Is everything okay?"

Of course, Pablo had considered this possibility, and he had several lines prepared in his mind. He briefly weighed up which one might best assuage this curious little man with the wiry wrinkled face leaning right up to his window. He wondered how some men managed to shave their faces, yet miss bits quite obviously for many days at a time, leaving little wiry tufts which somehow seemed to indicate a low IQ. He answered confidently.

"Mate, this is a bit sensitive, but I'll be straight up with you, fellah. I think my wife's having an affair with a guy in that block. I'm just trying to find out if I'm right or wrong. I just need to know, you know?"

The man suddenly stood bolt upright, as if shocked by something. Then he leant back to the window as closely as he could.

"Oh, I'm so sorry. No, I understand that, mister. I'm so sorry. I just wanted to make sure you're not a burglar or something. I can see that you're not. I'm sorry. I didn't mean to pry."

"No, it's okay. You're just being sensible, but please, don't say anything to anyone, okay? I don't want my wife getting wind that I'm onto her, okay?"

The man stood bolt upright momentarily again, then leaned right up to the window again. Pablo got the impression that if he were to open the window fully, the man would stick his nosey little scrunched-up face right in.

"Don't worry, mister. Your secret is safe with me. The bitch! You can't trust women, you know?"

"I think you might be right. Are you married?"

Again his upper body flew backwards emphatically, even more than last time.

"No. I'd never get married. You can't trust women, you know. Would you like a cup of tea or anything whilst you wait?"

Pablo smiled at him, pleased that he had assuaged him so easily.

"No, really, that's very kind of you, but I'll be fine. I just need to sit here quietly for a little while longer if you don't mind."

"No, that's absolutely fine my friend. You take as long as you want. If you need my help with anything, I'm just over there. Number 83. I can keep an eye on the place for you if you want."

Pablo suppressed a chuckle.

"That's really kind of you, mister, but really, that won't be necessary, but thank you all the same."

The man, quite satisfied now, disappeared off to number 83.

This little interlude made Pablo wonder if it was time to abort the mission, but just as he was wondering, a taxi arrived at the front of the building, making quite a splash in the puddle by the kerb. He lowered the nearside window which faced the building to get a better view. He saw Sean emerge from the cab, followed immediately by a young lady in a short black dress with flowing, long blonde hair. He stared at them intently as they dashed in the rain to the doors. He hadn't expected that, and then, as he raised the window, he questioned himself. Why hadn't he expected that? Sean was a popular young man. He had just been out on the town, and he had pulled. Why hadn't he considered that? Just because he had never had such a lifestyle himself? He was cross with himself. He couldn't afford to overlook obvious scenarios. Therein lay the likelihood of getting caught out and failure. Now he sat wondering what to do next. It might be the case that the young lady had simply shared a cab with him and that she lived in another flat, but he couldn't know, and there was no way to know. He had to presume that she would be with him in his flat for the night. He would wait for a while, just in case something unexpected happened. Fifteen minutes later, he was rather absent-mindedly watching the phantasmagoria of streetlights dancing in the raindrops running down the windscreen, observing the streaks of blue flashing in tandem with the oranges and yellows. Pretty little dots of water imprisoning little spurts of light, skipping down the windscreen, as if in a race, making a multitude of mini-splashes, like a hazy sky of tiny kaleidoscopes. The blue shards of light became ever more noticeable.

A police car with wildly flashing blue lights suddenly pulled up in the road right opposite the building entrance. Pablo slunk back in his seat, alarmed. Had someone phoned up about him? Surely that wouldn't warrant a blue light response. That would have been a quiet, stealthy, slow, spying crawl along the road to catch him in the very act of suspiciously loitering. He watched two male officers get out of their car and jog to the building. They didn't even switch off the blue lights in their haste. They must have known the code because they entered the lobby very quickly. He thought that maybe it would be a good time for him to leave the vicinity, but that small still voice in his head told him to wait. A mere ten minutes later, the officers emerged from the building with the young blonde black-clad lady in tow. They clearly weren't detaining her, yet she approached their car with them and got into the back. The officers both got into the front. Finally, the flashing blue lights were turned off, and the car drove away slowly.

Pablo could only wonder what had transpired, but what he did know was that Sean was now home alone. He waited for another ten minutes to make sure no more police cars were about to turn up, and then he drove off to the next side street to find the first discreet parking space. He found one. He was out of sight of the flats but was still close enough to walk there quickly. He got out of his car and stretched briefly. His heart was beginning to beat faster, and he could feel the adrenaline starting to surge. He pulled up the collar on his jacket, and as he walked towards the building, he donned a new pair of black leather gloves and made sure his black balaclava was in his pocket. X6852Y! And 405!

Chapter 4

Pablo was minding his own business at home, mid-afternoon, on his computer, quietly concentrating on a bit of share trading. He'd spent most of the morning in the garden. It was late April and there was so much to keep up with as everything was bursting into life. There was a tap on his bedroom door. This was most unusual. It would be Costa, but why?

"Yes?" he answered apprehensively.

Carlos opened the door, holding the edge with one hand he leaned around rather sheepishly.

"Pablo, you've got visitors."

Pablo's face immediately reddened. This didn't feel good. Carlos turned as if to lead him out, and Pablo followed him along the long hallway to the stairway. At the top of the stairs, he saw two smartly dressed youngish people standing expectantly in the centre of the huge lobby. His descent was clouded by racing thoughts. Were they police? Was it to do with Bill? Sean? Hellion? He was going to say nothing.

He walked up to the visitors, but before he had a chance to say anything, the male proficiently held out his warrant card and stated, "I am DS Richard Pageant, and this DC Rebecca Hurley. Are you Pablo Pinkerton?"

"Yes, I am."

He was trying not to swallow, but already, he felt his throat drying.

"Mr Pinkerton, we'd like you to come with us to the station please. We'd like to interview you about an assault."

"Am I being arrested?"

He presumed that he was, but they hadn't actually said so. He was doing his best to feign surprise.

"Not at this stage, sir. We're investigating a very serious assault, and we have a number of people that we need to interview, but we need to do it at the station."

"Can't you interview me here?"

"No, sir. The interview has to be recorded, and you have to have the chance to have a solicitor present too."

"I'm not keen. The last time I got taken in for interview, just because my ex-wife was being a bitch, they kept me in for twenty-five hours. That was so out of order. I'm not prepared to submit to that kind of abuse again."

The young lady, Rebecca, spoke up.

"Mr Pinkerton, we can assure you that we will take you straight into interview. You won't be booked in as a prisoner. It will just be an interview."

Pablo examined her face. Did he trust her? Was she the sort of person who would blatantly lie to his face? He wondered if they had sufficient evidence to actually arrest him if he refused to cooperate. Hellion had had him arrested on this very spot almost a year and a half earlier, and that incarceration had been a nightmare. The boredom. The frustration. The impotency. He was sizing them up. Guessing at their abilities to detain a resistant prisoner and feeling like they would stand no chance against him if he chose not to cooperate. They would have to call for backup. He couldn't help thinking that way. It was instinctive, but it was also redundant. Of course, he would go quietly with them if he had to. He didn't want to make a scene in his own home, in front of Carlos, his landlord, whose goodwill he relied on to have a roof over his head. He turned his head to look at Carlos behind him. He wanted to gauge him too. He was standing there unobtrusively, just quietly and curiously observing the proceedings. He turned back to the officers, with a quizzical and pained look on his face.

"Can you tell me what this is about please?"

The male officer, Richard, took over again.

"Not at this stage, sir. We can only state that it is in relation to a very serious assault. We cannot reveal any further details until we are on record, after you have been cautioned and you have had the opportunity to have a solicitor present."

They both looked at him, waiting, hopeful. Richard's eyes were almost begging. The last thing that they wanted was for it to go to arrest with a physical confrontation with a man of Pablo's stature.

"And you can assure me that we'll go straight into interview, and I won't be banged up for hours on end?"

Rebecca replied, "Absolutely. We want to be as quick as possible. We have a lot of people to see."

That last remark perplexed Pablo. How could they have a lot of suspects to see? That would rule out his ex-wife Hellion making spurious allegations again and probably Sean too. Must be Bill. He would have had a lot of enemies. But why weren't they actually arresting him? They must have connected him somehow, in which case they must have enough evidence to actually arrest him, surely? He was puzzled.

"Okay, but I will want a solicitor present. Last time I dealt with you guys without one, and they really took the piss, big time."

"Mr Pinkerton, that is fine. Do you want to call one now?"

That caught him by surprise.

"No, I don't have a solicitor. Can I use the duty solicitor?"

"Of course. There will probably be one at the station already."

"Even though I'm not arrested?"

He was still sceptical.

"Yes. That will be fine."

Pablo decided that it would be best to get this over with as soon as possible. He turned to Carlos.

"Carlos, can you phone my work please, and tell them I might be in late. I'm due in at four."

Carlos was happy to do that for him. Pablo was careful not to fetch his phone. He didn't want it confiscated. He just asked Carlos to google them for the phone number, and then he walked to the front door. The officers led him to a rather plush BMW that stood regally on the enormous gravel driveway and opened the rear door for him. He got in the back with Rebecca, quietly. It was time to face the music.

The officers were good for their word. At the station, which was a huge central city one, Pablo was discreetly ushered through secure doors at the front of the building, not through the series of hidden-away cages at the rear. He was flanked by the two fob-wielding officers and was efficiently escorted along several corridors, up in a swish lift to the third floor, and straight into an interview room. The few people they passed along the barren corridors looked rather tired and weary, as they shuffled along in their creased suits or rather drab skirts, a lot of them carrying thick files of paperwork. As the officers passed each other, there were only the briefest nods of acknowledgement, but no conversations. Richard and Rebecca were clearly on business with a guest, and that guest had a slightly shifty, nervous look about him.

Richard ushered Pablo into the non-custodial interview room and shut the door behind them. Pablo automatically sat beside the huge old-fashioned recording machine dominating the otherwise empty desk, facing the door. Rebecca had gone off to inform the duty solicitor that her presence was required. In the meantime, Richard and Pablo sat quietly in the room, waiting. It was awkward. Richard didn't want to start up a conversation which might veer into topics which he needed to keep for interview, and Pablo was in no mood for small talk. Richard broke the silence in time-honoured fashion.

"Mr Pinkerton, would you like a coffee, or tea? And is it okay if I call you Pablo?"

"Yes. That's fine. A coffee would go down well. One sugar please."

Richard made a quick call on his mobile, then started routinely perusing some case papers which he had brought up from the car in his briefcase. A couple of minutes later, a young plainclothes officer appeared with one coffee, which he politely deposited on the table, and then silently left, with just that familiar nod. Now Pablo had something to do. He could slowly and contemplatively sip at a mug of coffee. A real china mug. They must trust him. Minutes later, Rebecca arrived with a mature plump woman.

"This is Mrs Dearly. She will be your interview solicitor. We'll give you a little time together."

With that, both officers left, and Mrs Dearly approached Pablo very confidently. He stood, and she shook his hand limply and confirmed her full name before settling her ample girth onto the rather small chair beside him. "Hi, Pablo. I'm Robbin Dearly, the duty solicitor. This is my card. Hang onto that. You might need it later. How are you today?"

"Nervous."

"Of course you are. I take it that you're not in and out of these places like a spring breeze."

"Absolutely not."

She began to talk him through the process, as he took stock of her. Middle-aged looking, but he suspected not nearly as old as her first impression implied. She had an air of neglect about her. Loose shoulder-length, thick brown hair was probably her most noticeable asset, but even that was rather unkempt. To make things easier for her, he let her know that he was in fact a retired police officer and that he knew all about the processes. She looked at him askew, lowering her bifocals, clearly surprised.

"Oh. That's very unusual."

She took a moment to process that rather significant piece of information. Then she asked curiously,

"Do you know what they've brought you in for?"

He knew that defence solicitors preferred to know as little as possible about what their clients may or may not have done. That made their job easier. Then they could just focus on the technicalities and mere points of law conscience clear.

"No. They said something about a serious assault, but no names, places, times or what they think my connection might be."

"Okay. Well, you know well enough that if you've got something to hide, you go no comment to everything, and I mean everything. If you pick and choose what questions to answer, you'll actually be helping them."

As she said that, she fixed a stern look on him just over the top of her tortoiseshell glasses. He liked her. She seemed professionally competent even if he didn't pay too much attention to her own appearance. After the rather dramatic pause, and him nodding at her, she continued,

"If you've got nothing to hide, you might want to answer their questions. It's up to you. As far as I can see, they've got quite a list of suspects to work their way through, and I hope that they're just doing their bit to eliminate you."

She looked at him askance again, smiling.

"From their inquiries, I mean."

"Of course."

"I will make sure they don't pressurise you, or bully you, and that they don't just go on a fishing exercise, and if I think the interview is going badly for you, I will ask for a break and an opportunity to discuss matters confidentially with you, okay?"

"Sounds good to me."

"The same goes for you. If at any time you want to stop the interview for a private chat with me, you just say so, okay? That's what I'm here for."

"Of course."

"I take it you know the law on assaults?"

"Do you want the definitions from the Offences Against The Persons Act 1861 sections 18, 20, 46, or 47?"

She gave a little titter and then dragged a bloated old leather briefcase, which matched her rather well, up onto the table and rummaged around in it for several

41

sheets of paper. He had to sign some of them before she could act as his official representative. He was in fact signing a contract with her firm. It all seemed a bit heavy just for her to represent him in one interview, but he did as he was asked. Everybody had to cover their own backs. Anyway, he was in a precarious situation, and he really appreciated having her there next to him, to support him. He happily signed. Then, she asked him a few final questions, and checked that he was ready for the interview to go ahead.

"As ready as I'll ever be I suppose," he answered somewhat dubiously.

"Okay, I'll get the officers in. She raised her heavy body out of the chair and poked her head out into the corridor. She returned, the officers shortly in tow. They all sat rather solemnly before commencing. Richard switched the tapes on and quickly covered the preliminaries regarding introductions and information about the tapes. He then stated for the record that Pablo was not under arrest but had attended voluntarily. That was a first for Pablo, and it felt good. Pablo was cautioned and then the questioning began." Richard looked directly at him and asked,

"Mr Pilkington, where were you on the evening of the thirteenth of this month?"

Pablo didn't feel like giving anything away.

"Pass."

Richard looked a little put out. He hadn't expected Pablo to be awkward so soon. He continued with plain bold facts.

"Do you know a lady by the name of Meiying Chan?"

Pablo wondered what on earth this lady had to do with Bill, but he kept his facial expression as neutral as he knew how to.

"No," he answered succinctly and certainly.

"Well, she seems to know you."

"Really? How?"

"She's got your mobile phone number on her phone. We've got copies of all her calls for the past two years, and as far as we can see, you've been in touch with her regularly over all of that time. Would you like to tell me about your relationship with her, please?"

Pablo's face blanched. The penny had suddenly dropped. The only woman he could think of who might have a name like that was Lucinda. He only knew her as Lucinda, her professional name.

"Is she a Chinese woman who lives in Mayfair Place?"

"Yes. Exactly. You know her then?"

"I'm not sure who you're talking about. I only know one Chinese lady, but I only know her by the name Lucinda. She's a masseuse. I suppose that the name she gives me is her working name."

He hoped that didn't make her sound like a prostitute. She wasn't a prostitute.

"Why? Has something happened to her?"

Momentarily, Richard was silent. He was wondering whether it was the right time to give this kind of information to Pablo. He decided that it was appropriate to give him some idea about the nature of their investigation.

"She's in hospital. Someone nearly killed her."

Pablo crumpled in slow motion. He folded his arms in front of himself and lowered them onto the table as he dropped his head and torso over them, face down. Then, he cried like a baby.

The next day Pablo was on the phone to Fatboy. Tim was pleased to hear from him, as always.

"Mate, you're a legend."

"More like a leg-end."

"You sorted him out, bruv!"

"Shut up, you dope. You're not supposed to talk about this."

"I can talk to you about it, can't I?"

"No, you knob. Not even to me. Your phone might be bugged."

"Don't be daft. I heard that he got a right good pasting. And you broke his arm!"

"Not me, you dumbo. Someone broke his arm."

"Oh, okay. Someone really messed up his face too. Anyway, bro, I am very grateful to you."

"Change the subject!"

"Did he give you any trouble?"

"Get serious. He was soft as blancmanche."

"Really? You were okay?"

"'Course I was. He barely put up a fight. He was simply no match for me by a very long shot. Seriously though, bro, shut up!"

"Okay. Nice weather."

"That's better!"

"So, what's up, bruv?"

"Something horrible has happened."

43

"You've got yourself a girlfriend?"

"As if. No, much worse."

"Go on."

"You know my Chinese lady, Lucinda?"

"The one who's been massaging your cock for the past five years?"

"Yeah. That one. Well, someone beat her up and almost killed her."

Tim went really quiet and answered slowly in a whisper.

"Oh no, Pablo. That's terrible."

Pablo heard the concern in his voice.

"What a shit! How did you find out about it?"

"They only feckin' nicked me, didn't they?"

"What? Why would they nick you?"

"They just went through her phone records and pulled in all of her recent clients."

"God job you're not married, bro!"

"I wouldn't have been visiting her if I was married, would I, you knob!"

"True. Do you know how she is?"

"Not really. They didn't give away any details, apart from the fact that someone tried to kill her with their bare hands. I've found out what hospital she's in, but they won't let anyone visit her. She's under some sort of guard for the time being. Anyway, It doesn't sound like she's in any fit state to talk. I just hope that she pulls through, Tim."

There was a pause whilst Tim considered the situation, then, as then he asked quietly.

"You alright, mate?"

"I'm really upset, fellah. She's the closest thing I've got to a girlfriend, but this isn't about me. I just feel so sorry for her. She's such a lovely lady. Why would anyone want to hurt her?"

"Fatboy, you know better than most that there's a lot of sick weirdos out there."

He thought some more about the complications, then,

"Have they got the bastard who did it?"

"I don't think they'd tell me, bud, but if I find out who did it, he's in for it."

"Mate, don't go getting yourself in trouble. It's not worth it."

"Fatboy, sometimes, it is."

A week later, Pablo was attending the hospital. He had a nice bunch of flowers in a hand-tie so that the nurses wouldn't have to worry about watering them. DC Hurley was accompanying him. That was the condition imposed by the senior investigating officer. Pablo had been eliminated early on, soon after his interview in fact, although it didn't end being an interview at all. He was too upset, but he had agreed to give them a DNA sample, and that hadn't been a match for DNA found at the scene. Since then, he had been pestering the CID almost daily, insisting on being allowed to visit Lucinda as a friend and trying to find out how the case was going. He was worried that no one else would have been able to see her yet. Apparently, she had been virtually unconscious for quite a few days.

"Just take it easy, okay? Don't put her through some kind of inquisition," Rebecca warned him. "We only came to see her ourselves yesterday, and she didn't want to talk about anything."

"Did you have an interpreter?"

"No. She's been living in the UK for eight years."

"Irrespective of that, her English is terrible. I don't think that she will feel comfortable talking without one."

"Oh." Rebecca was surprised. It hadn't occurred to her or Richard that they would need an interpreter.

"Do you speak Chinese then?"

"Don't be daft. Of course not."

"So, how do you converse with her?"

"Hand signals mostly."

Rebecca laughed. Pablo was a bit of a pain in the backside, but he was funny, and he was genuinely caring, and she liked that. They took the lift to the fourth floor. Rebecca had to show her badge to be allowed into the Recovery-from-ICU ward. Their temperatures were taken and of course they had to douse their hands yet again in sanitiser, as they hadn't done so for at least two minutes, and each of them had to don a fresh mask. There were eight beds in the ward, each one screened off from prying eyes. A nurse led them to bed number five and she opened the curtain sufficiently for them to enter, before closing them again. There were two plastic garden chairs next to the bed. Rebecca sat on one, but Pablo walked around the other side to be closer to Lucinda. He stood by her shoulders. She was lying on her back under several shining white sheets. A radio played away quietly behind her. All he could see of her was her face. Her thick dark hair fanned out over the puffy pillows. Her pretty features were still slightly swollen. Her neck was severely bruised just above the neckline of her nightie. A sickly mix of colours now, some purple, some almost brown and some yellow. Her eyes didn't look like they would properly open, as if the lids were resisting letting the light get into her eyes. Pablo's initial instinct was to cry, seeing her so poorly. It tore his heart out. But he fought the tears. He had to be strong for her.

"Hey, beautiful. It's great to see you."

He had to restrain himself from the usual automatic niceties of "How are you?" or "You're looking well."

She didn't manage a smile. She looked rather shocked to see him there even though the previous day, officers had asked her if it would be okay for him to visit her. She had nodded. Maybe she didn't really think he would come. He was merely a customer to her after all. He showed her the flowers, as if they were a big deal. She managed a weak smile for those, and that pleased him. He placed the bouquet on the table over the end of her bed, then stood next to her again. She gingerly took her left arm from under the sheets and gently reached for him. He took her hand in both of hers as she looked at him inquisitively.

"You're going to be fine, babe," he stated assuredly as he cradled her warm hand, so close to tears.

"You must help the officers find the man who did this."

He felt immediately guilty allowing the ex-copper in him surface so soon, but he so wanted the perpetrator brought to justice. Her eyes opened slightly more as she quietly spoke.

"I no know."

"It's okay, darling. All I mean is that when or if you can help them, you really must, okay? You don't have to talk about it now."

She repeated, "I no know," with a certainty that implied that there was nothing else to be said. Pablo looked at DC Hurley wondering what to say next. DC Hurley remained silent. This was not the time to question anyone. Pablo grappled to change the subject.

"Is there anything you need? Mobile phone? Charger? Food, drink?"

DC Hurley interrupted him.

"We've got her mobile for evidential purposes."

"Yes, of course you have."

He brightened up. He could be very useful.

"Hun, would you like me to bring you in another mobile phone?"

46

"Yes, dalin."

She held his gaze. That was so unusual. Normally, she was always so coy, never looking directly into his face except for a rare, quick-fire, glance. He continued to hold her hand for the ten minutes that they were there. It was hard for him to make small talk with her because he really knew so little about her, and although she probably knew much more about him because he had always been such a ready talker. She still seemed shell-shocked. Maybe now she was scared of everyone. He didn't really think that she would be interested in his news, but he made small talk anyway. She didn't say much, and after about fifteen minutes, they politely took their leave, Pablo reassuring her that he would be back the next day with a smartphone for her. She managed another weak smile of gratitude, but overall, her expression had been fairly blank the whole time. Pablo hoped that her spirit hadn't been broken. She had always been such a strong woman.

Chapter 5

Leonard Hathaway was sitting in the back of his silver Bentley Bentayga SUV, eagerly sucking on a cigarette. The car was so new, the rich leather smell had not yet been dampened by the regular heavy smoking. Harry was in the driving seat, also puffing away.

"That's a filthy habit you got there, Lenny. Open the window, mate."

"You open yours, you fucker."

"Nah. It's fuckin' cold out there."

"Suit yerself."

"But you're blowin' yer smoke all over me, ya tosser."

"What ya complainin' about. Yer' gettin' free smokes. Put the air-con on!"

Harry touched a sensor. Almost immediately, the fug started to thin out. There had been a late-season frost overnight, and the morning air still had an arresting bite to it, and the low sunlight was yet to touch their car. They were parked at the quiet end of a sprawling transport yard set in a huge industrial estate close to the workers' cars at the dead end of the yard, looking back into the busy part. Several articulated lorries were backed up to grey concrete platforms outside the huge warehouse. Relatively tiny forklift trucks buzzed in and out of their rear ends like termites entering and leaving a huge earth mound. Every now and then, another monstrous lorry would rumble into the yard and the driver would so impressively swing the beast around like he was just swinging his coat-tails, and would back it up to the one of the docks with such inch-perfect precision, that it impressed the loaders every time, even though they witnessed this magic time after time, day after day.

Lenny and Harry had become the best of mates over twenty-five years earlier, when they used to bunk off school together. They smoked together then, and found that getting smokes and drugs into school to sell at a handsome profit was very lucrative. They weren't drug users themselves. They were both too astute for that, but they were absorbed by the money-making power of illicit drugs, and over the years moving drugs had made them a great deal of money. They had left school together, aged just sixteen and with no qualifications between them. They saw no point in studying or taking exams. They had already found their lucrative vocation in life, and with the passage of time, they had gone from strength to strength. They made a good team. Lenny was great at logistics. He was a numbers and ideas man. He hadn't been interested in algebra at school, but he could calculate percentages in his head at lightning speed. He could work out the combinations for a required score on a dartboard before anyone else could. His mind was like a calculator. And not just numbers. He could see the best way to organise complicated processes with ease. Harry was not gifted at anything academic at all. He seemed very much like Mr Average really, quite an ordinary chap in most ways, but his gift was that he was a people person, and therein lay his talent. He was a good judge of character and was great at winning people over to his way of thinking with his personality and ability to persuade. He was warm and ingratiating. He was also a bit of a dab hand on the guitar. Lenny maintained that a business was only as strong as the brains behind the outfit, whereas Harry said that a business was only as strong as the team that made it all happen on the ground. They complemented each other perfectly. Essentially, they were partners, but because Lenny had the sharp business mind and the numbers acumen, he was treated as the boss by everyone, including Harry. Nevertheless, to Lenny, Harry was his equal partner. They were best mates. They dressed similarly. Subconsciously, they wanted to reflect each other. They did smart casual. Suits, but not garish ones. Never a three-piece. They only wore ties on special occasions, basically only for events held inside a church. Never bowties or cravats. They both avoided appearing pretentious.

A rather plush Jaguar saloon car drove elegantly through the yard, taking care to give the lorries plenty of leeway, in case they should suddenly start to lurch forwards. It carefully parked next to the Bentley, and a small dapper Indian man in his fifties, in a smart suit with a tie, exited the car and got into the rear of the Bentley, and started coughing immediately. The air was still too smoky for him. Lenny turned towards him and held out his hand.

"Shivay, my old son. How the devil are you?"

Shivay's petite hand felt like a moist kipper inside Lenny's imposing leathery gorilla hand.

"All is very well, Mr Hathaway. Very well indeed."

Lenny kindly lowered his window.

"Hello, Mr Goldsmith. I hope that you are very well."

"I'm fine, me ol' mucker. Thank you for asking."

Harry was straining to lean around as much as he could to see Shivay over the solid, large, sculptured leather seat, which was prone to keep him embedded in the front-facing position. This was not the way they normally met. Lenny and Harry were legitimate businessmen, and usually, they would meet Shivay in his office, or in one of theirs, but every now and then, they would meet like this. Surreptitiously, away from prying eyes, ears, and possible bugs, to discuss the shadow side of the business. Shivay was pivotal in the success of the business, being the company accountant. He worked for no one else, only Lenny and Harry. They kept him busy enough, and well-oiled in terms of remuneration.

"Any problems?"

"No, sir. As you well know, the lockdowns hit our footfall on the high street, but we compensated with extra activity elsewhere."

Shivay went on to explain which businesses were compensating for others. Lenny knew all of this already. There were no surprises. That is what Lenny wanted to hear, just confirmation. He was always looking over his back. They had a lot to hide, but they also had a lot of ways to hide it. He kept these covert meetings as infrequent as possible, but with some topics, he was wary of talking on the phone or meeting in an office. To stay safe, he made an assumption that his phones were all bugged. He was sure that customs and excise and the police were always looking for an opportunity to bust him, and he had to be one step ahead. There had been occasions in the past when external audits had been carried out, but they had never found any evidence of anything underhand. But he knew they suspected him. He and Harry had built up a lot of legitimate business fronts over the years, just like this huge haulage depot at which they were unobtrusively parked right now. They were jointly respectable company directors. They drew salaries and paid their taxes. Their companies submitted accurate accounts every year and always paid all their dues on time. There was a lot of money involved, yet the really big money was all illegal, and hidden. Shivay was the mastermind who made all the dirty money appear clean. The haulage businesses, hairdressers, betting shops, gambling and games arcades, pubs and massage parlours, were all profitable in and of themselves, but their real purpose was to process dirty money into clean money, and that's what Shivay so expertly oversaw. He inflated the activity and takings of all the legit businesses to soak up all the drugs money, whilst always keeping it realistic and untraceable. The irony was that they could make a good living now from just the legit businesses, but the drugs business is what had catapulted their success to the place where they were today, and neither Lenny nor Harry ever contemplated walking away from it. It was in their blood. Lenny interrupted Shivay.

"Yeah, I already know all that, mate. I just want to know what's new. Are the trends we talked about last time continuing, or have there been any changes?"

"No, sir. Same trends, but now the lockdowns have largely stopped, we are picking up again in traditional areas, so we have a bit more slack."

Shivay was always very formal with Lenny, and Lenny liked that. It was a sign of respect.

"Have we still got enough leeway to soak up our invisibles, or do we need to expand any of our legit businesses?"

"No, sir. We're fine."

As always, Lenny's take on matters financial were spot on. Finally, his most pressing concern, as always.

"Any undue interest from the revenue?"

"No, sir. All normal and in order there."

"Great, but you let me know if anything starts to look a bit unusual, okay?"

"Of course sir."

"We have a considerable slush fund to help things go our way if anyone gets nosey. You know that, don't you, Shivvy?"

"Yes, sir, I am well aware of that."

"Speaking of slush funds, is everything okay with Gregory?"

"Yes sir."

"Payments untraceable?"

"Of course sir."

Shivay wasn't paranoid like Lenny was. He honestly believed that all the far-reaching anti-laundering measures that the government had put in place in recent years were not in fact to help fight crime, and certainly not organised crime. They were just a front to enable government departments to spy on ordinary law-abiding people and to make data more easily available to themselves and ultimately to gain leverage over ordinary people. As far as he could make out, the government actually deliberately attracted dirty money from all over the world into London, with the resultant very useful rise in London property prices.

Their business was quickly done. Shivay bade them politely farewell and got back into his own car, and moments later, it purred off through the concrete expanse. The strangest part of the situation was that Lenny and Harry had so much money stashed away which they more or less just ignored. They had no use for the excess. Harry was a family man with a lovely supportive wife and three teenage daughters whom he doted on. He already had all the trappings of wealth that he needed. The big house, two new cars, two not-so-new for the girls and anything his wife or daughters needed was a forgone conclusion. Lenny by contrast was a single man, but he compensated with regular lavish dinner parties. He lived in a huge ostentatious house set in its own grounds. He employed security, cleaners, cooks. To an extent, his employees were his family, and he was relatively happy. He still regularly met up for dinner with his childhood sweetheart Christina, but their paths had separated long ago. In her early twenties, she had chosen to marry someone else, not because she didn't love Lenny. She did. She was a very strong-willed woman, and she wasn't prepared to tolerate his illegal profession. She had given him an ultimatum, and he had chosen his way of life in the world of business over his love for her. However, over all these years, they had remained close. She remained his only real female friend.

Now, Harry silently fired up the Bentley. Business was done, and as it throbbed though the yard Lenny spoke cheerfully.

"Harry. Time for a pint! Nag's Head here we come!"

Pablo climbed up the grey concrete stairs of Leicester Square underground station and queued up to feed his ticket into a ravenous machine, which, when it was his turn, instantly freed its barrier for him, and him alone. It was midday, and he couldn't imagine how much busier this place might be during the rush hour. He was virtually swept along by the throng outside into a very busy Cranbourne Street. He took refuge from the meandering stream of tourists and blinkered businessmen by pulling himself over very closely to a shop front, and he rescued a rather crumpled street map of the area out of his pocket. It was a beautiful day in mid-May, and the sunshine had already warmed up all the concrete around him. He took his outer top off and tied it around his waist, and then scrutinised the map he had printed it off the internet two days earlier. He was close to a crossroads, and there were street signs, so he quickly confirmed his location. As soon as the lights went red, masses of casually dressed tourists rushed from either side of Cranbourne Street to cross Charing Cross Road, and he readily joined them. This was the first time he'd set eyes on the London

Hippodrome. It looked huge and impressive, and outside on the pedestrianised side, there were two rickshaws touting for business. He was surprised to see them, but then realised how close he must be to Chinatown. He meandered along the pedestrianised part of Cranbourne street, taking in the sounds and sights. It seemed like a never-ending stream of restaurants, pubs and cafes, and each establishment had made the best of securing outside seating spilling busily into the wide car-less street. It was of course big-city imposing. The buildings were a mixture of grand and utilitarian, but they were all four or five stories high.

He soon came across Leicester Court on the right, which was little more than a glorified alley. However, it was still wide enough to get a vehicle along, but two huge concrete barriers would prevent that happening. Hostile vehicle mitigation barriers were all over central London nowadays. There were no shops in this lane, but it was still bustling with colourful people keen to get somewhere else. When he got to the junction of Lisle street and little Newport Street, he noticed that the street names now had additional Chinese symbols on them. To the right he saw that the shop signs were mostly in Chinese. To the left and ahead, vibrant streams of bunting flapped overhead, creating the sense of being somewhere special, and fun. At this junction, the mouth of each street was coned off with removable but locked metal cones. More evidence that vehicles were now the enemy. He stepped forwards, squinting at his map. He should now be in Newport place. Yes. There was the street name high up on the wall in both English and Chinese. He walked along it, and as all these roads were short, he soon found himself staring at the tall metal Pagoda that marks the entrance to Gerard Street on his left. Half the people scurrying around him appeared to be resident Chinese. The other half were tourists taking their time to take photos and selfies in front of garish Chinese shop fronts and the pagoda. Chinatown for real.

He wandered down the street looking for numbers. The premises all appeared to be restaurants or food shops. Occasionally, he saw door numbers, and not far down on the left, he found the one he was looking for. Initially, he was a little embarrassed. The ground floor windows presented garish red electric signs advertising 'Massage'. A big blue banner was draped along the entire length of the black metal railings which were just feet in front of the building, advertising Chinese medicine and acupuncture. He looked up to the first-floor windows. Each pane had a giant red Chinese symbol in them. The next two floors looked plain and ordinary. He pressed the intercom. A high-pitched female voice soon answered in Chinese. Of course he had no idea what she was saying. He loudly stated his name and that he was here to see Lucinda. The voice rambled on in Chinese. Pablo repeated what he had said the first time only more slowly and loudly. The intercom went dead, and he stood there waiting. As he waited he noticed for the first time, two very imposing concrete animals on plinths outside the next building along. He wasn't sure if they were meant to be glorified ornate lions or some kind of dragons, or maybe a mixture of both. They appeared to be on guard, watching fiercely over the bustling activity of Macclesfield street right opposite them. The door opened, and a tiny Chinese lady in her fifties or sixties opened the door. She was impressively smart, no not smart. That word wasn't sufficient. She was adorned in a beautiful tight red dress that went from her calves right up to her neck, and the dark, rich red was festooned with innumerable gold emblems. Classy. Elegant.

"What you name?"

"Pablo. I'm here to see Lucinda."

She looked puzzled. He explained.

"I think she has come to stay with you for a while whilst she is recovering from some injuries. Lucinda. Meiyang!"

"Ah! Meiyang!"

The penny had dropped. Lucinda was expecting him, but this lady knew her only as Meiying. She emphatically indicated for him to enter.

"Please, enter, enter."

She led him up two flights of steps in spritely fashion, leaving him behind rather. He had to duck the occasional red or gold paper lantern. He joked about his tardiness.

"It's the old knees you know. Not what they used to be."

He didn't think that she understood him. She led him into a lounge. More garish red and golds caught his attention only momentarily, but he soon saw Lucinda sitting at one end of a couch and he went straight over to her. She stood and they hugged meaningfully. She simply chided him for making all this effort just to come and see her. She was always so demure.

"Babe. I care about you. I want to make sure you're okay."

"You no need worry."

He held her at arm's length and looked at her. The bruising on her neck had almost entirely cleared up now. Her eyes had gone back to their normal shape. She had beautiful dark olive-shaped eyes. The hostess, Chenguang, offered him food which he gratefully accepted, and she scurried off to get it. He sat with Lucinda, with his arm around her, making small conversation about life in Chinatown. It felt so lovely to be so close to her, and he wondered if she was a little bit less cautious with him today. When the food was ready, they sat at the red Formica dining table at one side of the room. It was a kind of mixed stew dish, with plenty of crispy noodles, which he loved. It was quite spicy but not too hot, which suited him perfectly. In between mouthfuls, he and Lucinda made small talk alongside the energised bursts of high pitch Cantonese firing sporadically between Lucinda and Chenguang, who sat on the sofa. Apparently, she was married to a Chinese man, but he was out, working as a chef in a nearby restaurant.

Eventually, Pablo got around to the topic he had really come to discuss. Following his own interview, he had regularly contacted DS Pageant and DC Hurley to see how the investigation was going, and predictably, they had told him that they weren't at liberty to disclose information to him. So, he had obtained written, signed authority from Lucinda as soon as he could for him to receive updates on her behalf, which was acceptable to all concerned. What he then discovered was that one of the suspects, whom they wouldn't identify to him, had gone no-comment during his voluntary interview but had subsequently been arrested following a DNA match from the scene of the crime, from semen. Whilst arrested he had gone 'no comment' again, and the officers had sought an identification parade. Unfortunately, Lucinda had refused to cooperate.

"Darling, the investigating officers told me that you weren't willing to take part in an identification parade."

She looked a little embarrassed and simply but firmly explained.

"I no interested."

"But if you successfully identify him, he should get convicted."

"I no interested," she repeated quietly, but just as assertively.

He knew her well enough. She has said those very words to him so many times over the years, and he well knew that she was completely intransigent. He wouldn't be able to change her mind. Perhaps she didn't want to go through all the hassle of attending loads of court appearances. Perhaps it was something to do with Chinese philosophy or culture. He had no idea, and she wouldn't explain. Quite some time later, when he left, the pervading thought inside his head was that there was more than one way to skin a cat.

Chapter 6

Lenny and Harry were having a quiet liquid lunch at the Nag's head, outside in the beer garden. It was an old city centre pub, full of character and pastiche, with a pinched-in beer garden at the rear, nestling between the dusty, faded rumps of ancient, grandiose houses. There was enough space for several chunky picnic tables, complete with unerected canopies sprouting through the table centres like small dead fir trees. Of course, these were used more for keeping the rain off rather than the sun, but today they were trussed up. It was a boxy garden mostly devoid of flowers, fenced in with faded wooden panels. The only stab at the horticultural essence were the few clematis plants scattered periodically around the fences. They looked rather sad and straggly, but amongst the thin, dry-looking leaves, the bulging flower buds were full of early summer promise. The men drank out here, even though it was cloudy and rather cool, so that they could smoke. Copiously. Most tables were, in fact, quite busy. People were enjoying the freedom of a pub while they were allowed to. They were in between lockdowns again, although no one knew exactly when the next lockdown would be imposed. Two other business associates, Richard and Charlie, were joining them, as they often did. Lenny was holding court. In between large gulps of beer, he was expounding on his favourite topic.

"Do you know, me an' Harry here will soon be as old as Pablo was when he was gunned down."

They knew he meant Pablo Escobar. Lenny had a fascination with the drug cartels of Mexico and Columbia, particularly the ones of the '80s and '90s.

"Well, let's hope you don't get gunned down when you get to forty-four!"

They all laughed. There was very little chance of that. Both Lenny and Harry were staunchly anti-violence. It simply wasn't in their nature, and besides, it would be hugely counterproductive. The last thing they needed was to attract police attention to their operations because violence was bringing them to prominence. They were at the top of their tree. They brought drugs into the country in bulk. Then they sold them on to high-level distributors for a very handsome profit, and being anonymous was paramount. They had built up a seamless operation, but as the business snaked its way down the ever-widening chain to the sad, desperate, damaged individuals on the street, where the violence did occur, they were completely hands off. They had no need for violence at their level and encouraged all their contacts to eschew it too. If one of their contacts let them down, they would just cut them out of the business. No retribution. Just no longer easy money.

Richard asked curiously, "Why the fascination with Pablo, Lenny? You're nothing like him."

There were giggles as the others tried to imagine him with a pistol stuck into his broad waistband, a spivvy moustache on his face, and a garish sombrero on his head. He shook his head meaningfully.

"I disagree. Pablo may be remembered for his violence, and his flamboyant lifestyle, his zoo, his enormous wealth, but really, he was also a logistical genius. I like to think that I share a bit of that genius too. Obviously, I'm not as clever as he was, but I do admire him."

"Zoo?" Richard blurted out, confused.

"Yes. Zoo. He owned tons of properties, so he could hide all over the place when he needed to, but his main abode was his ranch, 'Hacienda Napoles', which he made into a wildlife park. Illegal of course. Illegal animals smuggled in from Africa. Apparently, the hippos are still there to this day, not the same ones he bought necessarily, but apparently they have bred copiously. Today, his ranch is a theme park for fuck's sake!"

They laughed, bemused at Lenny's obvious disgust.

"Hippos? How the hell do you smuggle live hippos into a country?"

"That just goes to show what a clever guy he was."

Harry chipped in realistically and chuckled.

"I think the fact that he was one of the richest men in the world helped."

"Oh yes, that too," Lenny conceded, "but how did he acquire all that wealth in such a poor country?"

"By killing anyone who got in his way?"

"Well, he was absolutely ruthless at getting his own way. His motto was 'lead or silver'. Very few people stood in his way. They either went on his payroll, or they got shot. Simple as that. There was absolutely no leeway with him."

That sent a shiver down Charlie's spine. He responded as he blew out a huge cloud of cigar smoke.

"That's not genius Harry. That's just pure violence. I thought that you weren't a violent man?"

"I'm not, Charlie, but that's not how he made his money. That was how he broached no opposition and terrified a whole country. No, he made his huge wealth because he saw opportunity, and he knew how to organise to exploit it. His genius was an organiser and a planner. His ability to navigate all the complexities of moving illegal merchandise from one continent to another, in vast quantities, even though, theoretically, the authorities were trying to stop him. I think that the violence aspect of it was more to do with their culture than his nature. His downfall was that he wasn't big enough to take on the USA."

"What did they have to do with it?"

"Charlie, I didn't know how thick you are."

The others laughed.

"He had his own country in his pocket. Police chiefs. Army. Politicians, of course, and even presidents. He was so incredibly wealthy that he could bribe or blackmail everybody. In fact, he even entered politics himself at one stage, hoping to become the actual president! Other presidential candidates who were genuinely planning to clip his wings got assassinated. Kind of sad, I know, but that's Columbia for you. And Mexico. Violence is endemic and gruesome out there. It seems to be their way of life."

He had had this kind of conversation many times, with various friends, which spawned conversations about whether all criminals had to be violent and whether some crimes were actually victimless. Why were some countries so different from others in terms of violence and corruption? He carried on explaining.

"But what he couldn't do was bribe the whole of the American system, and they were truly pissed off with him. Because of him, thousands of miles away in Columbia, they were having massive problems in their own country with drugs, and drug-related crime, and huge sums of American currency were illegally leaking away into Columbia, and it was all his fault. He became public enemy number one."

He stared vacantly at the grey walls sixty feet away over the other side of the fence. It appeared that someone was in a bathroom. Maybe it was a gorgeous, naked female. He would never know. The textured glass deprived him of sight and knowledge.

Richard asked him, "Lenny, why do you think they're so bloody over there?"

"Dunno, mate. It's just their culture, I suppose. They have a weird way. They'll cross themselves and pray to God, just as they're about to blow some poor fucker's brains out."

He giggled at the craziness of it, and his jowls wobbled.

Richard was a little confused.

"So, the USA got involved with bringing Pablo down?"

"Big time. Dick, haven't you watched any of this stuff on Netflix? Its' educational. It's real history."

Richard frowned. He didn't like being called Dick, but he held his tongue.

"Can't say that I actually have," he replied a little sheepishly, as he raised his glass to his thin lips to take the attention off him.

"They pumped massive resources and cash into making the Colombian government take him down. It wasn't easy because he was a hero to a lot of his own people, and most people in the Colombian government were on his side"

Harry laughed. "Even though he killed four thousand of them!"

"Shut up, Harry. It's a different way of life out there. We can't really begin to understand it."

"I understand being alive or dead." He chuckled.

Charlie tried to sound knowledgeable. "So, Lenny, do you have a high regard for other people like him, say El Chaopo?"

Lenny looked at him sternly. "Wash your mouth out! That's like comparing Muhammed Ali with Frank Bruno!"

They all laughed.

"Yeah, he was also very good at organising, but he was more of a psychopath, I think, and he was only carrying on what Pablo had started. Pablo was not only a master of transporting the stuff; he set up factories in the Columbian jungle to actually make it too. A different league, I think. El Chapo's thing was to build lots of tunnels under the border and then to shoot all the poor peasants who dug them out, so's no one knew where they were."

Richard opined again.

"Well, I'm glad it's not like that over here. I don't think any of us would last very long."

They laughed together and raised their glasses to a loud clunk over the table.

"Cheers! To a long and bullet-free life!"

Pablo was not a happy bunny. "I don't fuckin' believe it. You're tellin' me that not only has the relevant paperwork gone missing but that the actual specimen has gone missing too?"

DC Hurley was embarrassed on the other end of the phone and was pleased that Pablo couldn't see her expression and her skin reddening. He preferred talking to her over DS Pageant. She was much more forthcoming.

"Don't ask me how that happened. I really can't imagine, and I probably shouldn't even be telling you this, but you're such a pain in the arse. Anything to get you off my back."

She didn't believe that Pablo was out to make waves for them, so she wasn't overly cautious with him, and he was Lucinda's official representative, after all. Now, she had told him that without Lucinda attending an identification parade, they had no case against their suspect whatsoever. The crucial physical evidence they did have had now gone mysteriously missing.

"Who was the guy?"

"He's a Mr big."

"I mean, what is his name?"

"Pablo, you know I can't give you that. You don't need to know that."

"So, nothing happens?"

"You know the score. Sometimes, we just can't proceed. Not enough to satisfy CPS."

"But you had enough."

"I know. Look, we're all not only hugely embarrassed about this, but we're outraged, too. To say it's disheartening is an understatement, but there will obviously be an inquiry. Maybe something will get sorted, but right now, the case is a dead duck in the water."

Pablo verbalised his exasperation some more. "How can you lose such crucial evidence?"

"Someone has got a lot of clout. That's all I can presume at this point in time, Pablo. I'm sorry."

An awkward silence followed. Pablo carried on, "So, are you saying that your suspect bought his way out?"

"Pablo, you know I can't make that sort of statement, but use your loaf. You know what the job is like. You've done your time."

He was gutted. He just about managed to thank her for her help before terminating the call, in a 'thanks for nothing' kind of tone. His mind was racing.

He felt a burning desire to avenge Lucinda, his peculiar love, but how and against whom?

Lenny escorted Christina out of his car and led her from the private car park into the adjacent restaurant. It was plush. They felt the substantial carpet pile in the entrance hall through their highly polished shoes. Once inside the dining area, the floor changed to a highly polished glistening marble. The waiters and waitresses were very smart, dressed purely in black and white, with neat jet-black hair and impeccable manners, bowing copiously and oozing deference at any given opportunity. Lenny and Christina were led to a large table at the end of the floor, where there was a smaller exclusive area, a few feet higher than the rest of the restaurant. The lighting was generally low, even though it was getting dark outside. The decor was dark too, with lots of blacks and golds, with red lanterns shedding rather dull light on the black nodding cats and the thick rubbery Crassula plants. A couple of musicians were playing on one side of the main floor. This was not a performance as such, just top-quality background music. Two Chinese ladies, in very similar attire to the waitress, were skilfully enticing beautiful sounds out of their instruments in perfect unison, one on a rich dark cello, and the other with a dull looking but vibrant violin, and they were good, very good. Lenny and Christina had dined here many times previously. It was one of their favourite restaurants, and he loved it when they had live music. Such a wonderful ambience.

They were decorously handed menus, and it didn't take them long to make their choices. As they awaited their starters, they sipped Bollinger champagne together. Christina never allowed him to spend more than one hundred pounds on a single bottle of wine or champagne. She felt that would be rather obscene and she would have been embarrassed.

"So, my lovely, how is life treating you?" he almost growled.

She smiled. She knew his interest was sincere, and she loved him for that.

"Same old, same old. Always far too busy with the school, I suppose, but if I'm honest, I do love it. I just get a bit bogged down with all the paperwork."

She chuckled a little.

"And how's my little darling Monica?"

Christina's eyes lit up. "Oh, she's just as adorable as always. She's the biggest ray of sunshine in my life by far."

Lenny looked a little crest-fallen. Christina noticed the look he was trying not to give.

"What? She's with me every day and has been for twenty-two years. Darling, I am lucky to see you once in a blue moon."

Lenny said nothing. He totally understood her viewpoint, but he was disappointed that he had not become more significant to her over the years. Christina had become pregnant with Monica in her late teens and Monica was probably the main reason that she had rushed into an early marriage to Steven, who was presumed by all to be the father. Steven had seemed like a great prospect though. Good A levels, then a place at university doing business studies with all the prospects ahead of him to carve out a glittering career in the world of commerce. She herself had struggled with university, having to juggle her studies with childcare before it had become so universally accessible. Monica had Down's syndrome and people presumed that that was the reason that Christina never wanted any more children, but that wasn't it. She loved her very much and found her a constant source of joy and affection and she would have loved to have had more children. Her reservation was purely to do with Steven. Once he got out into the business world, his drinking became heavier and heavier, and Christina saw the writing on the wall, that her marriage wouldn't last, and she didn't want to complicate things further with more dependents. She struggled on with him for fifteen years before she finally and irreconcilably declared that enough was enough. Now, she had been a very independent divorcee for six years.

Effectively, in the early days, she had chosen Steven over Lenny because of her principled stand over Lenny's elastic morals on drugs. She couldn't countenance supporting him in any way whatsoever while he was pursuing his dream to become the next Pablo Escobar. Then, when she became pregnant, her hand was forced and she had to make a choice. She made the sensible, principled choice, but Steven proved to be such a disappointment. That was probably why she had put her heart and soul into her career, and now she was a financially independent headmistress of a large secondary school. Lenny had stayed in touch right from the beginning. He never lost his admiration for her strength and aptitude. Many a time, he had implored her to throw her allegiance in with him and to live the good life, but the sticking point always had been, and still was, his line of work. Christina had remained a very principled person.

They wouldn't be having that argument, yet again, tonight, the one about his responsibility for some of the suffering of thousands of faceless Mexican or Colombian peasants, who were mere slaves of some dreadful, bloody cartel whose lives were dispensable, constantly held over some precipice as a threat to other slaves. She wouldn't be challenging him again about the damage that illicit drugs wrought on young people and the way they could ruin lives. Lenny had lamely presented his plausible deniability many times previously – that if he wasn't helping to make the trade happen, someone else would be. He didn't make people choose to use drugs, so it made no reasonable difference as to what he did. That these peasants didn't have to do the work that they did. None of these nimble, self-justifying evasions of truth ever washed with her. She would ask him how he would feel if he was told that someone was about to shoot his kids if he didn't comply with cartel orders. He would answer that he didn't have any kids. Deep down, he knew that he never really weighed on the moral issues. He just conveniently ignored them. This was his personal version of cognitive dissonance. To his mind, everyone chose to believe what was merely convenient to them, and so long as that worked for them, that was okay. The evening passed pleasantly enough. Great food, beautiful music, intelligent conversation, and Lenny did make her feel very special. He was always pursuing her, hopeful that one day she would relent and chance becoming his wife, but until that elusive day, she held him tantalisingly at a safe distance, yet so close, too. Theirs was a strange but lasting love.

Pablo didn't have much to go on. Rebecca hadn't even described the suspect to him other than 'he's a very big man', and Lucinda had refused to talk about it. Finally, when Lucinda's mobile was released to her, he did manage to talk her into giving him the assailant's phone number. She had been very reluctant, and it had taken all of his powers of persuasion to get it out of her. She was worried about what he wanted to do. He had only convinced her by lying that he wouldn't escalate anything. That he just wanted to know who this man was, in case anything else happened to her. Now, he had a dilemma. He needed to do searches to ascertain the phone owner, and he had no idea how to do that as a private individual. Second, in the modern world, every action leaves an electronic trail, and he couldn't afford to be traced making these kinds of inquiries, not if he wanted to beat the offender to a pulp and get away with it.

He made an appointment to visit a local private investigator. The office was accessed via a nondescript doorway between small shops. There was no security on this door, which led straight to a flight of steps. At the top of the stairway was a secured door with a choice of six intercom buttons. He pressed the button for

'Covert Solutions' and announced his name. A constant buzzing sound indicated that he was being granted entry. He pushed the door open and found himself facing a corridor with several doors on each side. At the far end, a man appeared half hanging out of the doorway waving at him. Pablo quickly made his way there and found the man holding the door open for him, smiling profusely.

"Please come in Mr Pinkerton and take a seat."

He sat on one side of the man's desk, facing the street. All he could see through the window were the orange bricks and windows of the second and third stories above the shops opposite.

"We spoke on the phone. My name is Derek Chesterfield. You just want to identify the owner of a particular mobile phone number. Is that correct?"

"Yes."

"You understand that for us to work for you, I am afraid that we have to satisfy ourselves as to your identity. It would be unprofessional of us not to."

"Yes," he replied flatly.

"You don't have to explain to us why you want those details, but if, as a result of our disclosure to you, a crime is committed, the police can get a warrant to force us to disclose information if they think there is evidence of a link to that crime. Do you understand that?"

"Yes, if you say so."

Pablo looked at the man keenly. Early fifties. Unkempt long wiry, wavy hair. Thin build. Smiley face with a nine o'clock shadow, and he dressed like an estate agent. Brown cords with a tweed jacket and a cream small-checked shirt. He certainly looked geeky.

"Well, this is a very routine inquiry for us. Is it likely to lead to any further investigations on your behalf?"

Pablo felt like the man was telling him that for them to be interested, it would be good if there was a bit more work to do.

"Well, I suppose it would be good to know a bit about him. Where he lives, what he does. Just some basic stuff. Like maybe what car he drives."

As soon as he said that, he regretted it. How hard would it be for him himself to discover what car this bloke drove if he knew where he lived or worked? He didn't need to pay someone else for that.

"Okay. Well, our sign-up fee is one hundred pounds, then we charge sixty pounds per hour, but don't worry, we can get a lot done in an hour."

He smiled reassuringly.

"This shouldn't take more than a couple of hours, I reckon."

More smiles. Pablo provided proof of identity, signed a contact, and provided card details. Then, he asked a question.

"You always say 'we'. Who's 'we'?"

Derek smiled broadly.

"You'll never know, I hope. I'm the public face of this company, but I have colleagues who work alongside me, but their anonymity is paramount to the ongoing success of our business."

"Oh, yes, that makes sense."

"When we've got what you want, we can send it to you through a recorded delivery post, or you can collect it in person."

Pablo considered this question for a moment, then, "I'll collect it if you don't mind. I might have some questions."

"That's perfectly understandable, Mr Pinkerton. Face-to-face is always best. I'll send you a discreet text when we're ready. It won't be long."

Harry was suddenly woken by his mobile phone. If Rachel had been at all roused by it, she didn't show it. The sound of her deep, slow breathing indicated that she was still virtually dead to the world. Harry was instinctively alarmed. He couldn't remember the last time he had been awoken by his phone during the night. He sat up, grabbed it, and switched it on as quickly as he could, so as to minimise the disturbance to Rachel. The first thing he did was look at the time. 2. 37 a.m.! The sudden brightness assaulted his eyes, which just seconds ago had been wallowing in dark nothingness. It was a withheld number.

"Yes?"

A polite female spoke. "Is that Harry Goldsmith?"

"Yes."

He had no superfluous words. He just wanted to hear why he was being phoned at this unearthly hour.

"Mr Goldsmith, this is the A and E department at the Royal hospital. I believe that we have your daughter Caroline here."

He didn't even ask a single question. He knew that something bad had happened. He dropped the phone by the side of the bed, briefly shook Rachel, and threw off the quilt.

"Rach, get up. We've got to go."

Chapter 7

Pablo found himself standing expectantly a few inches from that solid oak door again. To one side, he was aware of the beautiful rambling rose-flowers furling themselves up and over that side of the door. The scent was so sweet and pleasing, and the colour was warm and lush. The door opened and the vivacious Cynthia stood there beaming at him, dressed in smart black trousers with a rather dazzling bright white jumper. He stepped in and she showed him to the counselling room. He knew where to sit, and she offered him a hot drink, which he refused. He didn't want to waste her time making hot drinks. A fresh glass of water sat on the coffee table, should he need to wet his whistle. After a little settling small talk, she asked him how he was feeling.

"Yeah, okay. I felt good after our last secession, you know, where we looked at what I had done right, but that didn't last long. I went home to an empty room with my empty heart. No one to talk to or share my life with, and I felt like, really, I was a failure."

"Pablo, you are basing that feeling on a situation that is largely the result of how other people behave. You are not responsible for the way other people behave. You are only responsible for yourself."

She handed him his sheet of paper.

"Here's the record you made last time, of your core values."

He politely took the paper, quickly looked at it, and then said solemnly,

"They're all different now."

A sudden quizzical and confused expression captivated her face.

"Just kidding."

He had her for a moment there. He smiled his cheeky smile. She laughed, relieved and then composed herself.

"Maybe today, we can look at some of the important issues outside your circle of core values."

"What do you mean?"

"Well, last time we explored your core values, and how you had stamped them on your role as a father and a husband, and we acknowledged that you had achieved a great deal of what you had set out to achieve in those roles, but that external events robbed you of your comfort, and how you suffered terrible shattered assumptions, yes?"

"Yeah."

"And now, maybe we should focus on where you are going in your life next?"

Pablo was curious.

"Go on."

"Well, sometimes, changes which we think are horrible can change the dynamics in our life for the better. For instance, if you're in a long-term relationship, you focus on the things that are good for both of you. You choose colours for the kitchen that you both like, but you can lose sight of what is good for just you. Now you are in a position where you can choose what you want to do with your life rather than focus on what you need within a couple relationship. This could be quite exciting."

"It doesn't feel very exciting. It feels kind of lonely."

Cynthia looked at him sympathetically and asked poignantly,

"What are the things that you like about your current life?"

Pablo weighed things up in his mind.

"I'm chuffed to bits that I get on so well with all my kids, although the past year and a half has been a nightmare with all the lockdowns, etcetera, but then that has affected everyone hasn't it?"

"Of course."

"I like my job and where I live, and it's great to be getting back to dancing, obviously, but even that is fraught with problems."

"In what way?"

She looked genuinely perplexed. She knew from her own experience that dancing was just end-to-end pure fun, escapism, really. Pablo looked subdued.

"The last time I saw Hellion, my second wife, at a dance, was at the end of 2019, and she had me arrested for stalking her."

Cynthia looked shocked. Her face was a picture of astonishment.

"Oh my goodness! Why?"

"Because she could. It was pure vindictiveness, taking advantage of the police's positive action policy towards domestic violence, but now I'm worried that she'll do it again, at some other dance. Nothing came of it, of course, but it's still horrible being banged up in a cell for twenty-five hours."

"I can't imagine. So, have you not had the chance to discuss any issues with her?"

"Not at all. She went to work one day and didn't come back, and that was it."

She was disguising her shock.

"And you said that was five years ago?"

"Almost."

"So, do you think that you might be broken-hearted?"

He smiled. That was such a quaint old-fashioned term.

"Define broken-hearted."

She settled into 'carefully unravel' mode.

"A broken bone creates pain, as we all know, but psychological studies on the brain show that the same amount of pain can register in the brain from emotional pain, too. Emotional pain is just as real as physical pain. People really can die of a broken heart. Research has found that when a person loses their partner, the muscles in the heart physically weaken. One can literally die of a broken heart."

Pablo felt sad. He would have liked to have died of a broken heart in his eighties or nineties after being married for sixty or seventy years. He didn't like the idea of nursing one now prematurely, just because both of his wives had run off. He silently mused on the subject for a few moments, and then he answered.

"Yeah, you often hear of an old person dying of a broken heart just weeks or months after their lifelong spouse passed away. I don't have a broken heart for my first wife anymore. I did! Of course, for a long, long time, but now that she's been gone for thirteen years, I have definitely come to terms with that, and also, what helps enormously, is that we get on great now, but with Hellion, yes, I do have a broken heart. I felt like we were made for each other, and when she disappeared, I was shattered."

He looked a little tearful, but he stayed steady. Cynthia expanded.

"It can take a long time to heal a broken heart, and there can be a lot of anger mixed in there, too. Sometimes, one needs help expressing it. Do you think you are also nursing anger?"

Again, he was pensive. Then, "Yes, I suppose so."

"At her or yourself?"

"Both, although probably when I think about it, more at myself for not understanding her."

"Yes, you said last time that you had repeated some of the mistakes you'd made in your first marriage with her, too."

She gave him some silence, and he pondered some more as he stared at one of the flickering candles. He was sure that this one was a different colour from those of his last visit, and he wondered how quickly she got through them.

"I'm angry at myself for cocking up, unintentionally, of course, but I'm also angry at her for not communicating with me. If the tables were turned, I would have explained to her what I was unhappy about, and I'm angry that she couldn't do that for me. I would have done anything for her, although now, I can see how she didn't know that."

Cynthia felt his frustration. She had seen it so many times in so many people.

"Maybe she tried communicating with you, but she didn't think you were listening."

He looked at her drily. She had said that during the last session, too and was probably right, but he didn't want her to be right. She carried on,

"It also depends on things that you have no control over, like how she had been brought up, how conflict had been dealt with in her family. Maybe their habit was to sweep things under the table. Maybe talking about things was discouraged, or just led to fights. You don't know, but you can't blame yourself for those things."

Pablo resisted the urge to talk. He picked up the glass of water and drank slowly. That was his way of disciplining himself to just listen. He knew that he was prone to jump into any conversation too quickly. He was a poor listener. She continued,

"Sometimes cut and run is the way people deal with things because they are afraid of what might come out of confrontation. They might not be able to deal with someone who becomes angry or upset. Not many people, when there is trouble in a relationship, can have grown-up conversations. People don't listen properly. They get defensive."

Pablo was saddened, not just for himself but on behalf of the whole of humanity.

"Why is that? In our society, have we missed something crucial about learning about relationships and important stuff like that? Is it because we have been programmed by Hollywood to have unrealistic expectations of perfection and never-ending romance, and 'happy ever after'?"

"I think that people have been conditioned to focus on one relationship too much, and have ignored all sorts of other loves in their life. I also think we've not been taught about the art of conversation. Learning to really listen and understand the other person. People quickly put up their boundaries because they feel like they are being attacked. The ego gets in the way. The ego is a big thing, isn't it?"

"Depends what you mean by ego."

He actually had no idea what she meant by 'ego'.

"Ego... if you really want a good relationship with somebody, you put aside how you're feeling, and you listen to that person with clarity, and you really try to understand them. If your reaction is that they're just criticising you and making themselves sound better than you, then that's just your ego getting in the way. To move forwards, we have to get the ego out of the way."

His frustrations surfaced. "Cynthia, the problem for me is that she has never given me the opportunity to talk to her, so I'm either guessing or confused about everything. How does one move on in this situation?"

"If you're still in love with someone, there's no magic wand that will just make you suddenly fall out of love with them. All you can do is open new doors, and that's really important, but firstly, there needs to be an acceptance that maybe you will never get closure from her. The next stage is opening up your life to new loves and new activities."

She gave him a notepad and invited him to note down what loves he did currently have in his life. The obvious ones came first. Family, some friends, dancing, playing the piano, gardening, but soon, he ran dry. She set the bar high by telling him that there were very, very many more types of love. He then wrote down: 'blonde women, dark women, Asian women, Indian women, big women, little women, fit women, funny women, black women, Hispanic...'

She laughed. She knew he was just being comical. "I'm not talking about relationships. If you try to just move forwards with another relationship, without having closure, and whilst still having a broken heart, you will take your issues into the new relationship, and they will probably lead to more failure. You need to find peace away from a relationship first."

She paused, giving him time to process, and then, "What other things might you find fulfilment in?"

Pablo thought harder and wrote down more ideas.

"Reading, writing, nature, travel…"

Again, he stalled, and she commented.

"You are picking activities which are lone activities, but activities where you mix and meet new people would be good, so if you like reading, could you join a reading group? If you enjoy nature, could you join a rambling group? If you want to travel, could you join a party of singles? Could you do some charity work? You're single. What is to stop you going abroad to work? It's a big world out there. You can always come back here for holidays to see the grandchildren."

He quietly mulled over the magnitude of making such big changes. She carried on, "You like dancing. Would you like to learn another type of dance? What about going to Buenos Aires to learn tango?"

Pablo laughed. This was too much. He was too set in his ways.

"Why are you laughing?"

"It seems like such a crazy idea!"

"But that's what the growth mindset is. When we're either depressed or stuck, it's time to look outside of our little box. We live in little box houses. We drive little box cars. We work in little box offices. It's about entertaining new ideas and plans. It might mean just making plans to start with. Making new goals. Putting a little money aside each week to save up for being able to one day embark on a new dream."

She then returned to practicalities and asked him to rate each of his loves out of ten. When he had finished that, she told him that during their next session, they would work on a plan for each one of them to see how a nine could be made into a ten, an eight into a nine, etcetera.

"You can expand your life and become more fulfilled in other areas. Then I hope that you will be able to look at yourself with kindness, compassion and forgiveness, and that will help you show Hellion the same emotions. These are healing emotions."

Again, he left the session, not condemned or judged, but greatly encouraged. She made him feel like there was always hope.

Pablo had returned to see Derek, the PI who assured him that the mobile phone in question belonged to one Leonard Hathaway. He divulged his extensive business interests, where he lived, what he drove, where his main office was, family details, or rather a lack of them, and a little about his business partner, one Harry Goldsmith. He asked Pablo if he needed more financial details about the various companies, but that would involve more inquiries and more fees. Pablo assured him that he had already provided him with all the information he needed at this time and graciously settled the remainder of the bill. What Derek had discovered about Hathaway dovetailed nicely with the snippets of information he had gleaned from the police. Now, he would carry out his own PI work.

He spent some time mulling over the various businesses. He needed to work out Lenny's movements to find out what times he might be alone. Where he might be vulnerable. Of all the business, the pubs seemed to be the ones where he might best accrue some intel without seeming unduly nosey. There were five pubs to pick from. He decided to start with the one closest to Lenny's home.

On a Thursday evening, he entered the Fighting Cock and walked to the bar. It wasn't busy. He bought a pint and sat at the bar, trying to look casual. Of course, he didn't feel casual. He had a purpose. To try to uncover facts about this mysterious Lenny from people he didn't know. Snippets about his habits and behaviour. When he worked. When he travelled. What his hobbies were. Anything to start with.

Several large screens dotted around the place were all beaming out the same premier league football. The internal decor was grubby. The carpets were of a rich dark pattern that would disguise stains, spills and trodden-in bits of food. The lighting was dull and absorbed by the dark furniture. The fact that he wasn't a football fan wouldn't endear him to the other patrons, and he would soon be caught out if he pretended to know anything about football. People were clustered near the screens, although none of them seemed glued to the actual play as they chatted away jovially. He could just about observe the snooker table at the far end of the premises, and a few young lads were noisily enjoying their game there. He felt rather awkward and that he stood out like a sore thumb. He realised that he should have come with someone else. That would have looked much more normal. Apart from a few fleeting, vacuous remarks exchanged with the odd person, who happened to pass him as they briefly attended the bar or toilet, or as they trawled outside for a smoke, he made no meaningful contact with anyone during the two hours he invested there. It was a wasted effort.

Unperturbed, the following evening, he steeled himself to try again. This time at The Coach and Horses. This was much more promising, simply because, being a Friday evening, it was much busier. He had to wait to be served at the bar, even though most clients appeared to be ordering from their seats using their trendy apps. Having been served, he tagged onto the edge of a group, noisily following a football match. Again, he felt self-conscious because all of this crowd clearly knew each other, and he felt disingenuous trying to kind of tag along with strangers. Nobody spoke to him. He was trying not to look uncomfortable.

This was going to be harder than he thought. He wondered about the haulage businesses, hairdressers, betting shops, gambling and games arcades, pubs and massage parlours. *Would one of those be better for reconnaissance?* he wondered. Hairdressers were renowned for gossiping, but he had no excuse for going to a hairdresser. A massage parlour would be fun, but the girls there would probably have barely any command of the English language, let alone be privy to any useful information.

The next day, he tried again. A slightly different tack. He attended The Nags Head at lunchtime. He bought a pint and some crisps and went outside into the small beer garden and sat at one of the picnic benches, staring at his mobile, which was a perfectly natural and socially acceptable thing to do these days. The clematises were looking amazing, with their big blooms of pinks and purples. It was a warm sunny day and the garden was reasonably busy. Smokers would be coming and going, too. He felt much more confident about making contact with people this time. To his surprise, two gentlemen joined him.

"Don't mind if we sit here, do you, chum? Only it's a bit stacked out here."

"No, please. That's fine. I don't want to hog a whole table all to myself."

The one who spoke with a deep, gravelly voice was casually dressed, in his early forties, with curly brown hair that wisped around his ears. He oozed confidence. His smile revealed stained teeth from years of smoking. The second male was possibly slightly older, but he seemed quite reserved. He was tall and wiry and looked like the anxious type. His cheeks carried the pockmark scars of adolescent acne. He stayed quiet.

"You meeting someone?" the first man enquired. Rather boldly, Pablo thought.

Pablo hadn't really made his mind up about what story he would furnish for his presence today, depending on what kind of conversations he got into, if any, but the first-date notion was one of his possibilities. It seemed like a good idea to pursue that one now.

"Funny you should say that. Is it that obvious?"

73

The man laughed and simply asked what her name was.

"Claire, I think," Pablo chuckled. "I've been speaking to quite a few online. I hope I don't get confused."

The man looked at him studiously. He tried to be jocular.

"I tried a few dating sites a few years ago when the wife ran away with the milkman. Didn't work for me. Which site do you use?"

Pablo was beginning to feel like he was the one being investigated, but he focused on keeping his story flowing convincingly, and his demeanour untroubled. He blurted out the first site that came to his head.

"Match dot com," he answered confidently.

"You got a picture of her?"

This was too intrusive. He sensed that there was more to this than met the eye, and he started to get defensive.

"Why do you want to know?"

He didn't mean for that to sound aggressive, but it did. His prickles were up more than he had realised.

"I might know her."

"What, do you think it might be your girlfriend?"

He tried to laugh a little. They were verbally sparring with each other now.

"What time are you meeting her?"

Pablo looked at his watch. It was twelve forty-five. He was feeling very close to the point where he would tell this nosey guy to just fuck right off. One last polite answer, and then it would be 'Fuck off, you nosey cunt!'

"One O'clock."

"You're early."

"Wouldn't do to be late, would it?"

"Okay, pal. Good luck!" and with that, he abruptly got up and walked off.

The second man dutifully followed him, looking a little confused. Inside the pub, the inquisitor explained to his friend that he had noticed Pablo two evenings before, at the Fighting Cock, and that Pablo had been on his own then as well, and that something wasn't right about him. They casually kept an eye on him. Pablo realised that his attempt to gain information was going disastrously wrong, but he held his nerve and remained in situ, alone, until a quarter past one, hoping that his story might have seemed plausible. Then, as his imaginary date hadn't showed up, he left, but as he did so, he regretted having parked in the pub car park. He hoped that no one would take any notice of his car. However, it was well and truly noted.

Harry and Rachel had left the house as quietly as possible, and they had managed to do so without waking either Melissa or Sammy. Even the dog, Pluto, had barely roused on account of their unusual nighttime activity. He had grown lazy in his old age. Harry had quickly scribbled out a note on the back of a letter and left it prominently next to the kettle. 'As soon as you see this, phone us. Something has happened to Carrie and we are at hospital. – Love you xx'

His car was electric, so it left the premises silently, without disturbing anyone. He drove at speed. He didn't care if he went through a speed camera far too fast. Not in the slightest. He didn't mind breaking the speed limit at every single one. The roads were virtually empty. Rachel was upset that he hadn't found out any more details than he had done.

"Look, we'll know soon enough, and then we'll be with her. I didn't want to waste time on the phone asking loads of questions. I just wanted to get there as soon as possible."

"You could have at least asked what has happened," she stated, frustrated and upset.

Her stomach was in a knot. She almost felt sick. It was hard to be strong when you didn't know what awful thing you were about to face about one of your own children. At that time of night, and with Harry's breakneck driving, they arrived in just over ten minutes. He followed the signs for A and E, and abandoned his car on double yellow lines very close to the entrance. Concern over a parking ticket was no more significant than getting a bunch of speeding tickets. Anyway, he thought that he was unlikely to get a ticket in the middle of the night. They rushed into reception, ignoring the dozen or so casualties silently and tediously awaiting their turn to be seen, announcing their daughter's name urgently. The brightness and sudden contrast of the bright lights within the building offended their eyes.

"Mr and Mrs Goldsmith, Caroline is in Ward Beta, on floor 'C'. Please take the lift. It's just down there on the left."

The receptionist tried to look and sound caring, but she was tired, and this was what she did all day, every day, or all night, every night. She was glad to see them rush off. She might get some peace for a few minutes before the next lot landed. For Harry and Rachel, they had never known such an impossibly tedious long wait for a lift. Why did it travel so slowly? They both wished that they had taken the stairs. They would have leapt up them rapidly.

Long minutes later, the lift arrived on floor 'C' and they burst out of it frantically scouring the signs dead-ahead of them, the smell of disinfectant almost gagging their throats. Beta, to the right. Neither of them registered yet how clumsily they had dressed. Harry's flies were undone, as were his shoe laces. He had put on a T-shirt back to front, and he didn't even register the slight discomfort of it tugging at his throat. Rachel always wore tights. She felt that her forty-something legs no longer looked so good bare, and that was purely paranoia, but right now she was wearing the first skirt she had grabbed from the wardrobe, without tights, and with a jumper that didn't even remotely match it. Her hair was crumpled and ruffled from three hours of sleep. They both looked a mess, but none of that mattered. At the Beta reception, they noisily announced their names and whom they were there to see. The nurse checked her screen and then calmly invited them to sit down near the entrance. They didn't want to be kept waiting. They didn't want to sit.

"Can't we just see her, please? What has happened?"

Both of their minds were racing. Had it been a car accident? Had she been attacked? Was it rape? Had she fallen into a river? She had always been a very poor swimmer. Had she suffered sudden death syndrome, well, almost?

"Please. Sit down just here, and I'll fetch a doctor who can explain to you what has happened."

This was like torture. Reluctantly and impatiently, they sat, straining their necks to see if they could see anything of note down the corridor. The nurse disappeared into a side room, and just a minute later, reappeared with a stout female doctor who was a s black as the ace of spades. They both stood simultaneously and approached the doctor.

"Are you related to Caroline Goldsmith?"

What a stupid, annoying question.

"Yes, of course we are. We are her parents!"

No other people were in the vicinity, and the doctor felt quite comfortable informing them there and then in the corridor that their daughter was in a coma.

Their mouths dropped. That was devastating, yet they still wanted to know why and how. They wanted to be able to process this shockingly bizarre information.

"She was brought in unconscious from a nightclub. She has no other injuries, so we are presuming it's drug-related. We don't know what she's taken, but we are managing to keep her stable. Blood tests will be carried out soon."

The doctor looked coldly at them. She had enough injuries to deal with on every single shift without people harming themselves recklessly in the pursuit of decadent pleasures.

Harry and Rachel were stunned and silent, but then as Harry tried to process what he had just been told, he reacted crossly.

"But she doesn't do drugs!"

The good doctor looked at him with an air of superiority, armed as she was with the cold, hard facts. She resisted making a quip, tempted though she was, and then Rachel spoke.

"Stable? What does that mean?"

She was crying quietly, but she managed to speak softly.

The doctor turned her head towards her and allowed herself a small pang of sympathy for this devastated fellow mother as she looked at the torment in her face.

"It means that she could easily have died tonight. Her pulse was sky-high, her blood pressure on the floor and her organs were all shutting down. We have given her drugs to keep her in a coma whilst we try to stimulate her organs into functioning again. Hopefully, they will work."

"Can we see her?"

The doctor paused. There was really no point, but she knew they would insist. The nurse on reception was back at her desk.

"Speak to the nurse," she answered curtly, nodding towards reception, and then she walked off back into the ward and disappeared.

Chapter 8

Pablo was at his computer, gazing out of his bedroom window, wondering if he could write something therapeutically, when his mobile rang. The number displayed, but it was an unknown number. Normally, he rejected unknown numbers, but an instinct pushed him to answer this one.

"Hello?"

"Mr Pinkerton. You don't know me, but I know about you. Don't worry, I'm on your side and I want to help you."

"What do you mean, you're on my side? Who the fuck are you?"

"Please, I can't say too much on the phone. I would like to meet face to face, then we can talk properly."

Pablo was quite flummoxed. This didn't feel right. He felt a shiver of fear briefly shimmer through his body.

"Unless you explain yourself a lot better than so far you fucker, and quickly, you can just fuck right off, right now!"

"Look, I know this is out of the blue, but I have to guard myself. Can we meet please?"

"Not if you can't tell me what this is about."

The caller hesitated, then offered a bit more than maybe he was comfortable with at this moment.

"Lenny Hathaway."

Sudden thoughts shot through Pablo's mind. Lots of them, but one which stuck was that he had to keep himself safe too. He was a mixture of cautious and curious.

"Can I call you back on this number?"

"No problem."

"Ok, but I'll pick the time and place."

The caller was hesitant. "I might not be able to see you when it suits you."

"Tough shit!"

"I'll need notice."

"How much?"

"At least a day."

"What's your name?"

"You can call me Denis."

Pablo would occasionally phone Lucinda to see how she was getting on, and to find out if she was still in London where she had gone to recuperate after hospital. She was always very neutral, but she sounded well enough. He had learned very soon after first meeting with her years earlier that she had very close friends in London. She always went there for Christmas, and her one summer holiday abroad was with them too. His ulterior motive for calling was to encourage her to return home. He missed her badly. He missed her breasts hugely. In her absence he was back to visiting random massage parlours, but each experience lacked the depth and warmth of his connection with her, and he missed that terribly. His phone calls always ended with his heartfelt query about when she would come home. Her reply was always predictably the same.

"It no safe for me."

Pablo was very suspicious of this Denis fellow, but he had to check him out. He called him one Saturday morning and proposed meeting in a local cafe inside a large department store in one hour's time. This was just like in the movies, and no doubt he had been subconsciously prepared for this very event by the plethora of thriller films he had watched over the years. Denis sounded rather flustered over the lack of notice. That suited Pablo just fine. He didn't want him to have much time to prepare anything. If something went wrong, he envisioned himself making a rapid exit with a choice of staff corridors, stairs, lifts, escalators, with plenty of cover amongst the profusion of merchandise. A department store was the perfect place to lose someone. At the time of the meeting, he found a place to hide behind nearby clothes rails adjacent to the cafe, and he phoned Denis. He spotted a man in the cashier queue answering his phone.

"Are you alone?"

"Of course."

Denis looked around. He knew he was being watched, but he couldn't see by whom.

"Hey, all this cloak and dagger stuff is quite unnecessary, you know."

"I'll be the judge of that you fucker. I don't know who the fuck you are yet, do I?"

He took stock of Denis. A rather short, weedy-looking man, with cropped hair that had a silver sheen to it. Clean shaven. Well presented. He was relatively smart compared to the shoppers around him, because he was the only one wearing a suit and tie. He looked uncomfortable, knowing that he was being monitored.

"I just want to talk to you. What are you worried about?"

"What are you buying?"

"A cappuccino."

"Make that two."

Pablo watched him quickly retreat along the queue to pick up a tray. Shortly he placed his order, collected and paid for two coffees, and chose a table to sit at. Pablo phoned him again.

"Not that one, mate."

"Not what one?"

"That table."

He heard a sharp intake of breath.

"You're being ridiculous."

"I call it sensible. Move to the table right by the entrance and sit facing into the cafe."

Denis looked annoyed. He obviously didn't like being ordered around, or playing games, but he got up and did as Pablo had asked. Now he was looking around himself quite energetically. Pablo walked into the cafe and sat opposite him. Denis looked at him disapprovingly and pushed one of the cups towards him.

"One cappuccino as ordered," he announced abruptly.

Pablo took it and emptied one sugar sachet into it. He stirred it. Each man was waiting for the other to speak first. Pablo started.

"Go on."

"Go on what?"

"Tell me what you want to tell me."

"You're not very good at social niceties are you?" Denis scoffed.

"I'm only here to hear what you wanted to tell me, not to talk about the weather. Get on with it, or I'm gone."

"Alright, keep your hair on."

Denis looked around. The cafe was busy, but no one was paying any attention to them at all.

"This is all completely unofficial. I'm really sticking my neck out for you here."

Denis tried to put on an expression of generosity, but it didn't work. Pablo was not impressed.

"How?"

He looked around again. He didn't say anything, but he quickly flashed a police warrant card in front of Pablo. A piece of tape covered up the name.

"What's that supposed to mean?"

"It means that I'm a police officer, and that I shouldn't be here."

"So, why are you?"

"I know about your involvement with Meiying Chan, and I know you've been making enquiries about Leonard Hathaway."

Pablo just looked at him, and waited, quietly coaxing more information.

"Did Becky or Richard tell you anything about the assault case?"

"I'm not here to tell you anything," Pablo answered dryly.

"Christ, you're not being very helpful."

"Look bro. Tell me what you've got in mind, or I'm gone. I'm not here to play games."

Denis looked annoyed, as if he was in two minds, and then he continued.

"Ok, well, I'm presuming you know something about the case, and that nothing is proceeding. I'm also presuming that you think Hathaway is the perpetrator."

He looked at Pablo, expecting at least a nod, but Pablo just stared back at him blankly. He realised that Pablo was not going to make this easy for him.

"Ok, well, this Hathaway character is a slippery fish. There's a lot of officers who want to bring him down, but he seems untouchable."

"That doesn't seem right."

"No it doesn't. The least I can do is help you get at him, if I'm guessing right, and that's what you want to do."

He looked at Pablo appealingly. He wanted some confirmation.

"Maybe."

"That's where I can help."

"How?"

"I can help you get to him."

81

"How?"

"He's a busy man. He's always with someone. He's well protected, but I know his movements well enough. I know when he might be vulnerable."

"Go on."

"What's in it for me?"

"Fuck all, apart from he gets hurt."

Denis paused thoughtfully.

"I can give you a time and a place when he will be alone, and vulnerable, but you don't know me. You never met me, and if anything goes wrong, you won't be able to touch me I can assure you."

"Of course."

"Okay. I'll be in touch."

With that Denis got up and quickly walked away. He hadn't touched his coffee at all. Pablo moved seats, so that he could watch the adjoining sales floor and the cafe, and he drank both cups.

Harry was on the phone to Lenny. He and Rachel would be taking it in turns to provide a bedside vigil for Carrie. He was home now, having spent the night hours sitting with Rachel by Carrie's bedside, comforting and encouraging her. They had formed some sudden and drastic decisions about their future during the long night, full of anguish. On returning home he had been exhausted, and had managed to sleep fitfully, but now he was wide awake after just three hours of sleep. The body clock and anxiety would deny him any further recuperation. He was letting Lenny know about the events of the night, but there was more.

"Mate, I'm sorry, but this changes everything. If Carrie pulls through this, we've decided to quit England and go to Spain."

Lenny was aghast. "Harry, you can't make huge decisions like that under these circumstances. You're overreacting."

"No mate. We always saw ourselves retiring to the sun one day, but now it's more important than that, it's about protecting our family."

"You can protect them here."

"No Lenny, me and Rach have been discussing this all night. We need to make drastic changes to keep Carrie safe, and the others."

Lenny realised that Harry was acting out of character, and was under immense pressure, and that this was no time to argue with him. He relaxed.

"Bud, I just hope that Carrie makes a full recovery. Keep me posted. Just give yourself plenty of time to think about the future though, okay?"

"Okay," Harry answered uncertainly.

Pablo checked out the target venue in advance. In daylight. It was a large block-built windowless warehouse with a metal convex roof, at the end of an avenue of similar buildings, which itself was just a part of a sprawling industrial complex. There was a large car park in front of it, more for lorries than cars. It had one huge metal roller-shutter door to one side of the front with a normal door adjacent to it. Denis had told him that on Thursday evening at 9 p.m. Lenny's silver Bentley Bentayga would be parked outside, and that the small door would be unlocked. Lenny would be there alone, expecting a visit from a girlfriend, but unbeknown to him, she wouldn't be turning up. Denis refused to explain how that would be arranged, but Pablo had no choice other than to believe him.

Thursday evening arrived, and Pablo did his usual habit of parking some way from the venue, walking the rest of the way, partially hidden in his dark clothes and floppy hat. The industrial park was reasonably well lit, but there seemed to be nobody around to see him. He wished that he had a little doggy with him. People walking dogs never appeared suspicious, and most of these premises had notices placed strategically around warning that such and such security firms operated in this area at night. He'd never actually ever seen a security vehicle on patrol.

A few articulated lorries were dotted around the roads and parking areas, and some had their cab lights on, but their curtains were drawn shut. He walked nervously past them, careful to make as little noise as possible. Some of them might even have CCTV cameras recording their vicinity. As he approached Lenny's warehouse a passive infrared light suddenly beamed out over the forecourt. He couldn't let that put him off. He lowered his head and marched forward to the door where he stopped momentarily to swap his baggy hat for a balaclava. His heart was racing. He knew that Lenny was a big man, so his own advantage on this occasion had been to bring a heavy metal bar with him. It was tucked into his belt. His hand found the door handle, and he strode in purposefully. It was almost exactly nine O'clock.

Inside was dimly lit but as soon as he had taken a few steps inside, he was immediately aware of several large men around him. His heart missed a beat. Big burly men stood menacingly and silently around him. Adrenaline raced through his veins like an electric shock, yet he felt suddenly cold. He instantly knew that he was in deep shit. Deeper shit than he had ever known in his entire life. For a brief moment, his anal sphincter twitched and he focussed intently on squeezing it. Mentally, he had already surrendered. He stood impotently, awaiting an instruction. He had boldly walked straight into a trap. A very simple trap, but a deadly one nevertheless.

"Sit him down," Lenny growled from behind the men.

Two of them took him by the arms and frog-marched him fifteen feet into the cavernous, empty, hanger, whilst a third man roughly tore off his balaclava. He offered absolutely no resistance. He was totally defeated, and he knew it. He felt naked, weak and limp, overcome by his complete mental over power. No one spoke, and that only added to his sense of dread. Two old wooden dining room chairs were prominent by virtue of the absence of any other furniture. One chair faced the other. He was thrust backwards onto one seat. His arms were pulled behind him and he felt them get fastened together tightly in one quick efficient thrust. He knew that it was a plastic tie by the whizzing, rapid, grating sound of the plastic teeth dragging over the miniscule ratchet, and the thinness of the bond that immediately cut into his wrists. The men stood neatly spaced to his sides and behind him. They were formal, silent and disciplined. One noticed the metal bar protruding from his belt. He leaned forward and roughly tore it out. The atmosphere was weirdly echoey and menacing. It felt like he had just walked onto the set of a gangland movie, except that this was bizarrely real. Lenny slowly moved to the seat opposite him, which he turned the wrong way around, gathered up his long coat neatly around himself as he planted his bulk onto the ridiculously small chair, leaning on the back of the chair, facing Pablo intensely.

"I hear that you want to hurt me," he accused truthfully.

Pablo looked directly into his face searching for clues. Was this man a psychopath? Did he love violence? Was he going to be cruel? How much retribution would he carry out on a man who had intentions of hurting him? He said nothing.

Lenny took that as acquiescence.

"Well, I can't have that can I? What am I going to do with you?"

Pablo sensed a genuine dilemma in the big man. Lenny leaned forwards, his large arms perched precariously across the tiny chair back.

He looked at Pablo searchingly. "Why would anyone want to hurt me?"

Pablo answered dryly, but with purpose.

"You tried to kill my girlfriend."

Lenny had already been made aware of the connection with Lucinda.

"Your girlfriend? I understood that you were just a once-week-customer for a lady of the night."

The surrounding men stayed ominously still and silent. The air of menace and dread had not lightened one little bit. Lenny stared at Pablo, encouraging an explanation.

"I love her, and anyone who hurts her is my enemy."

Lenny chuckled. Pablo sounded like a little boy remonstrating with an authoritative adult.

"Well I'm sure that's very noble of you, but that doesn't change my dilemma. Do you want to get hurt?"

Pablo answered quietly, meekly. "Of course not."

"But you think you have the right to hurt me?"

The men standing around were beginning to wonder what the point of this interrogation was, but they wouldn't dare to interrupt their boss. He had his reasons, no doubt. Pablo watched Lenny's countenance carefully, noticing how very thoughtful he was.

"If you were to hurt me, what would that achieve?"

Pablo was embarrassed. What right did he have to be an avenger?

"You wormed your way out of justice. That's not right."

"That doesn't answer my question. I asked you what you hoped to achieve?"

"It just doesn't seem right that you should get away with it."

"So, you just don't want me getting away with it, is that it?"

Pablo didn't answer. He was embarrassed, and scared. Lenny looked at him curiously.

"What is justice?" he asked rhetorically. "If it isn't simply to decide which side has the better lawyer? Is that true justice?"

Pablo made no comment. He didn't want to be there, and by absenting his voice, he felt ever-so-slightly that he wasn't really there. Lenny looked up at his colleagues.

"Who's got my car keys?"

One of the men fetched keys out of his pocket and held them out. He looked rather perplexed.

"Me."

"Give 'em here."

The man gently tossed them over. Lenny caught them with some dexterity, and then he firmly ordered them all to leave. The men stood more or less still looking at each other perplexed. Had they heard correctly?

"Guys, please, I just want you all to leave. Go back to where you came from. I'll handle this myself."

Slowly the men walked to the door. There were quiet murmurings, but no one argued. One by one, the five of them took turns to shift through the doorway. The last man out shut the door with a loud thud, and the sound jolted Pablo. They were gone. He looked at Lenny, totally confused. Did he have a gun? Was he going to shoot him? And he didn't want any witnesses? Not even his own men? He waited. He couldn't help realising that his chances had just improved enormously. Yes, his hands were still tied behind his back, but no gun was evident yet, and now it was just one on one. He could stand up. His legs hadn't been secured. A lucky headbutt could save the day, and he could still kick, and run. But he sat still. Lenny also sat still. In any combative exchange, surprise was always vital for success. His mind was racing as to how best to proceed to save himself, but timing was of the essence. This was no time to be hasty and throw away the one good opportunity that might present itself, and one mistake would seal his fate. Lenny caught him by surprise, by asking yet another question.

"You sound like a nice guy, but you don't have a woman of your own?"

Why was he asking this? Pablo was perplexed, but conversation was good. It bought him time, more time to find that optimal opportunity.

"I'm waiting."

"For the right woman to come along?" Lenny laughed. "Not wishing to be rude pal, but you look like you've been waiting too long already."

Fair comment. Pablo defended himself.

"No. I've found the perfect woman, except that she's far from perfect of course. I married her but she fucked off five years ago."

Lenny laughed. He seemed to be enjoying this.

"And you're still waiting for her to come back?" he asked in disbelief.

"Yep," Pablo answered curtly.

"Why don't you just find someone else?"

Pablo got asked this so often. It was a compliment really. It meant that people really thought he was a nice guy, and was still attractive enough to get a new partner. What they didn't seem to realise, that his heart was spoken for. His heart was still full up. There was no room for anyone else.

"When you find someone really special and you fall in love with them, there can't be anyone else. Simples."

Why was he having a heart to heart with this guy? He had come here to beat him to a pulp. To break bones. To smash his face in. Lenny looked sad.

"You and I have a lot in common."

Of course he was thinking about Christina, but he wasn't going to explain. He continued quietly.

"So, this Chinese bird was just a stop-gap for you?"

Pablo resented hearing her diminished in this way.

"She's much more than that. She has been fantastic for me over the last five years. She's kept me going. Kept me sane. I'd love to be with her if I could, but she'd never have me."

"Why won't she have you?"

Pablo didn't answer immediately, but as he faced the truth, he answered quietly.

"She's like a machine. Weird, but true."

Lenny was contemplative. Pablo could see that he was deep in thought, and hardly preparing mentally for a physical confrontation. He was wondering if now was a good time to suddenly launch himself from his seat and place a thundering head butt right between his eyes. He was convinced that he could catch him off guard, and then, if he went down, he could kick him until he was unconscious. Maybe kick all his front teeth out too. He wanted to disfigure him.

"I'm sorry."

"Excuse me?"

Those words deflated Pablo's escalating energy.

"I'm so sorry."

"What for?"

"For hurting your woman."

Pablo was confused. Why was he saying this? Wasn't this the way this brute behaved towards women? Violently? How many times before had he done similar things? He didn't know what to say or do next. Lenny continued.

"I'm not a violent man. Absolutely not."

Pablo now was angry. How dare he try to evade responsibility! "Beating a woman nearly to death is extremely violent."

Pablo hissed his answer contemptuously, but he also found himself being drawn into the conversation. He still felt that the longer they spoke, the better he could time his assault. Or was he just putting it off? He was starting to feel actually confident that he would soon have the upper hand, but he was also feeling confused. Lenny buried his head in hands and started to cry quietly.

"It wasn't me."

"Then who the fuck was it?" Pablo demanded, annoyed at the confusion.

All he could see of Lenny's head now was the top of it. Lenny wasn't even looking at him any more. He was more or less defenceless, but the top of his head was not a good target. Far too solid. Pablo was more likely to knock himself out, and Lenny's face was unwittingly shielded from a knee-strike.

"I was stupid. One of my guys talked me into trying out this new Flakka shit. Said it would give me an enormous hard-on and loads of stamina, and I was tempted. So stupid. I'm a boozer, not a druggie."

"So, what are you saying? That it was you, but not really?"

"They call it bath salts. Sounds so innocent doesn't it? I put some under my tongue before I went in. It tripped me out. Must have used far too much, it totally tripped me out. I had no idea what I was doing. I'd never tried anything like it before. It was like a nightmare. When I came out of her place, I had no idea what I had done. I couldn't even find my car. I didn't remember what it looked like or even where I was. I just walked and walked for hours, until the drug wore off. How I didn't get picked up by the police, I'll never know. Fortunately I left her front door wide open, and an alert neighbour decided to check on her. That probably saved her life, thank God."

He cried some more. He was clearly remorseful, tormented even. He spoke quietly, as if he owed Pablo an explanation.

"It wasn't until a few days later when the old bill took me for questioning that I found out what had happened. I still can't believe it."

They both sat quietly. Lenny raised his head and faced Pablo. It was almost as if he was signalling a request for forgiveness. Pablo didn't know what to think. He had mixed emotions. Lenny's voice had become more gruff from the crying.

"If you feel so guilty, why didn't you just take the wrap?"

"Force of habit. Too much to lose. Cowardice. I bought my way out. Easy solution. One of the benefits of having so much money."

He looked at Pablo with purpose in his eyes.

"I'm going to cut off your cuff."

Pablo panicked a little. Did he just say cuff? Or cock? Lenny continued quietly.

"You do what you have to do. Maybe I deserve what you have in mind."

He stood, and pulled a small pen knife out of his pocket. Momentarily Pablo wondered if this was the ideal time to launch his forehead as hard as he could into Lenny's big face, but the impetus wasn't really there any more. Lenny walked behind his chair and cut the plastic tie. Pablo immediately stood up abruptly and faced him, trying to summon up his rage, but it had gone. Lenny poignantly and calmly folded up the pen knife and pocketed it.

"You do what you've got to do," he repeated, just feet away from Pablo.

They stood looking into each other's eyes for some seconds. There was a weird, almost spiritual connection. Pablo turned and walked towards the door. He couldn't attack this man now. He just couldn't. The man had opened up to him. He was clearly remorseful, and he was willing to risk Pablo's vengeance. Pablo stopped at the door. This was his last chance to change his mind. Lenny was on his own and he wouldn't get this opportunity again. He turned to look at Lenny who was simply standing looking at him, hands in pockets. He walked out. As he stepped through the doorway into the semi-darkness, an iron bar came crashing down on his head, and he was unconscious before his face landed heavily on the damp, gritty, concrete ground outside.

Chapter 9

D.S. Pageant leaned back on his seat, looking intently at the insouciant Mr Hathaway. He wished that this interview room wasn't so stuffy. No windows. No fresh air, just the dull whirring of the old air conditioner which seemed worn out. Sometimes he felt that his cognitive processes actually slowed down a bit in here. However, his senses didn't let him down. Like most officers, he had developed a sixth sense that told him if someone was lying. Of course, it wasn't a sixth sense at all. It was just the honing of the skill of reading body language, and conducting interviews was a fantastic learning ground. Mostly, interviewees had something to hide, and they would try to give nothing away, yet they sent involuntary messages via little facial tics, flicks of the eyes, fiddling with hair or fingers when they were lying. The ticks which accompanied honest answers were different. Often their made-up stories would end up tying them in knots anyway, which made it easy to challenge them.

The last time he had been interviewed, almost a month earlier, Lenny's solicitor, a Mr Graham Hattersley had advised him to go 'no comment' because he had been arrested on suspicion of attempted murder – a very serious charge which he didn't want Lenny giving them any possible extra clues at all. This time however, he was happy for Lenny to answer their questions if he wanted to. He knew that Lenny was savvy enough not say anything stupid. This time he had attended voluntarily, and it looked good for him if he appeared cooperative rather than defensive. But Mr Hattersley was dutifully there to shield him if necessary. Lenny was making a good job of appearing to be answering most questions honestly. But DS Pageant knew he was hiding something. He looked briefly at DC Hurley. That was her cue to continue the questioning, which she was eager to do.

"So, let me just sum up what you've said so far, Mr Hathaway. You attended your warehouse, alone, at nine in the evening, just after dark, to check that it was empty, and you found Mr Pinkerton lying in a pool of blood just outside the front door, and there was nobody else around, and you called 999?"

"That is correct miss. I was really shocked."

"And you expect us to believe that you, the big boss, would be running around late at night doing mundane tasks that surely ordinarily, you would be delegating to one of your employees?"

"I like to be hands-on when I can be, you know, to keep my finger on the pulse. Make sure nothing is going on which shouldn't be, and that things I am told are done, have actually been done."

He looked at her in all innocence, but the officers knew that he was lying about this, and yet they believed him when he said he had nothing to do with Pinkerton getting injured. His denial seemed quite sincere. Yet he obviously knew much more than he was letting on, and from their point of view, there were strange anomalies, like what was he really doing there? What was the real connection with Pinkerton? Yet it really was actually Lenny who called the ambulance, and the 999 recording of his call indicated that he was genuinely alarmed, emotional and terribly concerned by what he had found. He had sounded panicky, desperate and scared. And then there was the CCTV. None outside his warehouse unfortunately, but other cameras on the estate showed two other cars driving into the estate at the same time as he had entered, just after eight thirty, but they parked elsewhere, whereas he drove right up to the warehouse. The CCTV showed that the five men walked to his warehouse from those parked cars.

"When you found the unconscious man lying just outside the door to your warehouse, did you recognise him?"

"No, why? should I?"

"I don't know. That's why I'm asking you."

Lenny shrugged his shoulders. The DC continued.

"CCTV shows that when you drove into the industrial estate, two other cars were following you. It looks like you were all in procession. What can you tell me about them?"

"Nothing at all. I was alone, and I wasn't aware of any other cars. They are public roads, you know. Surely it's not strange that other cars were on the road?"

Rebecca looked at him, her eyes telling him that she knew he was lying.

"So, you're not aware of any other people being in that vicinity at that time?"

"None at all."

"From CCTV it appears that the men from the other cars walked up to your warehouse."

"I don't know anything about that. They must have gone somewhere else."

"Did you think it might be unsafe visiting your empty warehouse late at night, in the dark, alone?"

"That didn't occur to me at the time at all. It was only nine o'clock, although now, I can see that maybe I was taking a chance."

He gave a small conciliatory smile. Rebecca continued to question him for a few more minutes, but no clues were forthcoming. DS Pageant decided that it was time to play his ace card.

"Mr Hathaway, do you know about your connection with Mr Pilkington?"

Lenny tried to look surprised.

"A connection? But I don't know the man."

"You have a mutual contact."

"Well that is a coincidence. How bizarre. Is that relevant?"

"I think it probably is."

He felt hesitant at this point. He was unsure just how much he could reveal without potentially breaching data protection legislation. He had to be careful.

"Mr Pilkington had a connection with someone that you also had a connection with. Can you tell me about that?"

"Well I never! What a small world. Surely just a mere coincidence." Lenny was slightly overacting.

"Mr Hathaway, I don't think that's a coincidence. There is clearly a connection between the two of you, and I want you to tell me about it."

His solicitor, Mr Hattersley, interjected.

"Officer, I must object. My client has already told you that he doesn't know the man. You are trying to put words into his mouth, and I suggest that you don't."

He gazed intently at the DS and everyone went quiet. The officers were wondering what else they could ask. Lenny was waiting quietly. D.S. Pageant spoke.

"Ok, I think we'll wrap up here for now. Thank you for coming in. Mr Pinkerton is still unconscious in hospital. I hope he will make a full recovery, and that we will be able to interview him soon. Then I dare say we will have further questions for you Mr Hathaway."

His tone carried a slight air of menace, but as he examined Lenny's face, hoping to see a flush of fear sweep across it, he saw nothing.

Harry's daughter Carrie was released from Hospital after four days. The hospital staff had done a wonderful job tackling her physical trauma and bringing her back to nearly full health very successfully. The only ongoing effect was that her speech was slower than normal and was slightly slurred, and she walked with a very slight limp in her right leg. The doctor said that these things should improve with time, although there was a likelihood of some permanent brain injury which might have physical symptoms. Harry and Rachel had been making rapid arrangements to get out to Spain. They had been selling the idea to their other daughters as an extended holiday although their intention was still to make it a permanent move. Sammy was worried about her school work, and losing all of her friends. Melissa wasn't nearly so bothered. She had recently got a job as a legal assistant using her law degree, but she was already really bored with her work. She wondered if legal work in Spain might provide more interesting opportunities. She certainly liked the idea of a long midday siesta every day. The day after Carrie's release, they all sat down for an evening meal together. Harry and Rachel had yet to run the idea about moving to Spain to Carrie. Harry started.

"Carrie, your mother and I have been having a very serious chat about what to do next."

Carrie looked at him across the steaming plates of roast, alarmed at his tone.

"Do next about what?"

"Darling, we nearly lost you."

"Yes, Dad, and I'm so sorry. I made a mistake. It won't happen again. Please don't go all melodramatic on me."

She was embarrassed, and stared at her food. So far, everyone had just been making a fulsome fuss of her, so happy that she had survived and was now home again, but now the awkwardness of being confronted about what had happened, was about to start.

"We want to take the family all out to Spain for a while, you know, to get away from the temptations of life here."

"What, are we going to live in a tent in the desert or something?"

Melissa and Sammy sniggered. Carrie continued petulantly.

"I don't want to go to Spain."

Rachel spoke.

"Carrie, we didn't know if you were going to survive. When a parent gets that close to losing a child, believe me, they question everything. You girls are the most important things in our lives."

"We're not things."

"You know what I mean. You're more important than anything else. Much more important than things, money, or our way of life here. We want you all to stay healthy and be safe."

"Look, Mum, I made one mistake. That doesn't mean we've got to drag everything up by the roots and randomly chuck it over the ocean. Where do you want to go for God's sake?"

"Torremolinos. You all love it there."

"Mum, it's great for a holiday. That doesn't mean that it would be nice to actually live there. None of us can even speak Spanish!"

She looked imploringly at her sisters.

"I don't suppose Sammy and Melissa want to go, do they?"

Sammy and Melissa looked at each other guiltily. They were quite liking the idea. Sunshine, sea, sand, fit boys with great tans, and close to the city of Malaga. Sammy chipped in.

"Come on Carrie. It could be really good. All those water sports and hunky lifeguards."

Rachel frowned at her. She didn't like to think that her daughters reduced things to the lowest common denominator. She took up the conversation.

"There are great international schools nearby. You'll probably be able to do a similar course there to the one you're doing here."

"Mum, I'm not in school anymore. I'm at college."

"You know what I mean, darling, and we won't be far from Seville, and you know how interesting that city is, culturally, and Malaga is right on our doorstep, one of the oldest cities in all of Europe. You know how much you love history."

"I love reading about history, Mum, not living in it. What about all of my friends?"

She was at that stage of her life where friends were considered far more important than mere family.

"Darling, you'll soon make new friends, and your old friends can come and visit you for as long as they want."

Carrie looked aghast. "All this upheaval because I took the wrong pill at a nightclub?"

Harry took this opportunity to query her about her behaviour.

"I'm really surprised at you Carrie. You're the one in the family who's a vegetarian because you say we're not made to consume animals, and that it's bad for the planet of course, yet you're happy to stick unknown chemicals into your body without knowing what they might do to you?"

"Like you don't?"

Harry pulled a very quizzical face.

"You and Mum allowed the government to stick untested weird chemicals into your bodies which they pretended were a vax, but they were nothing of the sort, and you had no idea what risks you were taking."

"I think that's very different."

"Different how? Look at the adverse reactions they have caused. You're lucky you didn't grow two heads. Loads of people have died from them."

"We weren't taking it for pleasure, only to stay safe and keep everyone else safe."

Carrie pulled her best shocked facial expression. Rachel interjected. She really didn't want anyone arguing with Carrie about clubbing or drugs so soon after she had come home.

"Please. Can we have this conversation some other time? Let's just give Carrie room to settle back in and recuperate for now. She needs time to process our plans and what has happened to her. That's understandable."

She gave Harry a severe stare. That conversion was over now, and Carrie tucked into her roasted vegetables quietly, her pulse racing at the dilemma she now found herself in.

Lenny arranged to see Christina. As usual, he took her out for a lovely meal and a good conversation. Tonight was Italian, in an historic building with loads of exposed wooden beams, undulating floors and ceilings, and curvy walls. As he walked in, Lenny had trouble walking in a straight line, what with the uneven floor and low ceilings.

"Excuse him," Christina joked to the nearest seated diners. "He's already pissed."

Lenny chortled, holding his hands out to steady himself on the walls and chairs as he was led to their table. He apologised to other diners as he lurched his huge bulk uncomfortably close to them during his waddle. On their table an orange candle flickered in a beautiful old brown bottle, encrusted with a mass of solidified dripping wax. It looked like it had been there almost as long as the building itself. A small bunch of fresh flowers wilted slightly in a cut-glass vase. They sat, perused the menu, and made their choices.

"What brought this on? It's less than two weeks since our last date. Are you beginning to fall in love with me again?"

She smiled mischievously.

"Darling, you already know that I love you. I always have."

He offered nothing else. Her eyes almost watered. She composed herself.

"I can tell that something is on your mind. Well, I'm glad that you're happy to confide in me, Lenny."

She said that with obvious appreciation. Lenny looked awkward. She was right. He did have a lot on his mind, but he didn't really want to burden her with it, but who else did he have? No one.

"Things just seem to be going a bit tits-up lately, if you'll excuse my French."

Christina looked at him kindly. She wasn't going to pick him up on his 'French' when he was clearly allowing himself to be vulnerable and informative. She was just pleased that he was willing to confide in her.

"Go on."

"I've been interviewed twice by the police in the past month, and now Harry is talking about retiring to Spain."

She looked a little confused. She sipped her champagne as she gathered her thoughts. She knew nothing about either brush with the law, but decided to go with the easier option.

"What's unusual these days about someone talking about retiring to Spain?"

"He's not just talking about it; he's actually organising it. Now!"

"Oh dear. Yes, I can see that that would be a big blow for you, all those business interests that you share."

She looked pensive, then, "And the police?"

Lenny didn't mind her knowing that he had needed to fend off two investigations, but he didn't want to divulge any details.

"Oh, just some misunderstandings."

"To do with the businesses?"

"No, not really," he almost mumbled, unwilling to elaborate.

"So, what's the problem?"

He presumed that Christina knew that he used massage parlours and prostitutes, but these subjects were not for her delicate, prim ears. She looked confused.

"Well, I'm not in the habit of attending police stations with my solicitor to be interrogated, and then with Harry buggering off, it feels a bit like everything is falling apart."

"Yes, I can understand how that might be rather worrying. Maybe it's time for you to think about reaping the rewards of all your hard work and do some retiring yourself."

"What would I do with myself?"

"Ooh, I don't know, take up gardening, travel, learn a new language, golf, look after me! It's just a case of refocusing."

She was sad to see him troubled, but she was also excited. Maybe, finally, an opportunity would present itself for them.

"You know I would be able to do things with you if you weren't involved in the business you're in."

"You might have to give your up work too, depending on what opportunities presented themselves."

He was being rather vague, but she was quietly elated at the way new pathways were opening up broadly in her mind.

"That could be arranged if the right incentives were in place."

She gave him a cheeky smile, but felt a little guilty about blackmailing him a bit, but she really was excited. There were such great possibilities for the two of them. He didn't reply, and that meant that he was thinking about what she had just said. She pushed, hoping to strengthen his new broad mindedness.

"Sometimes life sends us messages, telling us that one season is over and that it's time to start a new one. Nothing lasts forever dear."

He took her hand with both of his and kissed the tiny bit of it that he could still see, in such a gentlemanly way, just quietly thinking, and then mused,

"I know darling. Maybe you're right."

She savoured the romantic moment, and then she got practical.

"If you sold up, how much would you be worth?"

"Millions and millions."

Her eyes glowed, and she smiled at him beautifully.

Pablo was receiving regular visits in hospital from his children. They took it in turns for one of them to visit each day. They would stand or sit beside his hospital bed and talk to him, describing the mundane events currently going on in their lives, about work, and how all the grandkids were getting on at school. The doctors had encouraged them to speak to him. He was in a coma, but they explained that people in comas are often aware of things being said, and any stimulus would be good for his brain. It had been explained to them that the traumatic head injury had caused a subdural haematoma, a serious condition where blood collects between the skull and the surface of the brain, and the resultant pressure on the brain could be fatal, or at least, very damaging.

Each one of the children were torn apart to see their strong, irrepressible, father lying motionless on a hospital bed, clearly so vulnerable and absent. Tubes wiring him up to so many machines, his head bandaged like a mummy, and his face so uncharacteristically devoid of any life or expression. His face was so pale. They had never seen his face pale before. That was almost as alarming as knowing that he had a fractured skull. It looked so wrong. They had been assured that the craniotomy, whereby a section of his skull had been temporarily removed, so that the surgeon could access his head and remove the haematoma, the lethal blood clotting, appeared to have been successful, but of course, there were no guarantees. Recovery was still a long way off.

Delilah also visited him. It was a long journey for her, and she would make the best of it by tying it into a stay with one of the kids overnight on the way home. When she was with him, she managed to keep her voice steady, but her eyes were full of tears. She wondered how differently things might have transpired if she hadn't left him all those years earlier. She felt partly responsible for what had happened to him now, even though that was completely illogical. She would hold his hand for almost all the time she was with him, stroking it lovingly, hoping to see a flicker of life somewhere on his pale, white-capped face. The nurses had given her permission to shave him. She well knew that he always gave himself a wet shave, but from her, it was electronic. No mess. If she was also with one of the children, they would talk gaily between themselves, about all and sundry, acting as if Pablo was included in the dialogue.

On one occasion when she was visiting with Sarah, she held back just as they were leaving. She leaned over Pablo and kissed him on one cheek. She whispered into a half-exposed ear, 'I love you', and squeezed his hand before turning to catch up with Sarah. She had never told him that in all the years they had been married. Or maybe she had. Maybe she had said that to him when he was asleep, like now. As she turned to leave, she didn't notice a solitary, glistening tear slowly form in the saggiest part of his lower lid, and suddenly tip over the edge and trickle slowly down his face.

Chapter 10

Melissa and Sammy were plunging in and out of the pool with three young, joyous, athletic, Spanish men they'd recently become acquainted with. It was lovely for Rachel to see them enjoying themselves physically, with the mesmerising restraints of an electronic device nowhere to be seen. The villa was on a hill about half a mile from the azure waters of the Mediterranean. The building and its garden had a clear view of the sea over the descending trees and orange roofs, arranged like giant stepping stones down to the waters. The outlook was glorious. The rich blue clear sky was becoming an expectation each morning, not a rare surprise. It was costing Harry a pretty penny to rent for the next few months at least, but for them all, it was absolutely worth it.

Rachel was indoors. Unless she was able to get in and out of the pool, she found the outside heat of the day rather unbearable now that it was close to forty degrees in the shade. She loved the outside during the cooler times of the day though. The inside of the villa was remarkably pleasant by contrast. The floors were all cool marble, and there were canopies or veranda roofs over all the windows, denying the piercing dry sunshine the opportunity of baking the interiors to a crisp, and lots of rooms had mysteriously silent large fans gently beating the air, to make it move around and create the illusion of almost cool breezes. She was in the kitchen quizzing Catalina about Spanish meals. She wanted to learn Spanish cuisine because she felt that in this different climate, there were good reasons why they ate different kinds of food. She was also keen not to lazily just import her familiar, stodgy old British culture. Catalina, a local woman, who knew all the best places to buy the best ingredients nearby, and was by all accounts an excellent cook, was being hired on an ad hoc basis for her expertise. For the time being, she was attending once a day, to further Rachel's crash course in Spanish cuisine.

There were several marble patio areas around the pool and villa, some on different levels to the others. They were partially shaded by small olive trees, and the occasional citrus tree which were heavy with small, green, unripe fruits, and the boundaries were now immensely colourful with Hibiscuses in full bloom. Bouganvilias blazed their rich pinks and purples all over the walls. For most of the daytime, one couldn't walk on the stones without some kind of footwear, or the soles of the feet would be scalded. Carrie was sitting under a huge sun canopy on the paved area just outside the rear of the villa. She was nevertheless hot in just a bikini, with a fine layer of perspiration coating most of her body. She was sipping cold wine to try to cool down. Sitting next to her was a lightly wrinkled retired expat, dressed in a very thin, airy, two-piece, who had moved out here a few years previously. She had a tiny chihuahua called Petal on her lap which she caressed unconsciously, always careful to keep her out of the searing sunshine, afraid that it could turn her into a hairy, frazzled crisp rather quickly. Rachel had been doing her best to network with the local expats, and she had met Dr Anglesy at the equivalent of a Women's Institution meeting several days earlier. It became apparent that she had in-depth knowledge of street drugs, having worked at one stage of her life as a consultant to a rehabilitation organisation, and of course, Rachel press-ganged her into visiting their home to subject Carrie to the benefit of her knowledge. Today was her first visit.

After Rachel had hastily shown her around the villa, she quickly stationed her outside with Carrie under the canopy, and after a brief introduction, she hopefully left them to it. Carrie had been warned, and had only agreed to this contact so long as it remained totally informal. Dr Anglesy made pleasant small talk with her to start with. She learned that Sammy was waiting to hear back from an international school in adjacent Malaga, and that Melissa was allegedly busy researching job opportunities in the legal field locally, although Carrie was under the certain impression that she was not trying very hard because she loved just lazing around in the sun, by the pool or at the nearby beach. The pet dog Pluto was still in England with friends awaiting his animal visa before coming over to quarantine. The good doctor discovered that their home in England had been cleared of personal possessions, some of which had travelled with them to Spain, and some of which had been put into storage, and that the home itself was now being rented out under management with a view to properly selling it if they did indeed settle down in sunny Espania. She asked how they were settling in, what was most enjoyable, and what had surprised them about parochial Spanish life. Carrie in particular had found the buzzing sound of the crickets at night strangely relaxing, but the dogs barking annoyed her. She didn't particularly want to have any conversations with anyone about drugs, but she had to do something to allay her parents' fears, and this old lady seemed pleasant enough. Finally, the cordial chat got around to the matter at hand.

"You know, I've found that the best way of demystifying drugs, and maybe robbing them of some of their allure, is to talk about how they work. Carrie, do you know how they work?"

Carrie looked nonplussed. She hadn't realised that this was going to be a knowledge test of some sort. After an awkward moment she stammered.

"I don't think I know what you're getting at."

"Well, why do people take drugs?"

"That's a bit of a huge question isn't it? There must be loads of different reasons."

"Yes, Of course, but I'm not intending to have a counselling session with you Carrie, as such, I just want to talk about the subject in general terms. So, in general, what do people take street drugs for?"

Carrie put on her best puzzled look. She screwed up her face, frowned, and disfigured her mouth.

"To get high?"

"Yes, okay, and what causes that high?"

Carrie really didn't like being put on the spot. She was expecting this lady just to explain the dangers of drugs, implore her to be sensible, and then to quietly go away, duty done.

She pulled her puzzled face again.

"What's in the drugs?"

She raised her tone at the end of her short answer to indicate that she wasn't sure.

"Not really."

Carrie looked disappointed, but Dr Anglesy smiled at her, happy that she had secured her entry point for the following explanation.

"Do you know how the brain passes all of its many messages around the brain?"

"Electrically?"

Again, she was most unsure.

"Yes, but also with chemical messengers. They work in combination. It's a very complicated and intricate process. The human brain is far more complex than the world's biggest computer."

"I'm not sure mine is."

Dr Anglesey laughed.

"Yours too, I can assure you. Well, let me just explain a little of how that all works. The brain is made up of about 100 billion microscopic cells called neurons. They look a bit like hairy tadpoles, the tail as it were, being called the axon, and all the hairy bits are called dendrites. Embedded in the ends of all those hairy branches are cells called synapses. Those are the most important bits."

Rachel quickly appeared from inside.

"Dr Anglesy, can I get you another cold drink please?"

"Please, do call me Marion, and yes, a cola with ice would be lovely, oh, and any chance of some water for Petal please?"

"Of course. You could just throw her into the pool for a while you know?"

Marion frowned.

"Just kidding. I'll get her some water."

Rachel flitted back inside, as Carrie called out after her.

"Mine's a white wine, a large one!"

They both tittered. The doctor continued with her discourse.

"So, all these billions of neurons are suspended in brain goo."

"Is that the technical term?" Carrie joked.

"It'll do. I don't want to blind you with science."

"You already have!"

"No, come on. You can keep up with my idiot's guide to the brain. No offence."

She smiled pleasantly and Carrie smiled back. This was going okay.

"These neurons are not actually connected, even though they are almost touching each other, so how do they pass on their messages from one to the other?"

"Bluetooth?"

Marion laughed. She stopped stroking Petal and used her arms to emphasise movement.

"The electrical part of the process is where a signal is released from the neuron and passes along the axon to the dendrites at the end of it, at 200 miles per hour. Considering that these cells are microscopic, that's virtually instantly. Then when they hit the synapse something very interesting happens."

Carries was actually looking quite interested. Biology had never been her thing at school, yet even at just eighteen years old, she wished that she knew more about how her body worked.

"Go on," she encouraged.

"Well when these electrical impulses reach the end of the line, at the synapses, they cause chemicals to be released into the liquid cavity around the dendrites."

Carrie watched her sisters diving heavily into the pool.

"Like people diving into a swimming pool?"

"Yes, exactly like that, and those chemicals then swim over to neighbouring dendrites, where they make contact with the neighbouring synapses, triggering a fresh wave of electrical signalling in that neuron, and so on and so forth."

"So, what's all this got to do with drugs?"

"I'm getting to that point.

The synapses have a variety of chemicals in them. Each single neuron has between one thousand and ten thousand synapses. That's an awful lot of messaging capability. The chemicals inside the synapses that do the messaging are called neurotransmitters because of what they do, obviously."

"Obviously," Carrie agreed.

"It's fascinating, don't you agree?"

Carrie shrugged her shoulders.

"The whole of the human body is fascinating, I suppose, if you understand what's actually going on inside it, but I'm afraid that I don't know much about it. Sorry."

"Please, no need to apologise. So, getting back to those all-important chemicals squirting out of the synapses. There are numerous neurotransmitters, such as testosterone, oestrogen, adrenaline, endorphins, oxytocin, serotonin and dopamine, and others."

"You're very clever, Doctor."

"It was my work, but I'm sure you've heard of most of those chemicals if not all of them."

At that point Rachel appeared with a small tray containing the cola, a large wine, and a Tupperware pot of water, which she placed close to Marion on the floor. Petal was set down, and lapped appreciatively before settling down in the shade of the table.

"Everything okay?"

"Yes, Mum. Everything's okay. I'm finally learning how my brain works. I'm avidly listening to the good doctor for you."

She rolled her eyes.

"Not for me Carrie, for you!" Rachel remonstrated, before adding, "Great. Well, I'll leave you to it."

With that she waltzed back into the villa and to Catalina.

"I can understand her being worried about you."

Marion smiled affectionately at Carrie, as she lifted her glass of cola to her lips.

"She's wildly overreacting."

"Maybe, but one never knows, for sure. Anyway, back to our neurotransmitters."

"Yes, I have actually heard of most of them."

"Oh I'm sure you have. The point is that when these hormones are released from the synapses, they affect our mood among other things. So, endorphins for instance, help diminish pain while triggering positive feelings. They induce feelings of pleasure or euphoria."

"Yes, I've heard that some people get them from doing loads of exercising. Doesn't work for me."

Marion laughed.

"Yes, I get what you're saying there, but then we're all different in small ways. Incidentally, the word 'endorphin' comes from two words spliced into one: 'endogenous morphine'. Endogenous meaning that it is produced within our own bodies, and morphine as you know, is a very powerful painkiller."

"Oh, that's clever. I like that. Semantics!"

Marion smiled. She was pleased that Carrie was engaging.

"Have you also heard of oxytocin?"

Carries eyes looked up, as if searching for the answer.

"Um, no."

"Well, oxytocin is sometimes known as the 'cuddle hormone' or the 'love hormone', because it is released when people snuggle up or bond socially. Basically, human touch makes the brain release it, and it makes you feel good."

"Ooh. I like the sound of that one. Got any more like that one?"

"Funny you should ask that. Have you heard of serotonin?"

"Don't think so."

"Well, that's the one which is most important in naturally regulating your mood. When your serotonin levels are normal, you feel happier, calmer, more focused, less anxious, and more emotionally stable."

"Sounds great. Can I get it over the counter?"

"No! Well, you can get synthetic versions geared to counter depression, but it has to be very carefully balanced by the body. Too little of it, and you will feel depressed. Too much of it, and it might burn out various parts of the system. You get it from listening to music or other things that make you feel good. And then there's dopamine. This is another pleasure inducing hormone. It mediates pleasure in the brain, and is released during pleasurable situations and stimulates one to seek out the pleasurable activity or occupation. It also affects movement, memory, behaviour, cognition, attention, sleep, mood, and learning."

"Wow! That's a busy one!"

"Yes, indeed. So, why have I explained all these hormones to you?"

Carrie looked embarrassed. She couldn't remember if Marion had already told her.

"I can't remember."

"It's okay, I haven't explained yet. The point is that our brain regulates all these reward hormones very carefully. They must be kept in a fairly precise balance for us to be mentally and emotionally stable. Okay?"

"Yes, I get that."

"Whilst all these hormones are stored in the synapses, we don't feel their benefit. We only feel the effects when they are released by the messaging system, usually as a reward for a certain behaviour, or even to an extent, or from a thought process. The brain even regulates how long they stay floating around being sensed in your brain-goo before they either decay or get reabsorbed into the neurons. Now, when someone takes a street drug like ecstasy, amphetamine, cocaine, flakka, or whatever, what does that do to the brain?"

"I've no idea."

"Well, to my mind, this is the interesting bit. None of these drugs actually add anything to the brain at all. What they actually do is hijack the brain's normal functions by stimulating the synapses to release their hormones more quickly than usual, or in larger doses."

"Isn't that a good thing?"

"Not at all. Yes, admittedly, the brain does get a temporary high, but it's a process of robbing Peter to pay Paul. Hormones like serotonin can't be replenished quickly, so if a stimulant causes the brain to release more than usual, there is a deficit for quite a while, and a deficit means feeling low, lethargic, depressed, anxious, upset or something like that. Another cost to the system is that certain organs get overstimulated by an excess of these hormones, so for instance, repeated use of cocaine, which admittedly provides a massive high temporarily, will eventually cause organs to burn out. You don't meet many old cocaine users. They have heart attacks early in life, or strokes. It all balances out in the end."

Carrie shuddered. Marion's words were impacting her.

"It's all about cost-benefit analysis. Yes, you might have a nice feeling now, but you'll pay later…"

"So, what happened to me?"

"Carrie, I've no idea. Do you know what drug you took?"

"It was supposed to be ecstasy."

"Well judging by what your mother explained happened to you, it might have been an excessive dose of a stimulant which damaged your brain, or it might have been a depressant. Those are drugs which shut you down, like Heroin, Ketamine, GHB or Midazolam, but those are another story. Maybe we'll talk about those another time."

She didn't want to overdo it and tire either herself or Carrie out. She could see that Carrie was at least a little alarmed. She had had the desired effect on her of making her think, and giving her more tools with which to weigh things up accurately. She wrapped up.

"Overall, these hormones all work together as part of the brain's reward system, which kick in after activities such as eating, drinking, sex, and maternal behaviour. They serve us to help channel us into healthy behaviour. We get rewarded for doing things that are good for us. Good for the human race. Think of eating, or orgasms."

Carrie looked at the old lady slightly aghast. She had surprised her. They sat watching the revellers in the pool, whilst finishing their drinks. Marion had one final parting shot.

"Your brain is the most exquisite, carefully balanced organ in your entire body. You really can't afford to abuse it. Mental illness or brain damage is not much fun."

With that, she politely excused herself, and found Rachel in the kitchen, who was smelling various herbs alongside Catalia, who was expounding their benefits

107

in broken English. Rachel broke away immediately, keen to learn how this ad-hoc counselling had transpired.

"How did you get on, do you think?"

"Quite well, I think. I gave her a lesson on the intricacies of the brain, and how wonderfully and fearfully we are made. I think that when one develops some awe and wonder for the complexities of our beings, and how finely tuned we all are, people tend to treat themselves with a bit more respect and a little less indifference or abandon. I've tried to demystify drugs so they don't seem so appealing."

Rachel looked very pleased.

"Oh that's great. Obviously I think that her experience taught her a lot, but a little education never hurt anyone."

Marion answered cheerfully. "Apart from those who were burned at the stake for going against the accepted incorrect norms of the time. Remember William Tyndale? He was burnt at the stake for translating the Greek bible into English so that common English folk could be educated."

Rachel looked at her askance. "I think we've moved on since those days."

Marion didn't look convinced and she only hmmmed before adding, "We don't literally burn them at the stake anymore, but if you go against perceived wisdom, your career might well go up in flames."

Rachel looked at her even more askance and wondered what stories this old lady might have to tell. They agreed to see each other at the next WI meeting, and she politely showed her out, hoping to have her around again soon.

Not long after getting home to recuperate, Pablo had another visit from his police acquaintances. It was now past the middle of June, but it was cool and raining, so he was disappointed that he couldn't have the meeting outside on the patio surrounded by his beautiful pots. He showed the officers into the lodger's lounge instead. D.S. Pageant and D.C. Hurley were attending again, because as they had interviewed him over the assault on Lucinda in the first place, so it made sense for them to be the ones to further the contact with him now. D.S. Pageant looked around the room in admiration.

"He doesn't do things by halves, does he?"

He was taking in with big eyes the plush settees, the huge glass dining table, the large dining chairs designed like thrones, the massive designer smoked glass coffee table, the stylish ornaments, and the garish art hanging on the walls.

"Well, all the rooms in this house are huge, and he loves to fill them with the best things he can get hold of. I don't know where he finds all this stuff. It is so unusual. I suppose it helps that money is no object."

"You're very lucky."

"In some ways, maybe," Pablo answered, gently caressing the lumpy fresh scars on his head.

He indicated for them to sit on the settee, and then politely offered them tea or coffee. They declined, so he turned one of the dining chairs around to face them, and sat down too. DC. Hurley started.

"Pablo, we're very pleased that you've made such a great recovery. We understand that it was touch and go at one point." Pablo smiled broadly. He felt like a champion. He had come through this ordeal well. He wasn't allowed to go back to work yet, or drive, but those measures were purely precautionary to ensure that there were no after effects, as yet unknown.

"Yeah, it seems so, but I have to wait to see if I get any kind of fits now. Apparently, after a blow to the head like that, or any brain injury, epilepsy is a strong possibility afterwards."

As he spoke, he felt inclined to jokingly feign a fit, but decided not to tempt fate. Instead, he caressed the top of his head very gently again. The joins felt lumpy to him, yet his skull had started to mesh back together well, but as he already had no hair on that part of his head, the scarring was always going to be quite obvious, but he was trying not to be self-conscious about it.

"Well let's just hope and pray that nothing like that happens."

Small talk over, the DS got down to his purpose.

"Mr Pilkington, is it okay if we call you Pablo?"

"Please do."

"Great, well, Pablo, we want to know what you remember about the night you were assaulted."

Pablo smiled a little. He didn't want to say anything at all about the events of that evening, although he remembered them as clear as day. "Richard, I'm afraid that I have no recollection."

"Do you remember what you were doing in that locality?"

"I'm afraid not."

DS Pageant looked down at his notebook, rather disappointedly.

"You were found outside a warehouse on the Michaelmarsh Industrial estate. Do you know it?"

"It doesn't ring any bells."

The DS thought for a while, wondering if there was any way of jogging Pablo's memory.

"Oddly, your car was about five or ten minutes' walk away from where you were found. Do you remember parking it that evening?"

"'Fraid not."

"Were you with anyone?"

"I really don't remember anything about it."

"What is your last recollection before the incident?"

"Nothing in particular. I have memories of my work driving the school bus. Of doing stuff on my computer. Of this place and all the stuff I do in the garden. I vividly remember our last interviews about Lucinda, but the next thing I remember is the dreamlike state I was in at the hospital. I don't recall what happened in between."

The officers looked quite dejected. They had been hoping for more. DC Hurley decided that it was her turn to try to prise out a memory.

"Pablo, can you think of any reason why you might have gone to that industrial estate in the first place?"

"No, I've got absolutely no idea."

"Or why you might have parked your car streets away from where you were found?"

"No idea."

Both officers looked rather nonplussed. Rebecca continued searching for clues.

"Do you know who owns that hanger you were found outside?"

"Of course not."

"A few weeks ago, you were very persistent with me trying to discover the identity of the suspect in the Meiying Chan case. Did you find out who that was?"

"Not as far as I can remember."

"Do you know who found you in a pool of blood that night?"

"No idea, but I'd like to find out. I possibly owe him or her my life."

"It was a man called Leonard Hathaway. Does that name ring any bells to you?"

Pablo appeared to be racking his brain for a few moments, then he looked directly at Rebecca as he answered.

"I don't remember ever hearing it before."

Rebecca and Richard looked at each other silently. They all knew that there was something very significant about that name. The officers realised that they were getting nowhere on this occasion, so Richard decided to wrap up for now.

"Pablo, you don't seem able to recollect anything about the assault, and maybe, given the injuries you sustained, that is understandable. If you don't mind, we'll come back in a week or two to see how you are then, and if your memory will have improved, but please, if you remember anything before then, do contact us, okay?"

"Yes, of course. Believe me, I want to see the perpetrator punished much more than you do." With that, he gave them a rather cheeky, knowing smile. He seemed so sincere but also so evasive.

Chapter 11

Lenny was on the phone to Gregory. He spoke briefly in a business-like manner.

"Greg, Harry's moved to Spain, and it just feels like the right time for me to offload. You just need to clear your desk. I don't know who's going to pick things up from me. They might contact you. They might not. It will be lots of different people. I'm not passing you onto anyone. Just make sure things are squeaky clean your end okay?"

Gregory was surprised and not a little alarmed. This was after all most unexpected.

"I always keep a clear desk. No loose ends! You know that."

He tried to sound oh-so composed. Even as he awaited Lenny's next comment, he was already unconsciously biting a nail.

"Okay. I'm just letting you know what's going on. Our business is finished. I'm getting out."

Gregory's brain was racing. What had brought this on so unexpectedly? He verbalised his considerable concern as mildly as he could. "Okay. This is all very sudden. Is there anything else I need to be aware of?"

"No. No problems. It's just personal stuff."

That was it. Nothing cordial, or personal, or particularly informative. Purely minimal business. The call ended prematurely as far as Gregory was concerned, and he was worried. Nothing had been said to reassure him. His initial involvement with Lenny had occurred almost twenty years earlier, when he had effectively blackmailed him for money, in exchange for 'losing' evidence against him, and had been on the take from him in one way or another ever since. He himself was due to retire from the police service in just a year's time, and he had built up a sizeable nest egg using the benefits of his association with Lenny, but now he felt more than just nervous. He sensed something portentous and calamitous. Was that mere anxiety? or was he being spoken to intuitively by a sixth sense? Lenny pulling out of a considerable business empire so flippantly just didn't feel right. Was Lenny going to use this as an opportunity to get revenge on him for blackmailing him all those years earlier? Could he hold a grudge for that long? The setup had always been a mutual trap. Once they had become involved with each other, neither one could afford to expose the other. If one went down, the other would go down too. Yet now, with Lenny distancing himself from his business world, could he confect an opportunity to betray him without sabotaging himself too? He didn't know, but the thought of losing everything at this late stage, after all he had been working towards for the past twenty-five years, terrified him, and he was far too alarmed and cautious to take that chance. His reprobate mind was already spawning a devious plan to safeguard himself. He would outsmart Lenny before Lenny outsmarted him.

Pablo had made it known at the Fighting Cock that he needed a meeting with Lenny, and it wasn't long before he got the call and one was duly arranged. They met at that pub a few evenings later, Lenny rather nervously, Pablo expectantly. Lenny ordered drinks at the bar and showed Pablo to one of the quieter corners of the saloon, where they sat at a table away from other patrons. Pablo noted that some of Lenny's minions were not that far away, and they looked very alert. Lenny opened the conversation.

"Pablo, you can't imagine how happy I am that you're okay."

He spoke with a sincerity that couldn't be faked, and Pablo had no reason to doubt him.

"Thank you. Me too. I just want to know what the fuck happened that night."

"It wasn't me." Lenny looked at him appealingly. He wanted to be believed.

"Lenny, I never thought that it was you. I wouldn't be sitting here having a cosy little chat with you if I thought that, would I? you plonker!"

Lenny chuckled, much more relaxed now.

"No, I suppose not."

Pablo looked at him very seriously.

"But I do want to know what the fuck happened."

Lenny shifted a little on his cushioned seat and took a large gulp of beer, as he considered his response. Then he put the glass down and looked over it, sternly meeting Pablo's gaze.

"Simples really. One of my guys over-reached. He took the initiative and made a bad decision and then followed that up with a big mistake. I pay these guys to do what I ask them to do, not to try to think independently. I'm sorry."

113

"So, what? he waited outside just in case something went wrong?"

"Yes."

"And me emerging alone meant that I must have hurt you."

"Yes."

"And he didn't think to question me first, or to see if you were okay?"

"Pablo, under the circumstances, he was very surprised to see you in one piece. Of course he presumed that something had gone disastrously wrong, and he just reacted. I mean, he shouldn't have even still been there. As you know, I asked them all to leave, but he decided to hang around, and under the circumstances as he saw them, he did the right thing."

"Who was it?"

"I'm not going to give you that Pablo. He acted in good faith, for me."

He stated that answer unswervingly.

"He almost killed me!"

"Pabs me ol' fellah. You walked into a trap which you'd set up for yourself."

He looked at him with disapproval and said piercingly,

"It was your own fucking iron bar, you know? The one you intended for my skull."

Pablo refocussed. He could understand and accept that Lenny wouldn't betray one of his men who had been acting in his best interests after all.

"That bent copper Denis really set me up, didn't he?"

"Of course. You already know this. I know him as Gregory. He uses different names and different phones for different people. He's very cautious. He has to be. I pay him very well to keep me protected, from the authorities, and loose cannons like you."

He smiled cheekily.

"And he got you off the hook with Lucinda?"

"Your Chinese bird?"

"Yes."

"Of course. Not that that sort of thing has ever happened before, but I do pay him handsomely to cover my back with the police, and although I despise him dearly, I have to say that he has always done a good job for me."

Pablo felt displeased and frustrated. He somehow wanted revenge, but at this point in time, he didn't know how, or even who to focus on.

"And do you protect him too?"

"Funnily enough, my relationship with him has finally come to an end, as I am having a change of direction myself."

"So, you're not protecting him?"

"To be honest with you Pablo, right now, I wouldn't even want to use him to wipe dog shit off my shoes, but at the same time, I can't afford to betray him."

Christina was getting excited. Each day, finally, a proper union with Lenny was getting closer. She had made enquiries about taking early retirement, and was weighing up her pension options. Her friends were telling her that she was mad, to sacrifice such a successful career in her early forties, for a man she didn't know she could trust. She had done so well for herself. She must be going completely mad! It was a mid-life crisis! They made all kinds of value judgments about Lenny, of whom they knew virtually nothing, and they were thinking for her in monetary and professional terms only. They had no idea how wealthy he was, and were taking no heed of her need for love, emotional support, and a yearning for really belonging with someone. Christ! They were even presuming that she would never want more children. She wasn't that old!

Her plans now were for her and Monica to simply move in with Lenny as soon as he was free of his illegal drug connections. She could rent her own house out for some extra independent income. More than anything though she just wanted to start a new life with him, the man who perhaps she should have been with all along. They were virtually childhood sweethearts. She was still standing by her principles. She always had, and she always would, but the end of the waiting was edging closer by the day, and she could feel the joy of anticipation beginning to seep through her mature and rather lonely tired bones. It was a wonderful feeling, full of promise, excitement, and fresh joyful expectations. A new start in life! The prospect of fulfilled love was making her feel young again.

Lenny was involved daily in intense discussions with solicitors, accountants and business associates. The first few deals had already been struck, but there were lots of different businesses to deal with, one after the other. There was still a lot of work for him to do. Harry was being kept in the picture by regular phone calls from him, whom he trusted implicitly, and now that he was in Spain, he was just looking forward to getting loads more money in the bank, to secure his family's future there for the rest of their lives, to live worry-free in luxury and sunshine. Things were looking sweet for everyone.

A week later, yet again, D.S. Pageant and D.C. Hurley were ringing the bell of Carlos's mansion. Carlos was in, and he answered the door. He smiled at the officers. He presumed that they were there again to interview Pablo about how he came by his injuries. Pablo had informed him that they would be back to reinterview him, because of his feigned memory failure. Pablo was summoned from his room. It was a beautiful sunny day, and he led the officers around the house to the rear patio. The garden was looking splendid, and he wanted to show it off.

"As it's such a glorious day, I thought you might like to sit out here in the sun, enjoying the ambience."

D.S. Pageant answered, "Thank you. I have to say that the garden is looking impeccable. Do you really look after all of this? It's huge!"

"Yes. Two acres, but don't forget that for me it's my hobby. I love doing it."

"Well, I have to say you've done a fantastic job."

"Thank you. It takes a lot of work, but it is worth it."

As they progressed deeper into the horticultural heaven, D.C. Hurley chipped in.

"These patio pots are looking amazing! How did you get them so colourful?"

"It's mainly the varieties you can get nowadays. They're so sturdy and floriferous. Calibrachoa, Nemesias, Diascias, Lobelias, Fuchsias, Petunias. They're all brilliant. They all flower for ages, and they've only just started."

She chuckled. "If you say so!"

"And I make my own compost, which helps."

She looked at him quizzically.

"How?"

"Horse shit!"

"Nice!" She chuckled.

"Old, well-rotted stuff. Stuff you don't mind getting all over your hands."

"If you say so," she answered with a distinctly distasteful expression on her face.

Pablo offered them both a hot or cold drink, but they declined, as usual. D.S. Pageant started the conversation off.

"So, Pablo, do you have any recollection now of the evening you were assaulted?"

"I'm sorry Richard. That evening is still a complete blank."

116

Pablo smiled politely, a definite crocodile smile. The D.S. looking rather sullen, pushed him.

"Are you sure that there's nothing else that you remember, not even one little thing?"

"Nothing at all. It's a complete blank," he quietly lied.

Richard didn't disguise the obvious disappointment in his face.

"Ok, well, there is another matter we need to discuss with you."

Pablo looked slightly worried. He had no idea what the man might be referring to, and he couldn't help fidgeting a little. He had sensed that their demeanour was rather serious, and Richard furrowed his brow, as if in slight pain, as he stated bluntly and coldly.

"Lenny Hathaway has gone missing."

Apart from disguising his genuine shock, Pablo sat there on the patio thinking that he was not even supposed to know that man, so why were they questioning him about this? He had to deflect.

"And you're telling me this because…?"

"Because I think you might be able to help us."

"How?"

"We can't help thinking that you two are connected in some way that we don't know about."

"Really? Can you explain?"

"Ok Pablo. I'll come clean with you. This all started with your Chinese friend, Meiying Chan being nearly killed by somebody, and we discovered that you were a regular customer of hers, and that Lenny also had a connection with her."

He still didn't feel comfortable revealing that the assault suspect was actually Lenny.

Pablo continued deflecting. "So? Presumably she has lots of customers and contacts."

Even as he said that he was reassuring himself that he was the only customer of hers that she really bonded with. Richard moved on.

"Then after that, you were pressing us to get as much information about the case as you could, in particular, details of our suspect."

"But I was doing that on behalf of Lucinda."

Richard looked at him quizzically. "So you say. Then you were found unconscious outside a warehouse owned by one Leonard Hathaway – Lenny –

and it was actually him who found you shortly after you had been assaulted, and it was him who called an ambulance for you. He probably saved your life, and now he has mysteriously gone missing."

He stared at Pablo as if to ask 'How can you deny knowing him?'

"I have to say, that does all sound very intriguing. Could it be just coincidence?"

"It doesn't feel like it. These things usually aren't."

Richard was certain about his presumptions. Pablo parried.

"How do you know he's gone missing? Sometimes people go off for short breaks on the spur of the moment."

"He has been reported missing by his girlfriend."

"I didn't think that he had a girlfriend."

Pablo had blurted out something without thinking first. He blushed slightly, as the officers looked at each, confirming with a gratified look that they had struck on something. D.C. Hurley took over.

"Pablo, you said that you don't know Mr Hathaway, so how would you know if he has a girlfriend or not?"

Pablo smiled. He had been caught out, and now he had to clumsily backtrack.

"You hadn't mentioned it before."

"So, what makes you think that he didn't have a girlfriend?"

"I don't know. I think I was just a bit confused."

"Pablo, you made that comment convincingly, in an unguarded moment. The more we speak with you, the more we are convinced that there is more to you two than meets the eye. Please, can you help us?"

"No, really, I don't know anything about him, and certainly don't know anything about him going missing. Honestly."

She gave him a contorted look, as his evasiveness actually discomfited her. The officers were both disappointed. The interview got them no further forward at all, apart from their suspicions about a connection between the two men being more or less confirmed. Richard stood up. He looked displeased.

"Pablo, you seem unwilling to help us with our enquiries, so we will go now, but please, do reconsider. Any snippet of information could be key. We are really worried about Lenny. This kind of behaviour is not like him at all. This is really serious. We have reason to believe that his life could be a risk."

Pablo looked guiltily at them briefly, aware that he hadn't tried to help them at all, but then a thought crossed his mind. Why were they so concerned about

Lenny going missing? As far as they were concerned, wasn't he a bad guy? Mr big in a criminal world? The enemy? He couldn't ask, because they didn't know that he knew about him. They were all keeping secrets from each other. He quietly walked them around the back and side of the house to their car. They all felt a bit awkward, so he was glad to see them leave.

Pablo had missed his last session with Cynthia some weeks earlier. She had left messages on his phone, and by email asking him to contact her after he had failed to show up, but she couldn't know that he was in a coma in hospital, unable to speak let alone deal with phone messages. Now he was back at her front door, hoping that she wouldn't make too much of a fuss about his head. He had a comfortable old beanie on. He wore that most of the time now. The beautiful roses around the front door had gone over. A few stragglers looked lovely, but the rest were gradually transitioning into dull, hard, listless rose-hips.

The door opened and the ever-bright cheerful Cynthia expressed her delight to be seeing him again. He hadn't explained on the phone why he had missed his appointment. In the comfort of the welcoming leather sofa, he removed his beanie.

"Oh my God!" she exclaimed. "How did that happen?"

She simply couldn't suppress her mild horror.

"I got assaulted. It was my fault. I ended up in a coma in hospital. I think I'm lucky to be alive."

"Oh my word! Yes, you probably are. That explains why I couldn't get hold of you. How are you now?"

She looked quite alarmed, but was doing her best to disguise her shock at the sight of the pink, stringy-edged, square in his head.

"Yeah fine really. I had to have a craniotomy, but it seems to have healed up really well. The surgeon told me I might develop some type of seizure though, like epilepsy, but nothing's happened so far, thank the good lord!"

"Oh no, let's hope not. How will they find out?"

"They just wait and see if anything develops. It would normally happen within the first few months, so I'm not supposed to be driving for a while."

"I see. So, how did you get here today?"

"I drove."

She suddenly looked a lot less sympathetic, and quickly and resolutely added.

119

"So, you'll be getting a taxi home then?"

That took him by surprise. He didn't expect her to be so strict. He flustered.

"Oh, do you really think so?"

"Yes, of course. Not only would you be putting yourself in danger, you'd be putting other people in danger too, and your insurance would be null and void."

She was most serious. After pondering the subject a little more she quizzed him.

"Why did you drive here?"

"Because I have a car?"

"Yes, but you've been told not to. How does this reflect on your attitude to society as a whole?"

Gaud! He was trying to sink into his chair now. He hadn't anticipated her taking exception to this like she was. She continued.

"If someone turned up here to see me in their car, and they'd clearly been drinking, I'd ask them for the keys. It's the same thing."

"Okay," he responded uncertainly. He didn't see it as the same thing but he wasn't going to argue with her. She was wondering if the blow he'd had to his head had in fact affected his thinking. Was he thinking clearly?

"What other times have you acted in a way that was dangerous to yourself or other people? Is this a pattern of behaviour for you?"

He could think of a lot of recent examples where he had acted in a way that was dangerous for him, but he wasn't going to say anything to her about them.

"Hey, I'm sorry, I didn't think it would matter. I suppose that I really don't think that I'm going to get epilepsy."

"But you don't know that for sure do you?"

"Okay, I take your point. I'm sorry."

"It doesn't matter to me if you're sorry or not, I want to know how much you treat your safety so casually. I'm interested in what this says about you. I mean, do you think that you're above the law?"

She was being very challenging. He took temporary refuge in grabbing his glass of water and sipping. Then, meekly,

"No, not really, but sometimes the law needs a helping hand."

He looked at her cheekily.

"Can you give me an example?"

He wasn't sure if he could trust her, but he felt he ought to give her something, but he tried to be fairly vague.

"Ok, well some time ago, some bloke did my daughter out of a load of money. He shouldn't have gotten away with it, but he did, so I went down and delivered some summary justice to him, and as a result of that, he paid his dues."

He thought that sounded perfectly reasonable, but Cynthia was considering the bigger picture.

"But that's not your job. That's why we have a court system. We don't live in a society where it's simply an eye for an eye. What gives you the right to take revenge?"

Pablo was stumped.

"Because I can?"

"So, if might is right, where does that end? Did you have any understanding of where your victim had come from in his own life's journey? What made him do the things he does?"

"I've no idea, but he was totally out of order."

"But what gives you the right to be judge and jury?"

"I was just protecting my own."

"But what happens if everybody does this kind of thing? It would just be anarchy and anger, anger, anger. In Psychology, we know that anger doesn't achieve anything constructive. Problems only get solved by communication and understanding."

"But is it right that some people just get away with their crimes?"

"That sort of thing might happen all the time, but if you take the law into your own hands, aren't you descending to their level? Is that kind of revenge behaviour not also destructive to you as a person?"

Oh dear. This is not what he wanted to be talking about today, but he was seeking her help, her expertise, and this is where she thought that he needed to examine himself right now, so he had no choice. She continued.

"If a man resorts to violence, doesn't he have to live with those images himself? Is that a good and healthy thing to have to live with? Look at the amount of post-traumatic-stress disorder that ex-soldiers have to deal with."

She looked at him with a look that she had perfected over many years which was a firm but gracious, challenging look. He didn't know what to say. After some silence, she carried on.

"What are you here for? Do you want to become a better person?"

"Of course."

"Only this is not a confessional. If you just want to just carry on beating people up, and then confess your crimes, counselling is not the place for you. You can go and tell a priest."

More silence. He regrouped.

"No, I do want to become a better person. Maybe part of the reason I'm here is that I do realise that my moral stance has become eroded and worn down lately."

He didn't like using euphemisms, but they had their place occasionally.

She waited for more.

"I think that when I initially came to see you, I was concerned about me hurting me, but I have turned that into me hurting other people who deserve to be hurt, instead, because I don't deserve to be hurt."

"Do you feel better about yourself if you are hurting other people?"

"Yes, for a little while. Yes."

"So, it's a temporary satisfaction, like when someone else might go and have a cream cake, or an alcoholic drink?"

"I suppose so."

"So, how does anyone deal with an incident where a loved one is harmed, and the offender is not caught. The act has happened no matter what you try to do afterwards."

"I don't know."

"How do all the millions of people whose loved ones have been hurt deal with it? Do they all go out and shoot someone or beat people up?"

"No, but do they just bottle up their resentment and die of cancer years later?"

"They all deal with it differently. Some go out and start up charities. Some get involved in victim support groups. Others get involved in fund-raising, or new educational programmes. Do you remember that pretty model lady some years back who had acid thrown in her face by a jealous ex-boyfriend. How did she cope with that? She had to have dozens and dozens of operations on her face and body, but she'll be disfigured for the rest of her life."

"That was terrible."

He didn't want to be aligned with the kind of beast who could do such a terrible thing.

"But how did she cope?"

"I don't know."

"She started up a charity to help other people with facial disfigurements. She became a spokesperson. She channelled her energies into something positive, not negative."

Pablo was feeling quite bad now. He had taken the easy, lazy, route.

"If you choose to extract revenge, where does it end? Will you want to get back at someone who served you a coffee that wasn't quite to your liking? How far do you take it? What effect would all this kind of behaviour have on you in ten years' time?"

He looked at her and carefully assessed her reaction to his question.

"Why are we focussing on this so much today?"

"I suppose that I can't work with someone who is hurting other people, or even an animal, or property for that matter."

She was very resolute.

"If you come here and talk about hurting people, no matter what they have done, and I don't challenge you, then it's like I'm in agreement with you, and I can't do that."

He was quiet. She was very principled, but that was a good thing.

"I can't condone that," she confirmed.

He considered that things were different for him now anyway, because of his injury, so he felt he could easily capitulate.

"Well, I can't carry on that way now. I can't afford to take even a small blow to the head. It would easily finish me off, so how can you help me to refocus?"

"Well, we could look at that word 'revenge' and look at what we can replace it with. Maybe gratitude. Gratitude that you didn't die, that you have a second chance at life."

"Yeah, that's a good way of looking at it."

"And with that gratitude for a second chance at life, might you feel like it's an opportunity to do something positive? What might you be able to do?"

Pablo had to think. This was new territory for him.

"I suppose that I could write to my MP, and complain how easy it is for people to get away with fraud."

"Yeah, you could do that. Maybe you could even get into politics yourself to try to make a difference. I Mean, you obviously have a desire to make changes, but you have channelled that noble feeling into violence, which is not very noble."

She laughed, then added.

"Maybe the MP would have some suggestions for useful things that you could do. How do you think you could channel your noble feeling into something actually noble?"

He mused. "I don't know. I suppose that I have taken the easy, lazy route."

She waited quietly whilst that notion sunk in. That was a bit of a light-bulb moment. He didn't like the idea of being lazy. He had always been a conscientious hard worker. Cynthia was feeling that they had covered enough ground, and at this time near the end of the session, she didn't want to delve into the very important notion of whether or not he was lazy. That could wait till next time. He was tired, and flagging. She had been very challenging, and now he felt rather drained. She felt that this was a safe place to finish the session. She summarised the important aspects of what they had covered, and she asked him to make a record of the session when he got home, for himself, to see what he remembered or had learned, and she asked him to email it to her. She didn't particularly need to see his recollection, but by asking him to send it to her would ensure that he would make the record. It made him accountable, and writing things down would help cement the learning in his mind, and it would also make a useful library for the future, when he could look back on the learning. He thanked her genuinely for her time and got up to leave. He wanted to leave. It had been a hard session.

"Aren't you forgetting something?"

He looked at her, puzzled. He was sure that he didn't owe her any money. He said nothing.

"A Taxi?" she added.

It took a moment for her point to sink in. He had forgotten all about her antipathy towards him driving at the moment.

"Oh, yes. Of course."

He sat back down, and got out his phone. He ordered a cab.

"Six and a half minutes," he informed her compliantly.

Chapter 12

The next day, Pablo received a text from Lucinda.

"Back home now. You can come?"

He was elated. He was dying to see her again. Thankfully his evening was free. He checked his watch and texted her straight back.

"Babe, that's great news! I'm so pleased. Can I see you this evening?"

"Yes darling. What time?"

"Is 8 p.m. okay?"

"Yes. C u later."

This was great news. As yet, he hadn't put two and two together. He was too preoccupied thinking about her soft, warm, naked, breasts.

Later, as he entered her abode and was politely directed straight into the massage room, as always, she almost immediately noticed his head injury. He was disappointed about that. He had stupidly hoped it wouldn't be so obvious, but she was horrified. She knew nothing of what had transpired. He assured her that he was fine now, although she remained most concerned. She wanted to know how it had happened, but he said little more than that it had been an unfortunate accident, and that it was nothing to worry about. He got quickly undressed and lay on the bed face down as always, whilst she scurried off briefly into another room to secure his fee. When she returned, he watched her remove her dressing gown. She had bare, thin, smooth legs, and was wearing a short skirt with a bodice style top. Her arms were bare. She never tried to act sexually, but she always looked divine. The anticipation of his forty minutes with her filled him with boyish glee. As she massaged him, she would occasionally run her fingers gently over the scars on his scalp, as if checking it was all in one piece still. He was anticipating so badly the part in the proceedings where she would just dangle her amazing soft, warm breasts over his face and let him play with them. That would make him feel a lot better.

"It okay?" she enquired caringly.

"Yes, babe. It's really not as bad as it looks. It's healing up really well."

He presumed that the officers would have also interviewed her about Lenny's disappearance. As he lay naked beneath her massaging fingers, he asked.

"Hun, Did the police interview you about a man going missing?"

"Yes."

"Were you able to help them?"

"No, of course not."

"Did they say why they were questioning you?"

"I no know."

"Come on babe, they must have said something to you."

"They say Chinese men take man from house. They ask me if I know. I say of course I no know."

"How do they know they were Chinese men?"

"I no know."

Pablo lay pondering. She had given him Lenny's phone number, without having a clue who Lenny he was. She really didn't know anything about him. She hadn't cooperated with the police. She had refused to take part in an identification parade, and they most definitely wouldn't have revealed their suspect's details to her either before or after that. He hadn't either. So, with regard to his tenuous connection to her, how did anyone find out it was Lenny? The police couldn't have released his identity without charging him, which they hadn't. He was genuinely puzzled, but what was interesting was their mention of Chinese men. From all the conversations he'd had with her over the years, he was convinced that all her Chinese friends were in London, and she hardly ever went to see them, and she had none locally. It didn't add up. He questioned her no more, but just lazily lay back intending to just lazily wallow in the rest of the half-hour's bliss. As he lay naked beneath her almost-naked body kneading her gorgeous breasts into his purposefully clean-shaven face, he suddenly had a thought. This was no time to be distracted, but his curiosity got the better of him.

"Babe, how come it's okay for you to be at home now?"

"It okay now," she reassured him.

"Yes, that's great, but how come it's okay now?"

"It okay now," she repeated, with a little more bite in her voice.

As his fingers gently squished and weighed her heavy breasts, he pushed again.

"But how do you know that it's okay now, whereas before, it wasn't safe for you to come home?"

"It okay now," she repeated, yet again.

This was her nature – not to commit to anything, to be simple and unassuming. He thought he might get away with one last question.

"Do you know what happened to the man who attacked you?"

"I no know."

He never got the impression that she had ever lied to him, but he did wonder if this answer was a half-truth.

The next day, Pablo was on the phone to D.C. Hurley.

"Rebecca, you want me to help you with your inquiry about Lenny, right?"

"Of course. Do you know anything?"

"No, but I might be able to help you if you help me." She didn't sound impressed, just disaffected. "Go on."

"I've spoken to Lucinda. She doesn't know anything, you know?"

"Are you trying to be helpful or just a complete pain in the ass as usual?"

He persevered. "She mentioned that Lenny was taken away by Chinese men."

"That is confidential information."

"But if you can give me something to work with, I might be able to help you."

"How?" she asked drily, clearly unconvinced.

"Because I've got Lucinda around my little finger, and I think that somehow, she is the key."

Of course, he was lying about how much influence he had over Lucinda, but Rebecca didn't know that, and she did know that in a very strange way, they were close. There was a pause.

"Do you think you can get anything out of her?"

"I've got a lot more chance than you."

Another pause. This was true.

"What do you want to know?"

"What can you tell me?"

"Okay, but I'm not going to give you any more than has already been leaked to the press. Lenny was taken from his home, probably at gunpoint, by Chinese men, the evening he went missing. His staff were witnesses. They were not harmed at all."

127

She paused for a moment whilst she considered carefully how much she could trust him.

"Actually, I'll tell you one more thing that's not been leaked, so you keep it to yourself, okay?"

"Of course."

"We've got a vehicle reg, and we have intel showing that it's linked to the triads in London, but we can't prove that directly."

He weighed things up for a moment, then.

"Why would they be interested in him? Business or Lucinda?"

"You know I can't give you that kind of information. All I will say is that if they were triads, I don't have much hope for his chances to live a long and happy life. I seriously don't think we're going to see him again."

Pablo thought about this for a moment. "You've implied that he's quite a wealthy man. Has there been a ransom request?"

Rebecca wondered if she should answer that question, but as the answer was simply negative, and she wanted his help if indeed he could actually provide any, she answered curtly, "No."

Another question surfaced in his mind. "So, if you knew all that, why on earth did you question me?"

"You know that it's unprofessional to follow just one lead. We have to explore all possibilities, and given the anomalies about your behaviour lately, we had every reason to suspect that you might know something about it. Anyway, timing had something to do with it as well."

"Didn't the staff report what had just happened?"

"Not initially. They were terrified and had been threatened to stay quiet. The first we heard of it was when his girlfriend contacted us."

"The girlfriend I didn't know about," he answered cheekily.

"Yes, that one."

"And she doesn't know anything?"

"Definitely not. Anyway, stop asking me questions. You see if you can find me some answers! Call me only if you've got something."

With that she rather rudely hung up, leaving Pablo racking his brains even more.

Harry was sitting at the kitchen table in Christina's home. It was a large kitchen-diner, modern, utilitarian, and rather devoid of heart because it was so clean and tidy, like Christina's life normally was. He looked overdressed for indoors, but he had already become somewhat accustomed to the hot Spanish weather. She was strutting around, unable to relax. In between pacing around aimlessly, she was supposed to be making him a cappuccino on her rather plush, glossy coffee machine that had pride of palace on the large, clear, onyx worktop. He was not settled either, but at least he was able to make himself sit still. He had returned from Spain as soon as he had learned of Lenny's disappearance, and having been friends with Christina for as long as he had been friends with Lenny, he took the first convenient opportunity to visit and console her. They too had all been at school together and had remained close ever since. She was still processing. With no answers yet, her mind would cogitate on every possibility that her over-active mind could confect. He tried to get her more grounded.

"I was googling stuff on the plane, Christina. Did you know that a person is reported missing in the UK every ninety seconds?"

She glared at him at his pathetic attempt to placate her with some irrelevant trivia.

"Oh come on Harry. That's mostly over-anxious parents calling the police when their little darling is five minutes late home after school detention."

Harry persevered.

"There are one hundred thousand adults go missing per annum."

"Yes, but for how long? Lenny's been missing for days! And the police have indicated foul play!"

"Come on Chrissy, we don't know that yet."

"He's been fucking kidnapped!"

Harry was surprised at her. He had never in all the years he'd known her, heard her swear. She really was under pressure. Her countenance was a picture of lined, strained, worry. He wanted to placate her as much as possible, but the rumours about the Chinese men had got around to him too, because he had already been to see the firm solicitor and Shivay. She looked at him crossly. Her life, her future, had suddenly inextricably disappeared from sight, and all he could do was spout out pointless, platitudinous statistics.

"I'm sorry Chrissy. I don't mean to be trivial about it. I know something bad has happened. Lenny would never just walk out on everyone, especially right now when we're selling off the businesses."

"Especially now that he's planning a new life with me!"

"Yes, that too, of course."

She grimaced and squeezed her hands so hard that Harry was afraid she might crack a bone.

"Love, it's hard for me to say anything that doesn't sound just like a hackneyed platitude, but really, getting yourself worked up achieves nothing. I love him as much as you do. Maybe things are not as drastic as we are imagining. I've been putting feelers out amongst our business contacts, to see if I can get to the bottom of this, okay? There has to be something we can do, okay? We just need some time."

She didn't look particularly reassured, but she did appreciate the concern he had for her.

"I'm sorry, Harry. I'm just so confused, and upset, and worried. It's just so horrible. If he suddenly shows up now, I'll bloody kill him!"

He stood and took her in his arms.

"Please Chrissy, please just try not to worry so much for the time being, please."

She melted into his arms, and sobbed like a baby.

Pablo was on the phone to his bestie. Whilst he had been off work recuperating he had been in touch with him a lot.

"Now what, Fatboy? Have you nearly killed yourself again?"

Tim laughed. He obviously didn't think anything might be wrong.

"No moosh, I have to be careful now. I am vulnerable. At risk. I have to act like an old man."

"You are an old man!"

More laughter.

"Fatboy, I'm so frustrated. I so want to get revenge on that bastard bent copper who set me up, but I'm no longer the fighting machine I once was."

"And don't you forget it! Your days of pretending to be the equaliser are well and truly over, mate. You're retired, you old bar-steward! Retired and *not* extremely dangerous!"

"Hey, you never came up to visit me!"

"I stayed in touch with Delilah. She kept me informed. She told me you were making a great recovery, and I didn't want to come and just look at your ugly mug when you were unconscious. It's not like I actually like looking at you bro."

He chuckled loudly, then added more seriously.

"I can understand you being mad at that cop though. I can't believe that he tried to get you killed."

"Well, to be fair, he didn't know what they were going to do to me, but he didn't give a toss what might happen, did he? Basically he sold me for thirty pieces of silver, the evil bastard!"

"You might just have to put it down to experience bro, and accept that there's nothing you can do."

"No, I'm not doing that!" he answered resolutely. "He can't just get off scot-free. There must be something I can do; I just haven't worked it out yet."

"Why don't you just dob him in to the cops. You know how seriously they take anything about bent cops."

"It's complicated. I can't do that without dobbing Lenny into the shite at the same time, and I don't want to do that."

"I thought you said he was probably fish food at the bottom of the sea somewhere by now."

"Yeah, probably, but I don't know for sure, and so I don't want to dob him in, just in case I'm wrong, at least, not yet."

"But I thought you wanted to smash him up for what he did to your Chinese bird?"

"Look, Fatboy, keep up. Remember my feelings changed because of what he told me about the drugs and stuff."

"Oh yeah, just before someone smashed your head in instead."

"Yeah."

"And that wasn't his fault either."

"Correct."

Tim laughed. "You know what Fatboy, I sometimes wonder if you live on the same planet as me. You're completely bonkers, as always!"

Then he changed the subject. "Speaking of madness old fellah, have you heard from Hellion lately?"

Pablo answered quietly and sadly, "Nah."

"She doesn't care about you mate. You were on your deathbed."

"Yeah, but how could she have known?"

"Anyone could have told her!"

"Nah, I think that's unlikely. I don't think anyone talks to her about me. Certainly nobody talks to me about her. We don't really have any common friends anymore."

Tim detected his friend's sadness, and pushed the subject no further.

"Ok mate. Well you never know. Maybe one day she will stop hating you."

Lenny rested his bulk into a well-worn black leather sofa. He really wasn't used to just loafing around during the day, watching TV, and he was aggravated by the indolence. He had never been allegedly so entertained during his entire life. The huge flatscreen gave access to Netflix, Apple-TV, terrestrial TV, Sky, and more, but he was overly sated. In fact, he was so bored with being entertained, he had even requested some books to try to read, even though he hadn't tried to read a book since leaving school so many years earlier. One of his guards fetched a bundle of mixed thrillers from a nearby charity shop, and he had managed to get halfway through the first one. He wasn't allowed out of course, and he wasn't allowed contact with anyone, and he felt his blood simmering with annoyance and frustration of it all, but he had to comply. The alternative was unthinkable.

He always had two minders, and they sat to one side of the sofa by the windows. He thought that the net curtains behind them were quite incongruous, but of course they served a purpose. He wasn't allowed near the windows, but the din of people outside, which was only occasionally drowned out by an occasional truck, indicated to him that they were several floors up, and were next to a pedestrianised area. He slept on the same sofa that he sat on all day. The only change of scenery was the regular visit to the bathroom. The lounge was large, but was only furnished rather sparsely. Just essentials. One sofa, a glass coffee table, a wooden dining table and chairs, and the huge TV. The dullness was slightly diminished by the red paper lanterns, the occasional nodding china cat, and a few large rather tired-looking, pot-bound Crassula plants. Pictures on the walls shouted of oriental temples or beautiful azalea gardens. The guards spent most of their time looking at their mobile phones and regularly broke out in cackles of laughter as they exchanged some hilarity on their screens. The watch was changed every three hours, like clockwork. They all conversed in some Chinese language, and they only spoke to Lenny when they felt they had to, or on the rare occasion he asked them something. Their accents were strong, and their English very ungrammatical, which often confused him. These men were of similar ages, in their late thirties to late forties. They all wore the same kind of dark suits with white shirts and dark ties, like it was their uniform. They all looked so similar. Short black hair. The suits. The similar, rather skinny, build. Lenny had begun to distinguish them by small individualities. Only one had a pencil moustache. Another had pock-marked skin. Two of them wore dark-framed glasses. One was considerably taller than the others at nearly six foot, though Lenny reckoned that he himself would weigh what any pair of them did together, but that didn't make them any less menacing. He sensed that they were men of violence. They were soldiers. Armed soldiers.

Apart from the first evening when he had been unceremoniously marched away from his front gates at home at gunpoint, no guns had ever been on show since, but he was in no doubt that each man was armed. He reckoned he could make out tell tale-bulges under the breasts of the jackets, which were never removed, and just occasionally he would hear the unmistakable hefty thud of a dense metallic implement being temporarily placed on the kitchen work surface, or on the bathroom floor when they were out of sight. The guards weren't directly menacing towards him. In a strange way, he felt that he was being treated as a guest, yet at the same time, he just knew that if these men were told to kill him, it would be done in business-like fashion, without hesitation.

During the journey of his abduction, he had the presence of mind to mention his business links with the triads. Unfortunately he himself had never directly contacted anyone in their organisation, but Harry had, and he had only ever mentioned a man called Gideon, so Lenny had dropped that name, with good effect. A silent journey quickly became a noisy garrulous one with phone calls being hastily made and noisy conversations engaged in. Lenny didn't understand a word of Mandarin, but he did perceive that the driver was given hasty new orders, presumably about their destination. By the time they unloaded him from the car it was dark, though with fairly bright street lighting, but they had put dark glasses on him and led him quickly into the building. The glasses weren't just dark, they were completely opaque. Anyone observing them would have presumed him to be a blind man being kindly assisted.

He knew very little about the triads, but as he killed the hours awaiting his fate, he mulled over his extensive knowledge of the cartels of Mexico and South America. There would be similarities, except that where the cartels operated, there was no real law and order. Might was right. Everything else was a sham. Their vast wealth meant that police, army officials, and politicians were routinely bought, but here in England, things were very different, thank God! If he were in Mexico in these circumstances, they would be torturing him right now just for sadistic fun, looking forward to a day or two later when they would be stringing

133

his headless or limbless corpse from a bridge or lamp-post, to remind the natives of their awesome, terrible, untouchable power. There, cartels made their violence clear and menacing, but here, in quaint old England, organised crime tried to keep a low profile. The British police were efficient and well resourced, and there was very little corruption. Venal officers like Denis were few and far between. As Lenny well knew himself, successful evasion of the law was secured largely by keeping a low profile and trying to stay under the radar. However, he didn't feel that much safer, simply knowing that if he were to 'disappear', it would occur as surreptitiously as possible, with bits of him disappearing without trace. These people would be just as ruthless, just a lot less bloody and much more secretive.

They were bringing him takeaway food, which he wasn't used to. His guts were bad, and his frequent visits to the toilet evoked much merriment from the guards. He was wearing clothes which they had brought for him, and they were ill-fitting. They had given him an electric shaver to use, but his habit had always been to have a wet shave. Electric razors seemed dusty and dirty to him. Even though his very life was in the balance, these minor discomforts nevertheless irked him. There was a knock on the door and a brief exchange of Chinese. After admitting three new guests the two guards quickly sunk back into the depths of the room by the window, where they stood like statues, having first placed three chairs in front of the TV, which they turned off.

Lenny felt it appropriate to stand, out of respect, but as he had been sitting for so long, his legs failed to activate efficiently, and he fell back onto the sofa rather embarrassed, as he hastily made a second attempt. He was stopped. The man in the middle of the three put his hand out as a sign for him to stop.

"Please, you may remain seated."

Lenny felt like the man was being polite, yet the way he gave the invitation had an air of authority which made it sound like more of an instruction. He thanked him, and sunk back into the copious sofa, wondering why he was thanking him. The visitors sat opposite him. There were no introductions, but as the proceedings went on, he wondered if this man was actually Gideon. He was going to think of him as Gideon anyway.

"You were going to pay for your attack on one of our family."

Gideon looked at him with an air of indifference. He was only a small man, but he carried an air of intimidation. Somehow his tight skinny features delivered a message of threat, and malice. Maybe it was the cold fierce eyes or the tight rigid lips.

Lenny was immediately embarrassed and ashamed. The accusation was not an easy one to answer.

"I am sorry. It was an accident."

Gideon looked angry.

"It was not an accident!"

Lenny backtracked.

"Okay, it wasn't exactly an accident, but I had made the mistake of taking some crazy drug, and I didn't know what I was doing."

Lenny was not in the habit of creeping. This was the best he was going to do. He looked at Gideon silently, impassively.

Gideon was not in the mood for excuses. His face and voice turned harsh.

"We were going to give you the ultimate punishment, but you are a business associate of many years. There is some honour in that, but you will pay a heavy price for your freedom."

Lenny was relieved and curious. "Which is?"

"Not so fast one with the round eyes and round belly."

His colleagues tittered. He gave a very wry smile.

"I am concerned about the man who betrayed you."

"Gregory?"

"I do not know his name, but he betrayed you to us. I am afraid that if you live, he will try to betray me, too."

"How could he do that?"

"I don't know. You tell me."

Lenny was a little bewildered. He hadn't expected the conversation to go into territory about Gregory.

"What do you mean?"

"He has betrayed you!"

He spat this out with utter contempt.

"Is he a threat to your business? and my organisation?"

Lenny mulled this over, then quietly.

"I really don't know. I don't know what he is capable of. I am shocked that he turned me over to you."

Gideon didn't look happy. He didn't want uncertainty.

"You will pay us one million pounds for us to overlook your indiscretion. For you that is small fry, but you will also give me this man, Gregory."

With that, he stood up to go. His colleagues stood up silently alongside him. Lenny was shocked by the imperious order. He too stood up, but by the time he was on his feet, Gideon was already by the door.

"Wait, how can I do that here, all locked up?"

Gideon turned to face him.

"You will be allowed to make a phone call."

One of the bowing guards opened the door for him, and he strode out, without any niceties, or helpful explanations, quickly followed by his cronies. Lenny stood there, mouth agape, wondering how on earth he was to comply with such a crazy order.

Chapter 13

Denis sat nervously at the same table in the same department store in which he had originally met Pablo. He looked around curiously. Clearly everyone around him were genuine shoppers, stopping for refreshments; young mothers with toddlers. Old ladies temporarily taking a break from carrying shopping bags or pushing old-lady trollies around. The occasional middle-aged couple. Some were just having coffees. Some were indulging in tasty-looking lunches. He reckoned that he could spot another copper at two hundred paces, and he was sure that there were none around. There was a general hubbub of contorted conversations and a sense only of normality. This could be some kind of set up, of course, but that was a chance he had to take. Not meeting Pablo as he demanded could be disastrous. At least by meeting him he had a chance to impact events and to properly gauge whatever challenge Pablo was going to bring him. He sat nervously, looking around rather skittishly, and paying no attention to the two cappuccinos he had just bought.

Pablo breezed in and sat down without invitation or greeting. He was wearing a large floppy hat, and was wearing a face mask. Clearly he didn't want to be identified. There was nothing unusual about wearing a mask, even in a restaurant. Lots of people still wore face masks all the time. The most catastrophised even replaced their masks between mouthfuls of food. They were quite mad, of course, but the mask had attained mystical powers for them and were attributed to possessing astonishing magic for warding off all kinds of nasty viruses and bacteria, and the vast majority of the population had descended into vague superstition. People repeated the official mantra that they were 'following the science' but they had become ignorant creatures of mere superstition. Any brief moments unshielded by the germ-ridden mask were moments of unguarded exposure to possible death. Denis fondled the rabbit's foot in his pocket.

Pablo was carrying a dark canvas holdall, with a light jumper carefully folded and placed across the top of it. He placed it on his lap, not on the floor. Denis looked at him inquisitively.

"What's this all about, Pablo?" he queried innocently.

Pablo was stern. He placed one hand under the jumper and stated authoritatively. "This is all about you coming with me!"

He nuzzled something in his bag so that Denis could clearly see part of it. Denis was staring at a gun barrel, and his mouth dropped open in sheer horror. His mind was racing. Could Pablo possibly just gun him down in cold blood? He had to decide, but he wasn't too keen on making the wrong choice. Pablo interrupted his mental deliberations and helped him to make his mind up.

"Stand up fucker! Let's go."

Pablo stood up first. His countenance was deadly serious. Denis was rapidly coming down on the side of yes, Pablo could shoot him in cold blood!

"Okay. Keep your hair on. Where are we going?"

"Maybe we are going to hell!" Pablo replied menacingly.

Denis got up and walked in front of him.

"Make your way downstairs to the entrance. Use the escalator."

Pablo walked a few paces behind him to minimise the chance of Denis trying to grab the gun. Denis turned half towards him and started the pleading.

"Look, I think you've got the wrong end of the stick mate. We need to sit down quietly, rationally, and talk this through."

"Just keep walking fucker, and keep your mouth shut. If you turn around again I'll take your kneecaps out!"

Denis walked rigidly ahead. He had never felt so attached to his kneecaps. Nobody seemed to be taking any notice of them, or were reacting to anything unusual about the purposefulness of their movements. Generally speaking, people were in a world of their own, contemplating their intended purchases, or going through a mental list of places yet to visit, or maybe just wondering if they could go another minute before checking their mobile phone. Pablo and Denis went down the escalator. Denis felt like looking back a couple of times, probably to check if the gun was pointing at him, but thought better of it. They walked in silence towards the front entrance.

"Pablo?"

The voice froze him. He looked towards the source and was shocked to see Hellion standing there looking at him most quizzically. She was wearing a light summer blouse, with a pale blue skirt, a summer hat, and was holding a large paper carrier bag. She looked exquisite but slightly different. He wasn't sure why, but he had last seen her two years ago, and something facially must have altered ever so slightly. His heart was already beating fast. Now it skipped a beat or two. She sensed that something very strange was occurring. Again, she asked, "Pablo?"

She wasn't sure. He had a face mask on, and a floppy hat. Of all the times! He had been so hoping to bump into her and find the opportunity to chat over the past five years, but not here, not now. The last thing he wanted was for anyone to recognise him. His eyes stared at her fiercely. He couldn't stop. He absolutely couldn't stop for any conversation at all. The last thing he wanted to do was to confirm to her that it was indeed him, so he said nothing and soldiered on. She just stared at him agog as he marched unfalteringly forwards.

"Who was that?" Denis queried.

"Shut up you fucker and keep moving."

They exited the building, and Pablo's mind was racing. He glanced back. Thank God Hellion hadn't followed him out. Would it make any difference that Hellion had seen him with Denis? He couldn't know. He would stick to the plan.

Nearby, a scruffy white Transit van was lingering by the kerbside on a single yellow line. It was an old model that lacked a side door. Pablo indicated the van.

"Get into that van."

"What, the back?"

"Yes, of course the back, tosser!"

The back door was unlocked.

"Open it and get in, rapido!"

Denis did so, and Pablo followed him in, discarding the holdall, and holding the gun in both hands, pointing directly at Denis's head.

"Lay down!"

"Mate, is this really all necessary? It's a bit Pinewood studios, isn't it?"

His voice was squeaky and nervous.

"Lay the fuck down," Pablo repeated, very sternly.

Denis lay down. The driver had come around to the back of the van, and he entered too, shutting the door behind him. As Pablo kept the gun focussed on Denis's head, the driver put plastic ties on Denis's wrists and legs. It took him several minutes as he was inexperienced at this sort of thing, and he was himself very nervous, and the light inside the back of the van came only from a pale-yellow light on one side, and was rather inadequate.

Denis queried nervously of the man he couldn't see. "Who are you?"

Pablo pressed the gun to his head. "What part of 'shut the fuck up!' don't you understand exactly?" he hissed quietly.

The man was Harry, but he made no reply to Denis, who asked no further questions. He was then gagged, and Harry returned to the driver's cab, whilst Pablo remained in the back, sitting on the floor.

"Let's go!" he shouted out nervously, and the engine raced as the old van lurched forwards into the traffic.

Later that day Christina was on the phone to Rachel in Spain.

"I was on the phone to him this morning. He seemed distracted. I got the feeling that he had discovered something but he wasn't telling me. Has he spoken to you Rachel?"

"No. I was just ringing you to see how you are coping. I couldn't get hold of him earlier, which is unlike him. If he's in a meeting or something he usually calls me back within the hour, but I haven't heard from him all day and it's nearly supper time."

Her voice brightened. "Maybe he has found out something, and has gone off to investigate or something, before he mentions it. You know, he doesn't want to raise our hopes maybe, in case it's a dead end or something like that."

"Oh Rachel. I'm just so worried. It's horrible just not knowing what has happened to someone you love."

She started crying again.

"I'm so sorry Christina. It must be so horrible for you. We all feel so helpless. I wish I could be there with you too, but you'll just have to make do with Harry for the time being."

She was trying to lighten the situation, but Christina was so deep in despair, she registered nothing slightly humorous. The doorbell rang. Christina jumped, and raced to the door.

"Rachel, It's Harry. I'll call you back."

With that, she unceremoniously dumped the phone and opened the door. Harry stood there smiling broadly, and she instinctively embraced him very tightly. This looked like it was going to be good news.

The next day, Pablo was at home feeling enormously nervous. He had hardly slept a wink due to anxiety. He was at home trying to focus on his internet trading, but his mind simply wouldn't focus. He was counting the cost of getting drawn into very serious criminal activity. His mind was dwelling on the fact that he could very well spend the rest of his life in prison. Nothing had actually gone wrong yesterday, but now there would now be an extremely thorough investigation. A police officer had gone missing, whilst on duty. That would be taken very seriously indeed. CCTV would be searched all around town. Before long Denis's car would be found, having overstayed its parking time somewhere, and that would narrow down the focus of attention. Pablo couldn't be linked to the van. That had been supplied by the Triad, and was said to be untraceable. The gun too had gone back to the Triad, but he might nevertheless be on CCTV. Given the amount of CCTV cameras everywhere these days, he was almost certain that footage would be found of him leading Denis out into the van. He could only hope that he was disguised enough not to be identified. Except for Hellion of course. Could she identify him? He kept trying to reassure himself that if the finger of suspicion ended up pointing at him, they would have no real proof, but he was simultaneously wondering what life in prison might be like.

His mobile rang. He didn't recognise the number, and wanted to ignore it, but then he would worry about who it was, so he gingerly answered it.

"Yes?"

"What were you doing yesterday?"

He was shocked to hear from Hellion. She hadn't phoned him for well over five years.

"Lovely to hear from you, darling. How long has it been? A day or two? A week? Five years?"

She bluntly maintained her focus.

"What were you doing in that department store yesterday?"

"Shopping?"

"You looked terrified."

"That's because I thought I might bump into you."

She ignored that remark, and he slumped in his chair. He realised that he had just admitted that it was him that she had seen, and he hadn't meant to do that.

"Who was that man you were with?"

141

"Hellion, why are you asking these questions? You walked out of my life five years ago, and now all of a sudden you want to know how I do my shopping?"

"I've never seen you like that, and I want to know what was happening."

He wondered why it was of such interest to her. She really had just spent years ignoring and avoiding him to her heart's content, and just when he wanted to be completely below the radar she turns up like a bad omen.

"Hellion, I don't get why you're interested, or what you're after."

There was a knock on his bedroom door. He looked up, surprised. Now what? "Yes?"

Carlos opened the door.

"Pablo, those officers are here to see you again."

Carlos carried that mildly curious expression on his face every time the officers showed up. Pablo nearly wet himself. His anxiety surged through him and made something close to his bladder quiver. He really felt like he might lose control of it. He couldn't think of what to say. He really didn't want to see them, but he didn't think he could ask Carlos to pretend that he wasn't at home. He just wanted to run away, or maybe just die.

"Did they say what they want this time?"

"No, but they look pretty serious."

He sat there quietly catastrophising. Carlos broke his distraction.

"Aren't you going to come down and see them?"

"Yeah, okay."

As he stood up he realised that he still had his phone in his hand and he could faintly hear Hellion talking on it. Gaud! He should have turned it off when Carlos came to the door. Now what would she be thinking? He turned it off now and flung it on the bed, and followed Carlos reluctantly down the long corridor, and eventually down the stairs to the front door. Carlos had left them outside. That was unusual. Did he instinctively know that they would be carting him off? Pablo stood in the threshold looking down the stone steps rather imperiously. As usual, it was D.S. Pageant and D.C. Hurley looking up at him inquisitively. Pablo tried to sound confident.

"Yes? What can I do for you this time, officers?"

"Pablo, can we come in and have a little chat please?" Richard enquired in a fairly friendly manner.

Pablo noticed that they weren't arresting him. That was a great relief. "Okay, come in."

He led them into the tenants' lounge, where they all sat on sofas. Pablo waited. He didn't even offer them a drink on this occasion. He just wanted to get on and face the music.

Richard explained. "Pablo, as you know we are dealing with matters relating to your friend Lucinda and a Mr Hathaway who as you know went missing recently."

"Yes."

"Well, early yesterday evening, Mr Hathaway mysteriously turned up back at his home, after several days away, in one piece strangely enough, and we wondered if you knew anything about it?"

"I'm pleased that he has turned up safe and well, of course, not that I know him or anything like that, but I am wondering why you are telling me this."

Rebecca piped up. "Come on Pablo. You're an ex-cop. You should be helping us."

"Whoa, you can't play that card with me. The job well and truly shat on me from a great height. I owe them absolutely nothing."

She looked disappointed that that tack failed so completely. Pablo continued.

"If anything, I should be well and truly anti-police." He paused to let that sink in. Then he continued. "But you may have noticed that I have in fact been very cooperative with you. Surely you've spoken to Lenny already?"

Richard picked up.

"Yes, we have Pablo, but he declined to give us any information."

"So, does it matter then?"

"Does what matter?"

"Whatever happened to him. If he doesn't want to talk about it, that's his choice isn't it?"

"Yes, of course."

"So, why are you talking to me?"

They both looked a bit uncomfortable. They were only fishing, and that was not a strong position for them to be in.

"Well, you already know that we suspect you to have a connection with him, and we thought you might be willing to help us."

"I really can't see what you think I might bring to the party, or what you're trying to achieve, or even why I might want to help you."

Their discomfort grew, visibly. "There are other very serious matters which might be related to this scenario, which we can't reveal to you, but it does mean that we do have a legitimate interest in anything you know about Lenny."

Pablo's mind wandered back to a few days earlier when he had got a call from a man he didn't even know, called Harry, who explained that he was a very close friend and business partner of Lenny's, and that Lenny was being held hostage by Chinese Triads at an unknown location, and that Lenny had been allowed one phone call to him to arrange the ransom, which would be a large sum of money, which Harry could easily arrange, and one bent police officer to be handed over to the Triads in exchange, which would not be easy to arrange at all. A life for a life as it were. His chest was still tight from the echoes of the anxiety he felt when Harry first described that Lenny believed that the best bet to lure Denis into some kind of trap was to use Pablo, hoping that he would want to exact vengeance on that man enough to help him, Lenny, out of his dire predicament. Pablo could still feel the complete weirdness he felt as he realised that he was bizarrely drawn into a pithy, film-like, real-life drama, as if he had no real choice. It was like he had to suddenly transcend everything that had been normality for all of his life. Strangely enough, it was only the fact that it sounded like Lenny would be killed if he didn't help, that really motivated him to participate. He couldn't hate any man enough to want to see him seriously harmed, but he would far sooner see misfortune happen to an evil, conniving, duplicitous, rotten, venal creep like Denis, and not Lenny, whom he actually quite liked. It had felt like such – bizarre and surreal state for him to find himself in – to be involved in deciding which man might live or die. He wondered if he could live with himself if he didn't help Lenny in his hour of need. He also wondered if he could live with himself if he assisted in the possible death of another man, even a man he had every reason to hate.

He focussed on the present again. "I'm sorry officers. I really don't think that I can help you."

Chapter 14

Pablo was still not sleeping well. His mind was alive day and night with thoughts of his treachery coming to light. He simply couldn't relax. He scoured the local news regularly each day. There were pictures of Denis walking out of the store with a suspicious-looking man walking directly behind him. There were appeals for witnesses to come forward. Did anyone recognise this mysterious man who seemed to be walking so closely behind Denis? Did anyone have any knowledge about the white van? There were pictures of that too, and it was using false plates. He had no idea how the investigation was going but they would have found Denis's abandoned car fairly quickly, and would be trying to piece together the few clues they did have. Fortunately for him, but he didn't know this, Denis had been a very private man, and the more his colleagues looked into his life, the more baffled they became. Pablo speculated constantly that the net would surely tighten in on him. He actually wanted to talk to Lenny for reassurance, but he didn't dare to phone him. Either one of their phones might be tapped. There was nowhere he could turn. He had to tough this waiting game out alone, try to learn to tune out the anxieties and literally hope for the best.

Just a few days after D.S. Pageant and D.C. Hurley had visited his home to ask about Lenny, he received another visit. Unusually he was the only one at home, so he answered the door himself. The door opened onto four stone steps which led down to the gravel driveway, meaning that the occupant stood at least eighteen inches higher than the visitor. This time it wasn't the officers. He stood on the top step looking down at Hellion. He couldn't believe his eyes. She was so tiny down there, but her presence was huge. She wore a serious demanding look on her face. "We didn't finish our conversation the other day."

He couldn't believe that she had the audacity just to turn up on his doorstep just like this, after ignoring him for so long.

"And?"

"I want to know why the police were here to see you?" He was exasperated. "Hellion, it's got nothing to do with you. Lots of things have happened over the past five years and you have chosen to be absolutely absent and uninvolved, so what on earth are you doing here?" He wondered if she had made some accurate deductions about the missing police officer. Had she seen the pictures in the press? Would she want to turn him in? or blackmail him? He had no idea, but he did know that she could be very vindictive, and that scared him. She scared him.

"Can I come in?"

Anytime over the past five years he would have loved for her to turn up and ask this, but not now. Not after the events of the past week.

"I don't think that's a good idea."

She looked at him fiercely. "So, you're not going to tell me what's going on."

"There's nothing going on."

"You're lying."

"And you're not welcome here. Please, just fuck off!"

With that he withdrew and shut the door. He rushed upstairs and looked out of the unoccupied spare bedroom window to see if indeed she would go. Her car was parked in the middle of the driveway. He watched her march defiantly to her car, get in with a glancing look of daggers towards the house, and drive away. One thing was for sure. She was still rich with attitude. Now he was even more nervous. He wasn't sure that he'd done the right thing, but he couldn't allow himself to get drawn into a discussion, yet the last thing he needed was her as his enemy.

It was clear to his colleagues that Denis, real name Orlando Sorrentino, who lived alone, had disappeared without having planned to. An inspection of his home revealed that everything appeared to have been left in place for later. A frozen meal had been left out to defrost on the sink. A nearly full two-pint bottle of milk was in the fridge, alongside fresh vegetables. The fruit bowl on the table was nearly full. There was no evidence of any clothes having been removed from the wardrobe or drawers. They were all reasonably full. Wet clean clothes were still in the washing machine. Some dirty clothes half-filled the dirty laundry basket. An empty set of suitcases were still packed away on top of a wardrobe. The set was complete. A shoe rack in the hallway was completely full. There was post just inside the front door on the floor. His computer had been left in sleep mode.

Door to door enquiries were made of all his neighbours, to discover if anyone had seen anything suspicious, or if he had mentioned anything to any of them. It became apparent that only his next-door neighbours ever spoke to him or vaguely knew anything about him. One was a sprightly retired solicitor called Herman Springer who had been there for many years, and on the other side were a young family, who hardly knew him. They hadn't been there that long. Enquiries were made of family, of whom there were very few, and other contacts, all to no avail. On the day of his disappearance, he missed two work appointments during that afternoon. He had said nothing to any of his colleagues about where he was going, or who he might be seeing. It was a quandary.

A couple of officers were assigned to go through all the cases he had been involved with over recent years to see if anything looked suspicious or useful to the investigations. He had been involved in several murder cases, lots of serious assaults, some fraud cases, and many more minor cases, but he had always been just one of the team, never playing a major role or attracting any particular interest. Nothing stood out. As a long shot the senior Investigating Officer, Detective Chief Inspector Denzil Higginsbotham, had applied to the courts for permission to access his bank accounts. That proved to open a pandora's box of several mysterious accounts, some offshore, with funds totalling far more than would be expected for a mere police officer to accrue. This made Denis even more of an enigma. The source of the funds were unknown as apart from his wages, they were all cash deposits made intermittently over all the years they went looking back through. The rumours soon started circulating that he was a bent cop, but no evidence was forthcoming. Maybe he was a gifted gambler, but there was no evidence to show that he gambled on the horses or in casinos. No legitimate sources for his extra income were established and the rumours persisted.

The lead officer DCI Higginsbotham was a burly middle-aged man of mixed race. His nickname was Stavros because he closely resembled Kojak's sidekick from the popular eponymous police series of the seventies. He was a very astute man and placed a lot of importance on intuition. He claimed that with the sheer volume of cases that police had to deal with these days, intuition played a vital role in honing in on the most promising leads to get things done efficiently. Time wasted was time not available for other precious enquiries. Time was always of the essence and had to be used as efficiently as possible. He had been granted a reasonably large team to carry out the kidnap investigation, and it included DS Pageant and DC Hurley because of their prior association with people whom Higginsbotham considered to be of interest in this inquiry. He took Pageant to one side.

"Richard, kidnappings in this country are virtually unheard of. It's not like South America, where if you have a few bob in the bank and you don't live in a guarded, gated community you *will* be kidnapped for a ransom. Now we've had two in about a week. Here in sleepy, semi-rural, not-South America England. There has to be a connection or I'll eat my hat."

"Yes, I agree, sir."

"I want you to bring this Hathaway fellah in and I want to interview him myself. Let me know when he's here."

Richard was a little hesitant. "Sir, do you think we've got enough to actually arrest him?"

The boss looked a little surprised. "Earlier in the year we had him for attempted murder right?"

"Yes, until the evidence went missing."

"And how do you think that evidence went missing?"

Richard was reluctant to answer. He hesitated.

"Come on Richard. Where did it go?"

"Someone took it."

"Obviously, but who?"

"We don't know."

"Richard, don't be obtuse with me. It was some copper. An inside job. Some bent fucking copper, and who do you think that might have been?"

Richard was still being guarded. "We don't know for sure sir."

"Richard, stop being a prat. We've just found a large stash of money in offshore accounts for one DC Orlando Sorrentino. Hathaway is a very wealthy businessman who we know is bent, and someone inside got him off the hook, here, right under our noses."

"Yes, sir, but isn't that all rather circumstantial at this stage?"

"Technically, yes, I grant you that, but do you think this Hathaway chump is going to relish us reopening the Chinese bird case?"

"I doubt it."

"Well then, he'd better not make too much of a fuss then, eh? Bring him in and let's see what we can turn over."

Pablo wasn't sure that he wanted to have another session with Cynthia, but really, anything to distract him from his predicament was welcome. He wasn't even sure that she could help him because there was little he felt that he could disclose to her about recent events. He could hardly admit to her that he had kidnapped a police officer, but he decided to see her anyway. She might have some good advice for anxiety, which was a new experience for him. Of course he took a cab to her place. He didn't want to get into trouble with her before he had even set foot inside the house. As always she warmly invited him in, and as she led him into the counselling room and the hot seat, she was perceptive enough to notice his discomfort. She didn't mention it, but she picked up that he looked very tired and worried. She herself was her normal bright and bubbly self.

"And how are you today, Pablo?"

"Not too bad, thank you."

"How's the head? Dare I ask?"

She wondered if his rather sullen countenance was because he had indeed started to suffer fits.

"Yeah, doing okay."

"Any fits?" she risked asking.

"No, thank God. I've been lucky, and the longer I go without one, the more likely I am not going to develop any."

"Oh that's great news."

She was really relieved for him and smiled happily. She wondered what it was then that was bothering him. The way she worked was not for her to have an agenda left over from the last session. Yes, there were topics which had raised their head for future discussion, but right now she would be exploring whatever was on Pablo's mind at this time. So, she invited him to divulge.

"Pablo, is there anything in particular you want to talk about today?"

He sat uncomfortably. He didn't know where to begin, so he started in broad terms.

"You know when you go on a work assessment of some sort where they put you in a group discussion where you all have to discuss a moral dilemma. You know, you're given a plane with six passengers in it, and one pilot, and the plane is about to run out of fuel at fifty thousand feet up, and there are only six

149

parachutes. You're given broad details about each person, and of course they're all very different. Age-wise, job-wise, ethically, family-wise etcetera, and you have to discuss the merits of why you would select the six that you do, and why the seventh person is the best choice to leave to his or her fate."

She smiled. "Yes, I think we've all had to do a few of those in our time."

"Well, something like that has happened to me in real life. I didn't choose to get involved or to be so crucial in the decision making. I had the moral dilemma thrust upon me. I had to choose between two people, as to which one might come to some harm, and which one might not."

As he spoke, his face was a mixture of alarm and confusion.

"Cynthia, I didn't choose to be put in this position, but it *was* my fault. It was other things coming home to roost. I had no idea what chain of events I had unwittingly started."

He looked at her appealingly. He wanted her to talk to him and not shut him down because he had maybe been involved in another crime.

"Do you feel like things have gotten out of control?"

"Definitely. And to be honest with you, I'm terrified of the possible consequences."

She looked very thoughtful.

"Are you willing to take responsibility for whatever it is that you've done?"

He hesitated. "Yes, I suppose so."

"And are you willing to make amends?" He didn't think that there was going to be much he could do to make amends with Denis, but he meekly answered 'yes' anyway.

"The trouble is Cynthia, that something bad has happened and I don't think that given your ethics, I am going to be free to disclose anything to you."

She pondered that carefully and before commenting. "When you start to keep secrets, that's when things start to eat you up. Voicing your truth on the other hand is the way to recovery. If someone has been hurt, someone has to take responsibility. If you can't reveal your truth to me, is there someone else that you can? The police for instance?"

He shrank in his chair. The last people on earth he wanted to be honest with were the police. He didn't want to go to prison. He obfuscated.

"Funnily enough, I have had a few chats with the police lately, not necessarily because I've done bad things, but because I've been on the periphery of a few incidents, and I actually have built up a bit of rapport with one office in particular, but I don't think I can talk to her just yet."

She thought of a different approach. "Is this incident which you were forced to make a moral dilemma decision on over now?"

"Yes, I think you could say that."

"And can you own what has happened and make restitution with the person who was hurt?"

He answered sheepishly. "No, I don't think so."

"Does that person have family members who are hurting? Could you help them understand what has happened. Could you give them answers and help them get closure and move on?"

"I don't know if this person has any family, but I know he has work colleagues."

"Well, maybe they are hurting and you could give them the answers they need. You need to be looking at ways of mending and healing in the situation."

He was frustrated. "It's so complex. It's like a seesaw. On the one side I've done good, but on the other side I've done bad. It wasn't my choice to get dragged into this. It was just an unfortunate consequence of other things I've done."

She continued purposefully. "Secrets get bigger and bigger. They have their own dialogue and they eat up inside of you. Any sharing of a secret is a release, and that release enables a person to move forward. I would encourage you to talk to that person concerned, to talk to his family and his work colleagues."

She looked at him expectantly. Inside though, he was squirming. He knew that he couldn't talk to Denis, and if he talked to anyone else, he would get himself into a lot of trouble.

"If I didn't feel ready to talk to anyone right now, do you think it could be a good idea to write stuff down for sharing at a later date?"

"That would be a good start, but what about people now who don't know what's happened. People who want answers now? Not having answers is so painful for people."

She really emphasised the 'so painful' part. "We need to be looking for growth in the situation. We know that psychologically, secrets hurt. If we want generational growth, we need to make hard decisions now."

Pablo sat there looking guilty. He was more concerned about protecting himself now and in the future. "To be honest with you Cynthia, if I was to be upfront with someone about my responsibility in something like this, I'd be afraid of the consequences."

"But that's cowardly."

That was very direct and she waited for his reaction. He just looked at her lamely. She carried on.

"Fear and harbouring secrets are destructive. The moral thing to do would be to be honest and to take responsibility. That would be better than just hiding under a rock for the rest of your life, whatever the consequences might be, wouldn't it?"

"What if the consequences were going to prison though?"

"That would be worth it."

That surprised him. "Because?"

"Because you would be taking back charge of your life. You would be taking responsibility and a path of forgiveness. You wouldn't be taking that bad action again. It would be drawing a line in the sand stating that you are not going to do this sort of thing again."

As usual she was being very challenging, but he looked at her unconvinced. Share carried on. "What would be the alternative? Hiding, living in fear? Looking over your shoulder for evermore? Wondering when you would eventually be caught?"

He was hearing her, but he was afraid of prison. Almost as if she had read his mind she asked.

"Might it end up in a prison sentence?"

"Possibly."

"Some great men have survived prison and have gone on to flourish. Think Nelson Mandela, Victor Frankl."

"I know Mandela's story, but who is Frankl?"

"He was an Austrian doctor who specialised in neurology before the second world war. At the age of 37 he was incarcerated in German concentration camps for the next four years. All his family members perished in the camps, but he survived, and went on to become an eminent psychologist after the war."

"People like that were exceptional."

"But wouldn't you rather be like them and not be a coward, hiding away from your truth?"

He said nothing. She carried on. "And what might that feel like? To be in prison?"

"Pretty damn awful I would imagine."

"But are you not in prison now, anyway, in your mind? Hiding? Not being real or true to yourself? You might have your liberty but are you not inside a prison of your own making?"

He knew that this was true after all the anxiety and fear he had suffered over the past few days. He did just want to hide. He was constantly living in fear of the knock on the door.

"You look at yourself in the mirror every day. Do you want to see a scared coward there every day from now on? Perhaps it would be better just to be honest and give your side of the story. There can be growth in prison, you know?"

He looked at her in disbelief. He regarded prison life as something vile and awful.

"How?"

"Because you would have taken responsibility for your actions, you would have explained your reasons, and you would enter prison with a clear conscience. You would be showing yourself to be brave and honest, to future generations."

"Cynthia, that all sounds very noble, but those are hard concepts to grasp. What man wants to give up his freedom in exchange for incarceration for the benefit of future generations? I don't see how that can be an exercise in growth."

"But what would the alternative be? Always being worried. Lies building on lies. What if you wanted to start a new relationship? Would you have to lie about this? Keep more secrets? What impact would permanent anxiety have on your health? Wouldn't a free mind be preferable?"

Pablo was challenged, but his fear of prison was still overwhelming. "But wouldn't those fears and anxieties diminish over time?"

"We know psychologically that they're more likely to grow over time. Likely to hinder your ability to form relationships. What if that just led to loneliness? We know that loneliness itself is a killer. What if the prison you went to was open and you had quite a lot of freedom in fact?"

She really was very convincing. She carried on. "Would it be so bad if you had exercise, TV, the internet, books and camaraderie, together with a free mind and a clear conscience?"

"Okay, you're making it sound not so bad, but there's still the fear of the unknown."

"Are you not living more with fear of the unknown right now?"

She felt that she had made her points well enough and now she got him to reflect back to her verbally on all the concepts they had just been talking about, to make sure she had explained herself adequately. He had retained well, and she asked him what the sticking point was.

"I suppose I wouldn't feel brave enough to face the music."

"But people have to be brave in all sorts of situations where they have become imprisoned. People can become imprisoned in a job or in an unhealthy relationship. To achieve freedom, they have to be courageous, courageous enough to make that decision to do something different."

Pablo had gone quiet. There was one more aspect of this that she wanted to cover.

"It's your choice Pablo, but if you choose to keep hiding and harbouring the lies, you will reflect that in your aura."

He looked a little guilty. He knew that this was true. He didn't want to damage his aura! She continued.

"People are attracted to authentic people. Being authentic is about being true to yourself, and being honest. You've mentioned your ex-wife and how she disappeared haven't you?"

He wondered where she was going with this. "Yes."

"Would you like her back if she was able to overcome her issues with you?"

"Possibly." Now he was remembering that she had just reappeared, and he had told her to fuck off.

"But if she came back now, she'd sense that you're hiding things. Your body is a signal. Our communication is eighty percent body language. She'd sense that despite whatever you're saying verbally that there are things that you are lying about. She will just know. Your body will tell her. She won't find that attractive. It will be carried in your presence."

"So, is that supposed to be a carrot?"

"Not necessarily. This will be the case with anyone you try to get close to. They will detect that there is a hidden side to you. Lies beget lies. Being honest and facing up to the consequences will enable you to have a free mind, and that's great for your character."

She laughed. He smiled. They had covered more than enough for one day.

Chapter 15

Lenny was arrested and brought to the station within the hour, and his solicitor Mr Hattersley joined him post-haste. The two of them faced DS Pageant and the DCI over the interview table. After all the preliminaries were carried out, and Lenny had been cautioned, it was the solicitor who opened the proceedings.

"For the record, I am Mr Hathaway's legal representative, Graham Hattersley, and I object to this interview taking place. No evidence has been presented to me to indicate that my client could possibly have been involved in the alleged offence of kidnapping. I therefore regard it as an unsanctionable fishing exercise and I have advised my client to go 'no comment' to all questions put to him."

Mr Higginsbotham sighed. "Yes, thank you for that Mr Hattersley. May we proceed now please?"

"Under protest."

The DCI gathered his thoughts for a moment. "Mr Hathaway, we are investigating the mysterious disappearance of one of our police colleagues, one Orlando Sorrentino. Do you know him?"

"No comment."

"Unfortunately we have discovered evidence that he might have been dishonest. Have you ever had any financial dealings with him?"

"No comment."

Mr Hattersley was shaking his head wondering how soon he should interrupt the proceedings again.

"You were arrested earlier this year as a suspect in an attempted murder case. Is that correct?"

Mr Hattersley exploded. "Officer, I hardly think that is relevant in this investigation, do you?"

"To the contrary M. Hattersley, I think that it is very relevant, and at this stage, I am giving your client the opportunity to help clear things up, if he can."

"My client was on bail for that inquiry until he received notification from the CPS that there was insufficient evidence to proceed. He was cleared."

Mr Higginsbotham chuckled. "Hardly cleared Mr Hattersley. Evidence went missing, and the CPS stated that they will take no further action unless or until further evidence comes to light, which I sincerely hope will happen. The case is definitely not closed."

Hattersley relented slightly. "Look, what is your point?"

"My point is that there is a strong possibility of a connection between our missing colleague and your client and I can assure you that I will get to the bottom of it."

He fixed his stare firmly on the solicitor who sat quietly waiting for the next question.

"Mr Hathaway, you recently went missing for several days. Can you please tell me what happened?"

"No comment."

"Some of my officers came to see you to make enquiries about your disappearance, and you didn't want to talk to them. Why was that?"

"No comment."

"Bizarrely, Mr Sorrentino went missing the same day as you mysteriously reappeared. I'm convinced that there is a connection. Can you please tell me what that is?"

"No comment."

"I have some pictures here, exhibits AG1 and AG2, which are believed to be the last known pictures of Mr Sorrentino as he appeared to be led out of a department store on the day he went missing. Do you recognise him?"

"No comment."

"Is there any possibility that you have ever seen this man before?"

"No comment."

The questioning continued in a similar vein for another five minutes, but with no answers forthcoming, the basic routine questions all dried up without spawning further impromptu questions and the interview was drawn to a close. In and of itself, it was significant that Hathaway had been asked all the relevant questions, and that he had chosen not to answer them. Mr Hattersley put in the final shot.

"Mr Higginsbotham, I will be putting a complaint in for unlawful arrest. You presented no evidence whatsoever during interview that my client might have been connected to the offence that you are supposed to be investigating."

He looked genuinely cross. The DCI dismissed him casually.

"Good luck with that one!"

Richard showed them both out of the building and returned to his boss.

"Boss, do you think they will put in a complaint?"

The DCI laughed. "Not in a month of Sundays. I can see that Hathaway is a man who likes to be discreet and keep a low profile. That has worked very well for him over the past twenty or so years. The last thing he will do is sanction another investigation which just might turn something up not in his favour. He's just going to want to go away quietly and hide as usual."

He was absolutely right.

Lenny was thoroughly enjoying having Christina and Monica move in with him. Christina was breaking her rules a little bit because she didn't know if he had ended his illegal activities yet, but she did know that he was in the process of selling off all the legitimate ones, and that when they were gone, the illegal ones would be gone too. Also, after the scare of him going missing so abruptly, she was willing to bend her rules just because she wanted so much to be with him now that he was safe. She wanted to keep him safe.

Monica loved the new house; it was so big! She was a very sociable person but she also liked having such a big bedroom with lots of lovely pink and fluffy things in it. In her mother's home, she hadn't been allowed to have a cat, but here, Lenny had actually bought her two kittens, and she adored them. Sometimes, they all went out together, but when Lenny and Christina went out for a date on their own, Christina would always organise for someone to be with Monica, not because Monica needed looking after, but simply because she wanted her to have some company. Monica loved people and didn't like being left alone. Christina was officially on school holiday leave, but at the end of the holidays, she would be actually retiring. She had started to volunteer two days a week at the occupational therapy centre which Monica attended most days, and she loved it. It was so unpressurised and organic. Lenny was consumed each day with marketing his businesses and tying up loose ends, but as the weeks passed by, he would end up with the novelty of leisure time, and Christina was exploring ideas to keep him, and them, busy and fulfilled. The last thing she wanted was for him to get bored and get lured back into his old ways. In the evenings they discussed the possibility of new hobbies. In time they would try golf, take up gardening, and maybe join an amateur dramatic group. They would go on frequent holidays to see Harry and Rachel in Spain. She had always fancied being part of a choir. Lenny liked the idea of taking up reading and playing snooker more seriously. Neither of them liked the idea of joining a gym, but a weekly swimming session or two appealed, especially as Monica absolutely adored swimming pools. The dilemma of wondering what to do with novel spare time was a nice dilemma for them to sort out.

Lenny dealt with anxiety much better than Pablo did. For starters, in his line of work, over the past twenty-five years, there were always threats of being investigated, caught out, arrested, prosecuted etcetera, and over those years he had learned to live with little dark clouds always hovering over the horizon, without giving them undue thought and giving himself ulcers. Furthermore, in respect of Denis's kidnap, he hadn't been directly involved. He'd only been the reason for it, not involved in the execution of it. He had much less to worry about than Harry and Pablo.

Harry had returned to Spain. He was pleased to get back to his family, but also, it was easier for him to let go of his fears if he was actually in another country. The escapade with Pablo has been as much outside his comfort zone as it had been for Pablo, probably more so, but the police would need some very reliable evidence if they were to succeed in getting an extradition warrant for him. The girls were still pleasing themselves daily in the sunshine. Cassie and Sammy had both enrolled into a local college, but term wasn't due to start for some weeks, and Melissa was rather enjoying researching the job market slowly and ever so thoroughly. She hadn't done nearly enough research yet to make an informed decision. Catalina had arranged for one of her teacher friends, Magdalena, to attend the house most days, to give them all informal Spanish lessons. They were all keen to learn the language, except for Harry, who sat in sometimes purely for amusement. He could never see himself learning a foreign language. He blithely explained that he had never had any academic capability and that he was an old dog unable to learn new tricks.

The weeks passed slowly by, and the investigation into Denis's disappearance went gradually further and further down the list of prominent investigations in inverse proportion to Pablo's confidence increasing. No body had been found, and without a suspect or motivation, that made it virtually impossible to turn the investigation into a full-scale murder enquiry. Mr Higginsbotham, however, was not leaving any stone unturned. The more dead ends they went down, the more avenues he looked for. He had officers make a detailed inventory of every single item in Denis's home. There was no particular reason for this. They had already discovered the incriminating bank accounts, but he had a hunch that something inside the house might give them a useful clue in time. So far, however, it remained just a fairly normal-looking list of domestic items.

Pablo started driving again for the school as soon as the autumn term started. He appeared to have escaped the threat of seizures due to his brain injury. Life was finally going back to normal. Thank God! He was just so thankful for normality and a quiet life. He wanted no more drama in his life. He had had his fill of violence, and had paid a high price for delving into that world. His phone rang. He was always nervous when his phone rang these days. That was one of the ongoing prices to pay for having big skeletons to hide, just like Cynthia had warned him. He inspected the screen; Hellion! Butterflies immediately swarmed through him. He collected his thoughts. This was only slightly better than the police phoning him. He hadn't heard from her since he had told her to fuck off on the doorstep many weeks earlier. Was she going to tell him gleefully that she had shopped him? He remembered the saying 'Keep your friends close, keep your enemies closer'. Guided by that ancient pearl of wisdom, he answered, cautiously. "Yes?"

"I want you back!"

A couple of days later he made the time to call his bestie.

"Hey Fatboy, you been managing to keep yourself alive lately?"

"Just about Fatboy." Pablo spoke quietly, with gravity. "Hey, moosh, you're never going to believe this."

"What? you've been arrested yet again?"

"No. Far more dodgy than that."

"You've taken up cage fighting? Playing Russian roulette with your dodgy head?"

"Not quite, but similar."

"Go on then, tell me."

"I'm back with Hellion."

His voice quivered with emotion as he said that. He was still feeling very emotional about developments. Tim's voice grew thicker and louder.

"You're friggin' crazy! How did that happen?"

"She just phoned up one day out of the blue. I knew she would one day."

"Mate, she's just gonna dump you again as soon as she feels like it. I can't believe that this has happened. Wait a minute. When you say that you're back with her, do you mean that you sent her a card and she didn't actually have you arrested again?"

Pablo chuckled. "No really. I'm back with her. Have been for two whole days."

Tim was genuinely astonished. He never thought he'd see the day. "I can't believe it," he repeated thoughtfully. "You're just setting yourself up for more pain and anguish. You do know that don't you? She's gonna dump you again, Fatboy."

Pablo laughed, perhaps a little nervously. "No, mate, I don't think so. I think we've both learned a lot whilst we've been apart, and this time we're determined to work through the issues."

"I know *you* are, mate. You never give up, like a mad dog, but what about her?"

"What about her?"

"You know, all that stuff about, what did you call it? Projection! Inner vows that made her walk away from love, her refusal to talk etcetera, etcetera, etcetera."

"Mate, she's willing to stop and talk about all that stuff now. That's what will make the difference."

Tim sighed. "Brother, I admire your optimism, but really, aren't you just dreaming?"

"No, bro', she's very real and still gorgeous."

He was feeling very pleased with himself.

"You said you'd never go back to her place. It was defiled and all that, so you haven't gone back, right?"

"Yeah, I did say that, but what with all that other crap that was going on in my life recently, I don't give a toss about how defiled it is anymore. I just want to be with her. I just don't think about who else has been in that bed."

"And you don't mind what she's been up to for the past five years?"

"Nah. It can't have been up to much or she wouldn't have come back would she?"

"You're not full of contempt for her because of all the other cock she's been having?"

"Come on, Fatboy. She's not like that. She's just been confused."

"Bro, I think you're the one who's confused, and you're incredibly forgiving, and stupid. She'll just chuck you out one day when the mood takes her. Please don't tell me you've given up your place at Carlos's?"

"Not yet buddy. It's still there if I need it, but I don't think I will. It honestly feels like love at first sight all over again, for both of us."

"Bro, you know where I am when you need me."

Pablo was back with Hellion just like they'd never parted. They'd had some intense discussions about commitment and what each one expected from the relationship. She'd been honest about wanting him to earn more money, and he had agreed to find a full-time job. She had accepted that there needed to be intimacy in their relationship, especially for him. Pablo made a point of kissing her regularly, and she had agreed not to make a fuss if his eyes were still open. She tried to be more tolerant in bed when he wrapped his heavy arms around her, and she felt like she might not be able to breathe. She had to be braver. And they both agreed to air concerns honestly and at an early juncture rather than sweep issues under the carpet. Challenging each other was to be seen as a good thing so that nothing festered.

It was a quiet cosy Sunday evening and they happily sat together on the sofa embracing as the warmth of their original love really had returned. They admired afresh the qualities in each other which had drawn them together in the first place. He was seeing that beautiful warm generous side of her again. He had always admired her delicate female beauty just as she had always adored his masculinity. The situation was feeling wonderful again for both of them.

"Pablo Pinkerton, I love you."

She looked forcefully at him as they sat snuggled up watching evening TV. He became a little embarrassed. When she was fulsome like this he wasn't as good at expressing his commensurate appreciation, but he was trying to get better.

"I know darling, and you know how much I love you," he replied, trying to telepathically remind her that he had waited five years for her to come back.

A black van reversed into their driveway its lights piercing the blackness of the night, its tyre crunching noisily on the gravel. Pablo got up and went to the door to investigate. They weren't expecting anybody. As soon as he opened the door he convulsed and fell to the floor clumsily, writhing uncontrollably. He was in great pain and had no coordination whatsoever. He tried to call out to Hellion but no words came. Moments later Hellion appeared at the doorway too only to see Pablo being carted off by three men in dark clothes and balaclavas. Just as she was about to remonstrate she was tasered too. She was not taken, just left quivering and jerking on the doorstep. Pablo was thrown into the back of the van where he was bound and gagged. The van drove sedately away, leaving Hellion convulsing and trying to regain control of her limbs for the next ten minutes. It was fully thirteen minutes before she was able to raise the alarm with her landlord next door.

Chapter 16

First thing Monday morning Hellion was sitting in her lounge being interviewed by DS Pageant and DC Hurley. It was tea all round, and after some polite small talk Richard got down to business.

"Mrs Brown, I can assure you that we've got a very experienced team on this case, and I know you've already made a full statement to the uniform officers who attended last night, but we are here because we know Pablo, and we might be able to tie up some useful links because of our earlier involvement with him."

Hellion was always boldly incisive. "How do you know him?"

Richard coughed a little. "I'm afraid that we can't disclose confidential information."

Hellion looked at him rather crossly. "But that might have a bearing on what happened last night."

"Mrs Brown, I'm sure it absolutely does, and that is why we are here right now, but we have to be discreet about what we disclose to you."

Hellion gave him a very dirty look and Rebecca felt that it would be good to interject at this point. "Mrs Brown, we don't know much about your connection to Pablo. Can you tell us what he was doing here yesterday?"

"He's living here now. We were married, you know."

Rebecca looked a little confused. "You never changed your surname?"

"I've changed it four times," she replied proudly with a wry smile.

"You were Mrs. Pinkerton?"

"Yes, and I changed it back to my maiden name after we got divorced."

"I see. So, when did you two get back together then?"

"Is this really relevant?"

"It might be."

Rebecca remained firm and waited for a response.

"A few days ago."

Rebecca suppressed her urge to titter. They were back together again. Two or three days!

"Richard took over."

"Do you mind if we call you Hellion?"

"No, that's fine."

"Okay, Hellion. Thank you. We've had some dealings with Pablo fairly recently, but he was living in lodgings elsewhere when we saw him, and as far as we know you weren't on the scene."

"We haven't been back together long, as I just said."

"I see, and has he said anything to you at all about any trouble he might have been in earlier this year?"

"No, nothing. Some weeks ago I was on the phone to him, when some police officers arrived to talk to him, so I knew something was up."

"I see. Did he explain what that was about?"

"No. I did ask him but he told me to fuck off. He was cross that I'd found out."

She looked at him politely, with her coy little smile.

"I see. We're obviously familiar with your statement from last night, Hellion, but have you remembered any other details, anything at all?"

"No. I told them everything that I saw last night."

"And you said that you heard Irish accents?"

"Definitely. It wasn't much. Just 'Come on you dozy fucker. Leave her!'"

She did a very impressive Irish accent.

"Do you know which one said that?"

"No idea. I'd just been tasered."

She smiled coyly again.

"Yes, I'm sorry. That must have been very painful and disconcerting."

"I've had more enjoyable experiences."

"And you're not sure if there were three or four men?"

"I definitely saw two men carrying Pablo, and one holding the van back door open for them, but I didn't see who tasered me, so maybe there was a fourth man. I suppose there must have been."

Rebecca chipped in. "Hellion, are you sure Pablo didn't say anything to you about any other strange things that have happened to him over the past few months?"

"Do you mean like how he got that wound in his head?"

164

Rebecca brightened up. "Yes, exactly like that."

"No, he point-blank refused to explain that at all."

"Has he explained to you about any new friends he has made recently?"

"No, but I wouldn't expect him to really. He's a bit of a loner."

The officers tallied for another ten minutes, but no useful information was forthcoming. It seemed that Hellion really didn't know anything of interest. Richard wrapped up.

"Hellion, thank you for your time. If you get any calls or other information relating to this kidnap, please let us know immediately."

The officers go up to leave. The word kidnap struck Hellion as so bizarre. "Why would anybody want to kidnap him? He's just a skint old codger who drives a school bus."

"That is what we are going to find out, Hellion, I hope."

He didn't sound very hopeful. Hellion saw the lack of conviction in his face. There was no confidence, only confusion. She didn't know that the sense of uncertainty they carried came from the fact that they'd got nowhere with Lenny's recent disappearance, and that over the past few weeks they had become quite despondent over the complete lack of progress in the Denis case. It seemed that kidnappings weren't really their thing. She pushed.

"Are you confident that you will find him?"

The officers looked at each other hoping the other would answer. After a short but tell-tale pause Rebecca stepped up to the plate.

"Mrs Brown, these kinds of cases are very rare in this country, but like any investigation, we will do our utmost to solve it and find Pablo. We can assure you of that."

Her reply was sincere but lacked that reassuring edge.

"I do hope so. We've only just started over again and I really do think we've got a rosy future ahead together."

Rebecca tried not to frown.

Later that day, Monday, a burned-out, empty black transit van was discovered in a quiet lay-by two hours away. It was suspected to be the one used in the kidnap, but there was absolutely no proof of that. It simply gave the police a potential clue as to which direction the abductors had gone off in if indeed it was the van in question. DCI Higginsbotham felt that it was likely to be their van given the timing, the unusual colour of the van, and the distance, and he put particular emphasis on any leads honing into that general locality.

Pablo was lying naked on a single wooden-slatted bare bed frame, his wrists and legs shackled to the posts with metal handcuffs. He was freezing cold and blindfolded, but if he tilted his head right back he could see slightly down the lower edge of the blindfold. He observed a single, bulky, hairy man sitting beyond his feet. He had been trussed up like this all the previous evening and throughout the night, alone, cold and terrified. This man had appeared a few hours after sunrise, and had torn off the two blankets that had covered him overnight, even though it was still freezing cold. The man talked to him in a mild, quiet Irish accent as he sat there, as if he had all the time in the world. Every now and then he would stand up and administer shocks using some kind of stun gun or taser. Pablo would scream out, hoping that someone would hear him. The pain was excruciating, and for ten minutes after the tasering his body felt like it had been taken apart and reassembled all wrong. Often he would be tasered again as soon as he had regained his composure. His interrogator was doing nothing to hide his identity. In fact, as he spoke, he was revealing many details about his life and that of his deceased father, who apparently had been a very active IRA soldier during the seventies and eighties. The man sounded very proud and admiring of his father and the violence he had eagerly dished out for the noble cause. Clearly, he didn't expect Pablo to survive this ordeal. In between talking about himself, his father and even his family, he explained how isolated they were on a very remote and private disused pig farm, and that there was no hope for Pablo of escape or being found. Then he would suddenly focus on his real quest and ask Pablo where she was. Where had he hidden her?

"I don't know what the fuck you are talking about."

Another taser and more writhing.

"I've got stronger ones you know. This is only two milliamps. I've got three and four too."

This was double-Dutch to Pablo who had never grasped anything about electronics. He didn't have the faintest idea what the difference was between an amp, a volt or a herz, or anything else electrical, but he was sure that they would all be unbearable. He decided early on that this man was deranged, the way he spoke to him like he was a friend, revealing details about his life, his history, interspersed with confusing questions about some little girl called Clodagh. His

166

back was feeling bruised from lying on bare thin wooden slats. He needed to move.

"I need a piss."

"Piss then."

"Are you going to let me get up?"

"No."

"So, I just piss here?"

"Yep."

"Isn't that rather disgusting?"

"You're disgusting."

"And if I need a shit?"

"Then shit, you piece of shit."

"So, you're not going to untie me for anything?"

"Nope."

"How will I eat?"

"You won't."

Pablo stiffened. He was going to be treated worse than any caged animal. This man obviously wasn't going to let him survive this ordeal.

"What do you want? I've got no money."

The man slowly got up and tasered him again. "Don't be impudent. You know what I want."

Pablo couldn't formulate words again for some minutes, and then he asked quietly,

"What's your name?"

"Eammon. Eammon O'Sullivan. Does that ring a bell?"

Now Pablo was sure he was going to die, not because he knew of an Eammon O'Sullivan, but because he believed that this man had furnished his real name, and he seemed to expect him to recognise it.

"Why are you going to kill me?"

The man chuckled. "You're thinking too far ahead. You haven't answered my questions yet. Where is she?"

"I don't know what the fuck you are talking about."

Another taser. As Pablo was slowly recovering, the man spoke softly but intently.

"She would have been seven by now you know. It's not only me and the missus who miss her dreadfully y'know. She has an older sister Orla, and a

167

younger brother Darragh. They really miss her too, y'know. You hurt a lot of people, not just her y'know."

Pablo stayed silent, even though he felt his ability to speak returning. Then, rather urgently he stated, "I really need a piss."

"Go ahead and piss then."

Pablo really couldn't believe that he was just expected to relieve himself where he lay. That was so degrading, but he could not help himself. His full bladder overcame his reluctance and he started leaking piss over his legs. It drained into an old-fashioned tin baby bath underneath the bed, which contained sawdust and lime. Eammon sat silently, insouciantly.

"Feel better now?" he asked mockingly. "Maybe you can tell me what you did with her now?"

Pablo said nothing. Another taser.

Monday afternoon DS Pageant and DC Hurley visited Lenny at his home. He was surprisingly hospitable despite his recent arrest and he kindly invited them in. This was after all, apparently, just a routine enquiry. He harboured no hard feelings about the arrest. They had just been doing their job, and nothing seemed to have come of it, and clearly, he wasn't being arrested again. He took them into his plush home-office where they sank into a deep dark leather sofa opposite his mahogany desk.

Lenny sat on his throne-like office chair behind the desk seeming rather superior. "Do I need my solicitor present?" he sensibly asked.

Richard answered. "I don't see why. We are here for your help really."

Lenny looked at them quizzically. "And do you think I ought to be helping you?"

"Mr Hathaway, that is entirely your choice. We can only ask."

Lenny was curious. "Go on then. Tell me what you want."

"It's about Pablo Pinkerton."

Lenny looked sheepish. He wasn't supposed to really know Pablo, apart from when he had found him unconscious that night.

"He's gone missing."

"Christ almighty!" Lenny was genuinely shocked. His mind started to flit around anything he could think of relating to the Triads and Denis but he only ended up confused.

"Describe missing."

"It seems that he was taken, just like you were some weeks ago."

The officers remained silent whilst that sunk in and as they studied his reaction. He asked a question, shocked.

"Chinese people?"

"No, not like you were in that sense, just that he's been taken. Not Chinese as far as we know. We don't know who took him. Obviously."

Then Rebecca spoke.

"Lenny, you know we believe that there's a connection between the two of you, which neither of you has been willing to admit to, but maybe now's the time to come clean. You might be able to help us to help him."

She looked at him imploringly. He was really confused. This made absolutely no sense. He would need time to process this, so he was going to say nothing right now. There were a lot of issues to weigh up, not least his need to protect himself in the Denis abduction case.

"Can you tell me what happened?"

Richard took over. He was the senior officer here, and it should be his decision as to how much information it was appropriate to reveal.

"Lenny, as you know there is always an issue of confidentiality which we have to carefully weigh up before we reveal anything. I think that the most we can reveal is that yesterday evening his partner reported that he had been kidnapped from her home. That will become public knowledge soon enough."

Lenny weighed this up. He would help if he could, without incriminating himself, but to reveal one small detail would be to open the flood gates. He had no choice other than to reveal nothing.

"Who is his partner?"

The officers wondered why he asked this. It didn't seem to be relevant. Richard answered. "I'm afraid we can't give out personal details of other parties concerned."

Rebecca got to the point. "Lenny, are you going to help us or not?"

"I want to speak with his partner."

"Do you know her?"

"No."

"Then how is that going to happen?"

"You're going to pass on a message for me."

"And why would I do that?"

"Because that just might help your cause."

Tuesday. Day two with Eammon. Pablo's voice was growing hoarse with lack of liquids. His back was feeling increasingly bruised, and his body was shivering from the cold. He had shat overnight and the stink of faeces was revolting. He probably wouldn't need to shit again, not if he wasn't being fed, but he needed drink desperately. He begged for a drink. Eammon needed him to be able to talk. He had bottles of water with him. He opened a new one for Pablo and held it to his mouth as he lifted his head up as high as it would go despite the shackles. That was just enough for Pablo to be able to swallow a few mouthfuls.

"Not too much. I don't want you pissing everywhere," Eammon commented cruelly.

"Are you ready to tell me about her yet?"

Pablo knew that he was about to be tasered again no matter what he said, so he just weakly told him to fuck off.

As he was recovering from the tasering, he acutely listened to Eammon rambling on about his daughter. He desperately hoped that something would be said which would help him understand what the fuck was going on here.

"You're a clever bastard. I bet you were involved in the investigation weren't you, busily hiding clues, muddying the waters."

Pablo thought, '*Investigation? Was this something to do with his days as a police officer?*'

He weakly asked, "Has this got something to do when I was a police officer?"

He got tasered again.

"Don't act stupid with me Pablo. That really annoys me."

When the convulsing stopped, and he was able to mouth words, Pablo pursued this line. He had the faintest hope that maybe this would get him somewhere.

"I left the service eleven years ago."

Another tasering.

"Don't lie to me you devious bastard."

When Pablo came around, he didn't risk speaking. He didn't want to escalate his punishments.

"She used to always wear that necklace you know. The silver one with the silver butterfly with the ruby-red body. The butterfly reminded me of her delicacy. The ruby reminded me of her hair. I got it for her third birthday. She loved it. She always wore it. I only feel slightly better knowing that wherever she is, she has a part of me with her. Do you remember that necklace, Pablo?"

No reply and another tasering.

"Now, you really need to tell me where she is."

Tuesday, late morning, Lenny's phone rang. It was the day after the officers had been to see him. It was not a number he recognised.

"Hello?"

"Is this a Lenny Hathaway?"

"It is. May I ask who's calling?"

"You don't know me. The police gave me your number yesterday evening and said that you wanted to talk to me."

"Pablo's girlfriend?"

"Partner," she corrected him proudly.

"Oh yes. That's great. Listen, can we meet somewhere for a chat please?"

"I take it that this is to do with Pablo's disappearance?"

"Yes, of course, but don't get your hopes up. I don't know anything but I want to help if I can."

She was unsure of him. The officers had been rather mysterious about him, but they had certainly piqued her interest. They seemed unsure about whether she should make contact with him or not which alarmed her considerably.

"What do you propose?"

"Just a meet somewhere. Nowhere too busy, but soon. This is urgent."

She agreed and within an hour they were making their introductions inside one of Lenny's old pubs over coffee. Lenny was surprised at how attractive she was. She was petite, birdlike, which belied her years and her face portrayed the exquisite arrangement of features which just seemed to luckily make up an arresting masterpiece. He also detected the strength of her character. He looked at her and smiled admiringly.

"I can see why Pablo was willing to wait for you."

She smiled slightly deflectively.

"Thank you. It wouldn't have taken so long if he was not such a slow learner."

She looked at him brightly. Her eyes were rich with insight, but she was ready for business now. "I believe that you might be able to help the police with this case. Is that correct?"

"Maybe. It's a bit awkward for me to deal with the police though. We've had a few misunderstandings ourselves lately."

171

He smiled mischievously.

"Okay, well, as I'm not the police, can you please explain to me what your connection to all this is?"

"No Problem."

He focussed, staring into nothingness as he concentrated his memory, and spoke thoughtfully, slowly.

"Earlier this year, something very bad happened by mistake, involving me. It wasn't supposed to have happened. Pablo took it upon himself to settle a score about that, but then something else very bad happened by mistake, involving Pablo, which also wasn't supposed to have happened. Then I got into trouble for the first mistake and Pablo wanted to help me deal with that by settling a score with someone else who had made the second very bad thing happen. As a result of that another very bad thing has happened and Pablo is in trouble because of that, by mistake, and I want to help him deal with that because he helped me to deal with the other bad thing that happened to me."

She looked at him very blankly. "Lenny, do you speak English?"

He chuckled. "Really, I can't reveal any more than that."

She looked at him askance. "Do you understand the meaning of the word 'reveal'?"

He smiled. He admired her spirit. She had a lot of spunk, and he could see why Pablo considered her to be so special, but he said no more.

Hellion sat back emphatically. "Right, that's cleared that up then. Now it all makes sense. Thank you so much. Clear as mud!"

He just looked at her and smiled again. He wasn't going to elucidate.

"Lenny, you're not the best at explaining things are you?"

He shrugged his big shoulders. "I tried."

"Okay, well maybe you can explain to me why I'm sitting here being totally confused and unhelped by you?"

He chuckled again. She amused him, and then he got serious. "I can't really help the police because there's too much at stake, but I really do want to help Pablo. I owe him, big time."

"I saw you rock up in a Rolls Royce didn't I?"

"A Bentley actually," he corrected her modestly.

"Are you wealthy?"

"Yes, I am."

"So, are you being blackmailed? Are they using Pablo to get money out of you?"

Lenny didn't answer immediately. He had to consider the implications. He hadn't received any demands. The only way anything like that could be orchestrated would be via Denis, and he really didn't think Denis was around anymore. The Triads didn't leave loose ends. Could the Triads be intending to blackmail him? No. Too much at stake business-wise. It would be counter-productive. Having thought carefully he replied.

"No. No one is trying to get money out of me."

"Are you sure? You took long enough to answer."

"I was just considering possibilities, and I really don't think that's what this is all about."

"So, how can you help then?"

She was still none the wiser and was beginning to feel disappointed.

"I can't help the police directly, but I can make my own inquiries. I have a wide connection of colleagues."

"And you think that you might be able to turn something up where the police can't?"

She sounded doubtful.

"Yes, possibly, but I need your help."

"How?"

"I need you to tell me everything you know, and I need you to tell me everything the police inform you about their investigation. I can only help if I'm looking in the right direction."

"Why should I trust you? You might be trying to cover up for someone else."

Lenny looked puzzled and after contemplating her question, he replied simply, "I don't know."

They both looked at each other rather blankly.

Chapter 17

Lenny had very little information to go on, but he did have a lot of contacts nationwide and a fairly wide network with shady drug dealers. He wished that Harry was here with him. He would be much better at this sort of thing – trying to get favours out of people on the phone. Hellion had given him where the black van had been found burned out, and that at least one of the kidnappers had an Irish accent. That didn't amount to much, but that afternoon and evening, he got busy phoning around anyway. He was asking people near that part of the country, confidentially of course, if they knew of anyone likely to be capable of kidnap and extortion? And did any of them have an Irish accent? He was asking exactly the same kind of questions that police investigators were asking. The difference was that he was far more likely to get someone to talk to him.

Following his meeting with Hellion, and spending the entire afternoon and evening phoning around one contact after the other, Lenny had made over fifty-six phone calls, and nobody had anything for him at the time, but one phoned back the following morning.

"Lenny, this has to remain totally anonymous, agreed?"

"Of course, you absolutely cannot mention my name, okay?"

"Absolutely."

"Okay. Well, look, I think you should talk to a man called Eammon O'Sullivan. He runs a few pig farms not that far away from where that van you mentioned was found. He is an elusive character, but he's into some pretty heavy stuff. He's got very close contacts with the real IRA and there's quite a big tight Irish community up where he lives. He's dangerous. I honestly don't know anything about recent kidnappings, but if you can get him to talk to you, he's your best bet. If anyone knows something up there, he will. Problem is, if you make contact with him and he's not happy about you, you might not live to tell the tale. He's that fuckin' dangerous, and cautious. You understand what I'm saying?"

"Yes, I think so."

"His pigs are very well fed and eat a very wide variety of foodstuffs if you get my drift."

"Ooh. That sounds nasty. A bit Mexican. Anyway, listen, thanks for the heads up. How can I contact him?"

"Are you sure you still want to?"

"Yes, I have to."

"I've got no direct details for him. Your best bet is to go to the White Blacksmith pub at Norton Sodbury and just mention you want a meeting with him, then wait, and pray."

He scribbled down the address on a notepad, at the ready.

"Bud, I'm so grateful. Thank you so much."

"Lenny, I hope this is worth it. Just trying to meet him is dangerous. Are you sure it's worth it?"

"Fellah, I have to do this."

"Okay, mate. It's your funeral, but no mention of me, please. I don't want to become pig fodder one day."

"My lips are sealed. Thanks bud. I owe you."

Police officers had trawled through Pablo's old police service record and his banking records. They had visited members of his family. They had interviewed all his recent employers and close work colleagues. They had made contact with fellow lodgers, new and old, and had interrogated his computer records and his phone. They found nothing of interest which they didn't already know, apart from his contact much earlier in the year with a private investigation firm called Covert Solutions. A Mr Chesterfield of that firm was duly interviewed, but of course he declined any information, and the police couldn't get a court order to force him to reveal any details, because Pablo was not suspected of committing any offences. Mr Higginsbotham considered that it was probably something to do with his ex-wife who had been giving him trouble about him sending her occasional cards, so he wasn't particularly interested anyway. Lucinda was interviewed, and she was very upset to learn of his disappearance and had nothing to offer to help them. She just gave them her stock answer 'I no know'. They were drawing a big fat blank just as they were in the Denis case.

DCI Denzil Higginsbotham liked to have regular cosy chats with his officers, individually. He felt that this was the best way for him to spot promising lines of enquiry. Sometimes officers were onto something without actually realising it, because they weren't seeing the bigger picture. Denzil liked to take the overview. He sought out DS Pageant and brought him to his office.

"Richard, how are we getting on?"

"You mean with the case, sir?"

"Yes, of course with the case Richard. I don't want to know about your love-life, your trendy exercise regime, or your latest fad for rap-music."

"I don't like rap music, sir."

Denzil just looked at him, rather sternly. He didn't like wasting precious time.

"Okay, well, sir, as you know, Rebecca and I have built up quite a rapport with Pablo this year. We interviewed him back in the spring about the assault on the Chinese woman, then about the assault on him outside Hathaway's warehouse, then about Hathaway's disappearance, then finally about Hathaway's reappearance, but we've found no evidence that anyone might want to harm him, and he hasn't got two pennies to rub together for extortion."

"What about someone smashing his head in?"

"That's still a mystery. Obviously somebody very nearly killed him, but we've turned up nothing about a suspect or a motive."

"Do you think they might have come back to finish the job off?"

Richard thought for a moment then, "But why now? And why Kidnap him? If they just wanted to finish the job off, a small bang on the head now would do it apparently."

"Why is he so skint? He used to be in the job, didn't he?"

"Yes, sir. It seems that he was doing alright for himself up to about eleven years ago when he left the job, and then his wife divorced him, and it seems that he lost all interest in making money or acquiring things. We've been through his bank statements for the last twelve years. He's just whittled it all away on a quiet, undemanding, rather lazy lifestyle. Now he just works part time and rents a bedroom."

Denzil mused. "Each to his own I suppose. Sounds a bit sad though, don't you think?"

"Yes, I suppose so, but on the other hand, he doesn't look like he's going to burn himself out anytime soon, and he's in great shape."

"What ya' sayin'?" Denzil gripped his spare tyre and wobbled it up and down comically.

"No implications intended."

Denzil stopped wobbling his belly before he started breathing heavily. "Have you found any interesting leads at all?"

"Not yet sir I'm afraid."

"You went and saw Hathaway again on Monday didn't you?"

"Yes, sir."

"Anything?"

"When we told him that Pinkerton had gone missing, he was genuinely shocked. I've interviewed him enough times to know what he's like. He's usually non-committal and unemotional, but when we told him that, he nearly fell off his seat."

"And you think that was genuine surprise?"

"Without a doubt."

"That's helpful in a sort of negative way. They're a strange couple, don't you think? We still haven't sussed out their connection have we?"

"Not apart from our interviewing them both in the Chinese lady case, and that in and of itself is a very tenuous connection."

"Hmmm. Anything else to offer me at this time Richard?"

"Not really sir. Sorry."

"Please. No need to apologise. Just keep your ears to the ground and your hands to the grindstone."

"Yes, sir."

With that Richard got up to leave.

"Hang on. Anything new on the Sorrentino case?"

"No sir. Nothing."

It was Wednesday and day three of interrogation for Pablo. He was feeling weak from lack of food, poor sleep, and the constant electrocutions. He really wondered how much more of this he could take. He hadn't had his shackles removed for anything. His wrists and ankles were chafed and bleeding from their constant metal restraints. His back was aching so badly that at night he could barely sleep. His shoulder and hip joints were giving him pain from being constantly set in one position. He was totally exhausted. Eammon had given him occasional sips of water, but that was not enough. This day would be exactly the same as the previous one. Eammon would eventually turn up, alone and spend several hours alternating between torturing him and speaking soporifically to him. Ramblings about family and life and the same old questions about Clodagh. Questions he couldn't answer even if he wanted to, no matter how often they were repeated.

Lenny headed off to the White Blacksmith within half an hour of his conversation with Hellion. Christina was quite distraught that he was rushing off on a mysterious mission, and couldn't tell her a blessed thing. He just told her that he loved her very much and went anyway. He dressed very smartly. This was going to potentially be a very important business meeting and he wanted to make a good impression. He needed to be a presence to be contended with. He even wore a tie.

Two and a half hours later his prestigious Bentayga swished into the rather tiny car park at the rear of the White Blacksmith, Norton Sodbury, an edge-of-town working man's pub. The car park wasn't really suitable for such large cars, but he managed to find a space where other cars could just about negotiate around his overblown SUV. It was cold, and he donned his caramel-coloured camel-hair overcoat with the black velvet collar and made a rather grand entrance through the side entrance. It was just after lunchtime and there was a small cluster of men at the bar chatting and drinking. The place immediately felt more like a working man's club as opposed to the more regular swanky up-market dining pub that were most common these days. The dart board and snooker tables were noticeable at one end of the bar, although they were currently redundant, and the whole place had a tired rather dirty feel about it.

The men all looked at him momentarily, before turning back into their huddle. Lenny strode slowly up to the bar where a cockney-sounding young lady with far too many tattoos and face-piercings took his order for a pint of stout. Before choosing where to sit, he spoke to the huddle of men.

"Do any of you gentlemen know a man by the name of Eammon O'Sullivan perchance?"

They went very quiet for a moment, then rather comically started asking each other. 'Do you?' with various vacant responses – 'No, me neither', 'Can't say that I have'. They soon went quiet again, just looking at him.

"No problem," he announced confidently. "I'll just go and sit over there and wait."

Ten minutes later one of the men came over to him with a pen and paper.

"Mister, we need your details for the track and trace rules, you know, in case someone comes in here with a cold and we have to let you know."

"Sure."

Lenny wrote down his name, address and mobile number. He had nothing to hide. He had anticipated that he would have to wait whilst they checked him out, very possibly until the next day. Hopefully he wouldn't be seen as a threat. He had the presence of mind to have brought a book with him. Christina had encouraged him to join the local library, and he had withdrawn his first book recently. *Lord of the Flies* by William Golding. He had chosen that one because It was one of the few he had heard of, and he was strangely vaguely aware of what the book was about. Perhaps he had seen the film in his youth. He couldn't really remember. He fetched the book from the car, and settled down opposite the bar in a cosy leather wrap around chair next to a small drinks table and started reading.

Back on the abandoned farm Eammon was sitting quietly, reminiscing sadly about his lost little girl. Pablo was fading. Eammon didn't know how much more punishment he could give him before his body weakened sufficiently for the spirit to decide to leave. He had witnessed that sort of thing before. Nurses in palliative care would also notice the final signs when someone was about to give up. They would whisper to other carers, "They've not got long now. Just make sure they're comfortable." Patients would possibly be moved so that their final hours were spent as peacefully as possible. Prescient messages would be sent out to close relatives. "You need to come and see them soon. They will be gone very soon." They'd seen the signs before, and they recognised them. Eammon didn't want Pablo to go yet. He hadn't revealed his secrets. Eammon still wanted answers. He gave him extra water, and less shocks today. He was surprised at how soon he had started to fade. He thought that he would have put up a much better fight. He had looked so strong, but he had tired quickly. His will to live seemed to be weak. He was already close to letting go, but Eammon needed him to hang on long enough to reveal the truth.

His phone buzzed. He checked the screen. An interesting visitor at the White Blacksmith, hoping to meet him. He had been checked out. He went by the name of Lenny Hathaway, had arrived in his own car and as far as they could discover, he was a wealthy businessman with a penchant for drug dealing. Eammon checked his watch. Maybe he could give Pablo an early night today. He might survive one more night and day. He gave him a final drink and threw the two blankets over him and promised he would be back to spend some time with him the next day.

Lenny had just finished his third pint of the afternoon. That was a bit dodgy, because now he was entering the over the drink-drive limit. He would need to eat a substantial meal before too long to help absorb the alcohol if he was to get back on the road. The gaggle of men were still at the bar, and other drinkers had started to dribble in and take up some of the vacant seating. It was still too early for food. He had found it difficult to focus on his book, yet he had sort of read almost half of it. It had arrested his thinking piecemeal. His thoughts had flitted between the story on his lap and the real-life story inside his head – Eammon, Pablo, Denis. Just as he was contemplating asking for the menu, a rounded, rather plump, middle-aged man entered the bar. He stood, looking contemplative. He appeared to be cold. His clothes were scruffy, his hair thick and rather wild, and sported a rather monstrous dark brown beard. He looked like he worked outdoors, and had acquired that rather weather-beaten look. The men at the bar all gave him a slight nod, as if to show respect. No one indicated Lenny, yet Eammon walked directly over to his two-person table, and sat right opposite him.

"I understand that you are looking for an Eammon O'Sullivan?" he asked in a soft thick Irish accent.

Lenny stood and went to shake the man's hand, but his hand was not proffered in return, and so he sat again. Eammon looked at him sternly. "I can't imagine why you would want to meet him."

Lenny steeled himself. He had to convince this man that he was genuine about his inquiry and meant him no harm. Somehow he had to earn his trust.

"I'm looking for a friend, and I think he might be able to help me find him."

"And how might that be?"

"I think my friend has got himself into some kind of trouble, but I think there's been a misunderstanding."

Eammon chortled. The bar lady came over with a beer for him and two packets of crisps and left without saying anything. He took several large gulps, and sat back, opening the first crisp packet.

"And what kind of misunderstanding might that be then?"

Lenny looked sheepish. "I don't know."

Eammon chortled again. "You don't seem to have much to go on, do you?"

"I know he's a decent man, and what's happened doesn't make any sense."

"I see, and what's happened then that doesn't make any sense?"

Eammon's expression had changed from annoyed curiosity to one of slight mirth. He was finding this larger-than life big businessman trying to explain something he didn't know about amusing.

"Certain things have happened, which do make sense. That's why I know that this is incongruous."

"So, you're going by your instincts?"

"Yes."

"So, you know this fellah you're looking for really well then?"

"No."

Eammon chortled again. "So, what makes you so sure then?"

"Admittedly, I don't know the man well, but from what I've seen of him, he is a man of integrity. I can't imagine why anyone would want to kidnap him. I think it's a case of mistaken identity." Eammon laughed out loud. "And do you have any evidence of that?"

"No."

Eammon looked confused. "If you hardly know him, what do you care?"

"I owe him."

Eammon was now beginning to look a little exasperated. "Mister, you need to start making sense or there's no chance of you meeting anyone you want to meet."

"I don't know how to do this. I've never been in a position like this before."

Eammon looked at him like he was a bit dense. "Maybe you can start by telling me who this friend is and how you know him, and why you owe him."

He sat back expectantly sipping his beer regularly. Lenny did not normally readily disclose sensitive information, but in this scenario, it was all or nothing.

"His name is Pablo Pinkerton. Our paths crossed earlier this year for the first time. I'd rather not go into that. It's extremely embarrassing for me."

He had succeeded in piquing Eammon's interest. "Go on."

"I'll be absolutely honest with you. These are not things I would normally discuss with anyone, but I have to do what I can to find Pablo if at all possible."

He looked Eammon in the eyes to convey his sincerity.

"I'm waiting."

"Okay. So, I made a mistake that annoyed the Triads in London. They took me for punishment."

He looked into Eammon's face to see if he found this too implausible. Fortunately the mention of Triads had really brightened him up.

"The triads, you say?"

Lenny felt confident to continue.

"Yes, indirectly I'd been doing business with them for many years. Anyway, it turned out that a bent cop who I'd been using for years had dobbed me in to them about the mistake that I'd made, and fortunately for me, him betraying me seemed to annoy them more than anything I'd actually done wrong."

Eammon looked puzzled. "Why would a bent cop who you'd been using for years suddenly dob you in?"

"That's a good question. What had changed, and admittedly it was a massive change, was that I had decided to retire and had begun the process of selling off my various interests."

"And he thought that you might dob him in the shit now that you were getting out of the business, so he got his defence in first?"

"Maybe. I don't know. I'll never know. All I can say is that he was an extremely cautious person. I never worried about him making mistakes, but him dobbing me in to the triads took me completely by surprise."

Eammon was keen to know what punishment they dished out.

"What did they do to you?"

"Well, to be honest, I think they intended far worse for me to start with, before they realised that I was actually a business associate of theirs, but they did a deal with me which kind of got me off the hook."

Eammon was trying to disguise his interest, but his eyes had lit up a little more.

"Presumably this bent cop didn't know you did business with them?"

"You know what it's like. You don't let one hand know what the other's doing."

Eammon smiled knowingly. "Go on."

"They gave me a big fine, and effectively would exchange me for this bent cop."

"How big a fine?"

Lenny saw the glint in his eye, and he most definitely didn't want to feed any notions of being blackmailed again.

"People know I've come here you know," he answered with a chuckle.

Eammon chuckled too, realising how that question must have come across. Then he looked puzzled. "Were you their prisoner?"

"Yes."

"So, how could you bring the copper in?"

"I had to rely on a very close colleague, but the only bait we had was Pablo."

Now Eammon looked really confused. "Why Pablo?"

"This bent cop had done the dirty on Pablo some months earlier, and I just hoped that human nature being what it was, Pablo would help me just to get revenge on the cop."

"How did you know that this cop had done the dirty on Pablo?"

"It's a long story."

"You don't want to tell me that bit?"

"No, I really don't."

Eammon laughed out loud. He could see Lenny's obvious embarrassment. Then he encouraged him to continue.

"So, to save me, Pablo was willing to set a trap for the cop, which he did, and it apparently went like clockwork. An exchange was arranged the same day, and all of a sudden I was a free man again."

"What happened to the bent cop?"

"I shudder to think."

Eammon smiled as he considered the possibilities. He astutely weighed up what he had heard so far, and then explained in his quiet, melodious, Irish accent.

"But you haven't explained why Pablo might have gotten into trouble with someone else."

"I don't know how that could have happened. Like I've said, all I can do is vouch for him as a person and that he just wants a quiet life."

"I don't give a fucking fig if he wants a quiet life or not. You clearly don't know what he might have done before he met you, what did you say, earlier this year? You've only known him for less than a year?"

Eammon was cross and Lenny looked at him rather forlornly. "I'm a good judge of character" was the best he could proffer, weakly.

Eammon's thoughts were back on his poor tiny daughter and that monster who had taken her. It was time to be honest.

"Mister, I don't think there's anything I can do to help you find your friend."

Lenny Looked hopeless and sorrowful. He was helpless. He didn't know what else to say. Eammon rapidly crunched his way through the second packet of crisps as he contemplated things. He didn't have a kind nature, but this man in front of did arouse his interest. He raised his empty pint glass momentarily, and within moments the bar lady was bringing him another. Lenny tried to seem hopeful.

"May I have another stout please?"

She nodded at him and quickly replenished his glass. The men sat in silence for a few minutes, then Eammon asked a question. He used to live in Lenny's area and he wondered if he might know the cop.

"What was that bent copper's name?"

"Detective Constable Orlando Sorrentino."

Eammon almost choked on his beer.

Chapter 18

It was half past five, and Lenny was standing outside the pub in the car park, hoping that DC Rebecca Hurley was still on duty. He didn't have a mobile for her, so he had to call Yewell Tree Road police station switchboard and ask to be put through. He presumed she was a nine-to-fiver, so he wasn't confident that he'd catch her, but he had to try. He really needed to speak to her urgently.

"DC Hurley speaking. How may I help you?"

"Thank God. I was afraid you'd be a nine-to-fiver."

"I am a nine-to-fiver only these days, it's more eight-to-sixer. Doesn't quite have the same ring to it, does it? Who am I speaking to please?"

"Lenny. Lenny Hathaway."

She was surprised to hear from him. "Lenny? What's wrong?"

"Becky, you've got to help me. I need you to find out about a letter for me."

He sounded excited and even a little breathless as he tried to rush out his words.

"Lenny. Slow down. You're not making much sense. What is this to do with?"

"Pablo, of course."

"Have you found him?"

"I don't know. I mean, no, I haven't, but I've got a feeling that I'm close, but I need something else."

"A letter?"

"Yes."

"What letter?"

"Look, Becky. This all has to be off the record, okay?"

"I don't know about that. I have a glittering future career to consider, and I'm not keen to throw it away for…"

She nearly added 'for someone like you' but realised that she didn't really mean that. It sounded too harsh. She adjusted herself. "You really need to explain more."

"Listen, I know what happened to Pablo."

"Shouldn't you be ringing 999 then?"

"No. That would seal his fate. With just a little confirmation, I think this could potentially save his life."

"Sounds fascinating Lenny, but it's still not making any sense to me."

"Sorry, my mind's racing a bit." He paused and gathered his thoughts. "It looks like Pablo has been framed for a heinous crime, something I know he couldn't possibly be capable of. Gregory has framed him. Gregory!"

"Gregory? Am I supposed to know him?"

"Sorry, I meant detective Sorrentino."

"Lenny, have you been drinking?"

"Yes, I have, but nothing excessive."

"Are you sure about that? You're sounding quite weird and you're still not making any sense."

"It's just that I'm feeling emotional, excited and scared, all rolled into one."

"Where are you?"

"I definitely can't tell you that."

"Are you safe?"

"I think so."

"Are you being forced to speak to me?"

"No. I don't find it *that* difficult."

She paused, then encouraged him. "Well, carry on telling me what you can."

Lenny drew a large breath and continued.

"I think that on the day that Sorrentino went missing, he arranged for someone to send a letter for him if he didn't return from some rendezvous, and in that letter he fingered Pablo."

"Why would he finger, Pablo?"

"I can't tell you that."

She was beginning to feel cross. She knew that both he and Pablo had been evasive about a lot of things, and from her point of view, things could make sense if they had been honest with her in the first place. She expressed her frustration.

"Why can't you two just be honest for once?"

"There's far too much at stake I'm afraid."

Rebecca searched for some understanding in this. "Why would Sorentino give his letter to someone else to post?"

"It looks like he only wanted it to be sent if something bad happened to him. Then, if he came back from his rendezvous unscathed, and nothing had gone wrong, he would have retrieved it and it wouldn't be sent. It could be saved for another rainy day."

"What rendezvous?"

"I don't know," he lied.

"Lenny, you're not making any sense. Either that, or I'm a lot more tired than I thought I was. Why would Sorrentino suspect that something bad might happen to him?"

"Because he'd been a very naughty boy, and matters might have been coming home to roost."

"Is this to do with him going missing?"

"Pass."

"Were you involved in that?"

"Pass."

"Was Pablo involved in that?"

"Pass."

"Lenny, you're really pissing me off."

"Off the record?"

"Off the record."

"That's okay then."

Lenny realised that he hadn't made his most important point. "Timing is crucial. I need to know exactly what day that letter got posted. If I'm right, it would have been the day after July the fourth, but I need confirmation."

"Why July the fourth?"

"That's the day I came home and the same day that Sorrentino went missing."

"Confirmation for what or who?"

"Can't say."

"Lenny, you really are a pain in the arse, just like your mate Pablo. You two make a great pair."

Again, she collected her thoughts. She didn't want her exasperation to cloud her detective mind. "Who would Sorrentino trust enough though? He was a bit of a loner."

"That's where you come in, Becky. I need you to find out."

"I'm about to go home. It's already been a long day."

"Becky, a man's life is hanging on this."

"Yes, but I'm tired, and anyway where on earth would I start?"

"You're the detective. You should know."

There was silence at the other end of the line, so Lenny carried on. "Look, he used to mention a solicitor friend occasionally. He never used his name, just referred to him as a solicitor friend. That would be a good place to start."

"What do you mean 'he used to mention'? I didn't know you knew him."

She sounded astonished, or was it annoyed?

"Becky, there are loads of things you don't know. You're not supposed to."

"But you expect me to help you when it suits you, though?"

She sounded quite angry now.

"It's not about me, Becky. I thought that one of the prime tenets of the police service was to preserve life. That's what I am asking you to do, please. It's not for me."

As he pleaded with her, her memory suddenly threw up Herman Springer, Sorrentino's next-door neighbour. She suddenly remembered that he was a retired solicitor.

"Listen, I'm not pleased that you hide stuff from us all the time, and then you expect us to help sort out your mess when you end up in the shit."

"Sorry. Life is complicated."

"What I will do is call by on my way home on a retired solicitor who I think might be able to help, but that's all. If I draw a blank with him, I'm going home for my Horlicks and to put my tired feet up, and you'll have to pursue this in the morning through official channels. No more secret squirrel with me, okay?"

"You're a darling."

"Anything else I should know about?"

"Oh yes. I need to phone you on this official police number in the morning at 9 a.m. to see if you found out anything."

"That's very precise."

"Yes, it has to be. Is that alright? Will you be there?"

"Yes, I suppose so."

She sounded uncertain, so Lenny expanded.

"The reason I have to be so precise is that someone else will be with me, listening, so don't say anything other than to answer my exact questions, okay?"

"I really don't like the sound of this, Lenny. Who will be listening in?"

"I can't say."

"And you think I should just go along with this chicanery of yours, and put my faith in you, just like that?"

"Yes."

"God, you're asking a lot."

She was mulling everything over and she thought of a question. "Remind me again, where did this letter notion come from in the first place?"

He replied slowly and certainly. "I've seen it."

Lenny didn't see the point of returning home if he had to be back in Norton Sodbury by 9 a.m. He phoned Christina.

"Hi darling. Sorry to dash out so unexpectedly this morning. Something very important came up."

"We missed our swimming session with Monica this afternoon."

She sounded so disappointed.

"I'm sorry darling. We'll do another one as soon as we can."

"What time will you be back?"

"Honey, I've got to be here first thing in the morning, so there's hardly any point in rushing back now just to rush straight back in the morning. I'm going to find a local hotel for the night."

"Oh!" she exclaimed. "Is everything okay, darling?"

"Yes, sweetheart. Trust me, this is important and everything will be fine. I'll be back tomorrow for sure."

"Darling I don't like it when you disappear like this. It's not been that long since you were kidnapped, and now I worry about you, and I don't know where you are."

"Really sweetheart. Everything's fine. I'll see you tomorrow. Say hello to Monica for me."

Rebecca knew where Herman Springer lived. It wasn't exactly on her way home, but it wasn't too much of a detour either. She found a parking place fairly close by and approached his front door purposefully, warrant card at the ready. She wondered if he would be at home. She watched as the hazy shape of a body expanded through the misted glass panel. Of course he was at home. He was a retired, single, old man. He appeared curious to see her, but as soon as she identified herself and explained that her visit was in connection to the

189

disappearance of his next-door-neighbour, he enthusiastically invited her in and sat her in the lounge in a big winged armchair. He offered her tea, and she actually felt like she really needed a strong one and readily accepted. As he pottered off to get the tea, she took in her surroundings in the lounge. All the furniture was very dated. The pattern on the curtains made her smile. It reminded her of old aunties homes she used to be dragged to as a child. The three-piece suite looked like something out of a seventies sitcom show. The pictures of old relatives on the mantelpiece were adorned within antique carved silver frames. She realised that he had been in this house a very long time. Herman appeared with a tray on which was a teapot under a cosy, two proper tea cups and saucers, a small china bowl of sugar with a matching milk jug, with three silver teaspoons. "Been here long then, Mr Herman?"

He answered proudly. "Oh, about twenty-five years. Never saw the point of moving really."

"Oh, that's nice. It gives you the opportunity to get to know the local community properly."

He pondered that for a moment before replying. "Yes, to a degree, except that most other people seem to be on the move every few years."

"Yes, I suppose there is that."

She took her tea and then got down to business. "Look Mr Herman, I really need your help."

"Yes, of course. I have already been interviewed by the police about poor Mr Sorrentino, you know."

"Yes, I am aware of that, but there has been a development."

"Oh that sounds promising, I hope!"

"Well, strictly speaking, it does involve Mr Sorrentino, but it's more to do with another missing person inquiry, but there seems to be a possible link, and I'll be honest with you Mr Herman, at this point in time it seems more pertinent to the other inquiry."

"That's fine, Miss Hurley. I'm more than willing to help if I possibly can."

He appeared to her to be a straightforward, upstanding, professional man. She decided the best way to approach him was to tap into his integrity, although she herself decided that a little bit of embroidering the truth on her part would be most appropriate.

"When you were interviewed, you never said anything about a letter that Mr Sorrentino might have given you."

She studied his face. She had gone straight for the jugular, and she saw him flinch uncertainly. He seemed unsure of how to respond. Perhaps his mind was not as quick as it had been in his heyday. She on the other hand was emboldened by his hesitancy and doubled down on the attack.

"Mr Herman, I have reason to believe that this letter from Mr Sorrentino has surfaced somewhere, and is now rather crucial to one of our other investigations."

He looked embarrassed, as if he'd been caught out stealing a biscuit from the biscuit barrel, but he didn't understand.

"Miss Hurley, I'm not sure that I can comment. I gave Mr Sorrentino my word."

Now she was certain she was on the right track.

"Mr Herman, I know that you are a man of integrity. I can see that, but please, don't be misguided with tunnel-vision. If you gave your word, I respect that too, except that now, something far more important is at stake than a matter of one's word. A man's life is at stake."

She was echoing Lenny's words with conviction, even though she did not know them to be true herself.

"Oh dear, that does sound serious."

"You know the law Mr Herman. The law says that it is wrong to break into someone's property, but if there was a fire in the property, and you believed someone inside needed rescuing, the law would happily allow you to break in, or even if it was only to save some bits of personal effects."

"Yes, of course. The principle of reasonableness and proportion, and common law defence."

"Exactly that, and I put it to you Mr Herman, that this is the situation you find yourself in right now. I can assure you that to break your word to a man who to all intents and purposes has disappeared completely, in order to potentially avoid fatal consequences for another man is totally proportionate and reasonable."

"Well, now that you put it like that, it does make me wonder."

"Mr Herman, I only need to know if you posted a letter for Mr Sorrentino. I don't need to know what was in it. Or to whom."

"I don't know what was in it. Oh dear, I feel very uncomfortable about this. I gave him my word that I wouldn't mention it to anyone, particularly the police."

She looked at him quizzically. "Did he ask you especially not to mention it to the police?"

He looked at her guiltily. "Yes."

"And that doesn't make you think that here's something wrong here?"

"But I gave him my word."

"Well, now we know about it anyway, Do you think that maybe he has tricked you? Taken advantage of your good nature? We have reason to believe that he was not as straight and honest a person as he would have us believe."

"Oh dear. That is disappointing."

They sat quietly, sipping tea. She thought she had said enough. She just needed him to let things sink in. She hoped that she had said enough to see his defence slowly crumble.

Chapter 19

Lenny didn't sleep well. How could he? His hotel room was fine: Quiet and well-equipped, but he couldn't quieten his mind. He wished he'd had the presence of mind to ask Becky for a mobile number, or to have asked her to call him during the evening. Then he would already know if his quest might be successful or not. Now he had to wait until nine o'clock in the morning, just like Eammon. All night long wondering. If she hadn't discovered anything, he would be sent on his way empty-handed, despondent and very sad. So near yet so far.

He was up early in the morning. It felt like he had stirred about every half an hour during the night, and now he felt almost exhausted, yet his sense of mission was huge. He didn't even know if he believed in a God or not, yet he found himself quietly begging him for a miracle today. He had plenty of time for a full breakfast and plenty of coffee. He was wishing the time away. He was only twenty minutes away from The White Blacksmith. He played with his phone. It still had plenty of charge. Fortunately it had been fully charged the day before in the car during the journey to Norton Sodbury. Finally, thankfully, it was time to go. He drove carefully, sedately. He didn't want anything to go wrong.

At five to nine, he knocked on the front door which was locked. The pub wouldn't be opening for business until 10 a.m. The girl with too many tattoos and face piercings opened up for him and brightly invited him in. He was surprised to see Eammon already sitting there in the same exact spot he'd been in the afternoon before. He was also surprised to see him nursing a pint of a very dark beer, probably Guinness.

"Early breakfast?"

"Can't beat it. Full of natural goodness," he purred.

Eammon looked at him with a strange look, like he hadn't made up his mind about him yet. "Did you get hold of your detective friend?"

"Yes, I did."

"Do you know how she got on?"

"No."

Eammon could tell from the look of uncertainty and wariness on his face that he really didn't know how this was going to go. He appeared nervous. Eammon had a piece of paper in his hand. On it was the phone number for Yewell Tree Road police station.

"Give me your phone."

Lenny dutifully handed it over. "What's your contact's name?"

"DC Rebecca Hurley."

Eammon slowly repeated the name a couple of times as he tapped the number into the phone. It rang. They both waited with anticipation.

"Yewell Tree Road police station. What extension do you require please?"

"Officer DC Rebecca Hurley please."

"I'll try her extension for you."

They both listened nervously to the extension ringing. Eammon tapped the button to put it on loudspeaker before hanging it back to Lenny.

"Hello. DC Hurley speaking."

"Becky, it's me Lenny. How did you get on?"

"Good morning to you too, Lenny."

"Becky, this is no time for formalities. How did it go?"

She sighed, then more brightly, "You're in luck. I found Sorrentino's solicitor friend at home."

"And?"

"Well he was very reluctant to break a confidence. Orlando had made him swear to secrecy. I had to use all my charms and wit to break through his misled integrity."

"What did he say?"

"Yes, on the fourth of July just before midday, Orlando came around to his place with a sealed letter, asking him to only post it the next day if he didn't come around to get it back in the evening."

"Did he say anything about what that was all about? I mean, he must have found that strange."

"No, he didn't seem unduly surprised because apparently, it's happened a few times over the years, but this was the first time that Orlando didn't reappear to collect it, so as agreed, the man posted it the next day."

She knew to remain silent unless Lenny asked her another question. Lenny gave Eammon a quizzical look. Eammon looked dispirited. He just nodded. He knew.

"Thanks, Becky. I'll call you later."

Without waiting for her response he turned his mobile off and sat just looking at Eammon, who had got his letter out again, and was studying for the hundredth time, very thoughtfully.

"He used me to reach out from the grave to execute his revenge, didn't he? He fucking used me, the utter, utter bastard. I hope he rots in hell."

He looked tormented. He put the letter on the table and shoved it towards Lenny for him to read.

"Do you agree?"

Lenny read it carefully.

"Dear Eammon O'Sullivan,

If you're reading this letter, that means that something very bad has happened to me and the man responsible is the same man who abducted and killed your daughter four years ago. I'm sorry. The case had been more or less abandoned by everyone else but I found irrefutable evidence identifying who the killer was. He is a retired police officer. Be very careful of him. He has a lot of sway with people in very high places. I'm sorry. I did my best but it seems that I may have paid a very high price in trying to bring this man to justice. His name is Pablo Pinkerton. He is undoubtedly the culprit in the killing of your daughter. He has her necklace.

Detective Constable Orlando Sorrentino."

Lenny felt for him. He had lost a very young daughter, and now someone was playing with his emotions and exploiting him.

"He was a clever guy. He knew how to tap your buttons and he must have known how ruthless you are. I think he has played you."

Eammon looked sullen, defeated. "I so wanted to find the man responsible, my determination blinded me."

Lenny didn't disturb his sad realisation. He did think he had been very gullible. The letter was, after all, pretty childish. Only someone desperate to believe it would have taken it at face value.

"You got a sat nav on that thing?"

"Yes."

Eammon got him to tap in a postcode.

"When it says you've arrived, carry on for about a hundred yards. There's a big, high, solid, metal, double-gate on your left."

He got a bunch of keys out of his pocket and took three off. He handed one over.

"This one's for the padlock. Drive up the track. It's a long one. Your Bentley should just about handle it. Eventually you'll come to a huge old hanger with a concrete building in this end of it."

He handed over the second key. "This one's for the door."

He then handed over the third. "This one's for the cuffs."

Lenny winced at the thought as a tiny shiver went down his spine.

"I don't know what condition he will be in today, but whatever you do, you don't call an ambulance or 999."

He looked at Lenny fiercely.

"Agreed."

"You don't take him to a local hospital. You take him back to where you two cunts come from."

"Agreed."

"Obviously, you say nothing to the police, and you make sure Pablo doesn't either. I take it that if either of you did you'd both be in the shit for this fucking bent copper, yeah?"

"Correct. We have to keep this as low-profile as possible."

"Just leave the keys on the floor when you leave. Be as quick as you can."

He started to get lost in his own sad thoughts again as he waved Lenny away.

DC Hurley was in a spot. She ought to report what she had found out to her supervisors, but at this point she wasn't sure of what exactly she had found out, and she didn't want to do anything to upset Lenny's applecart, at least not before she knew what the outcome with Pablo was. She decided to keep it quiet for now, and see what happened next. She was beginning to get strong feelings that Lenny and Pablo must have been involved in Sorrentino's disappearance. It was not a conclusion that she wanted to come to. She actually liked them both, but she had no proof, and there were too many unanswered questions. Who was the letter sent to? What did it say? She was mystified.

As Lenny drove up the muddy track he felt very alone. He wanted someone to be with him. He didn't know what he was going to find. It was very isolated.

Overgrown hedges lined the track, and wide empty fields stretched out to each side as far as the eye could see. The hanger slowly appeared in the distance like a dark, menacing monolith. He pulled up near the door and approached it with trepidation. He unlocked it. Inside was not very light with the only daylight coming in from two unglazed windows on the hanger side. He noticed the stench of urine and faeces but in his high state of adrenaline, it really didn't bother him too much. He saw a single bed with scruffy blankets on it. Instinctively he got out his mobile and started filming what he saw. He didn't say anything. He was too nervous. He filmed the room and the bed and as he pulled the blankets off, he filmed the shackled, spreadeagled body underneath them. He wasn't sure who it was. The face was gagged and blindfolded. Whoever it was, he was motionless and silent. Lenny found himself crying a little. It was a very upsetting scene. He stopped filming and fetched the cuff key from his pocket. Without saying a word, he undid the ankles cuffs and then the wrist cuffs. He hoped that the man would get up, but he didn't. He untied the gag. At this point he was close enough to think that this body was very cold. He started shaking. He couldn't help himself. He removed the blindfold. It was Pablo.

He spoke quietly, as if loud words might damage him in his frail condition. "Pablo! It's me, Lenny."

There was no response. He picked up the blankets and threw them back over him. He rushed outside and opened the rear door of the car, and then rushed back into the room. He gathered Pablo up as best he could with the blankets, and dragged him off the bed and across the dusty concrete floor. Pablo felt like a dead weight, but as he moved him, there were gurgling sounds. Pablo's eyes were shut, but there were some little reflexes in his arms as he was awkwardly dragged through the doorway. He was alive, not a lot, but he was alive. This was strenuous work for Lenny, and he struggled for a couple of long minutes dragging, pushing and pulling him onto the back seat. Eventually he crammed him onto the back seat and secured him with the seat belts, ensuring that he was covered as much as possible by the blankets before also throwing his camel-hair coat over him. He turned the car around and sped down the track as fast as he reasonably could, heater on full blast. He was heading for their hometown speedily, hoping he wouldn't draw attention to his driving. He didn't mind setting off speed cameras, but he really didn't want to get stopped by the police with an almost dead man in the back.

It was not until ten days later that DC Hurley found the opportunity to pay Pablo a welfare visit. She ensured that he was at home alone. She wanted to talk to him man to man as it were, without Hellion around, and off the record. She sat at his kitchen table whilst he made them both a cup of tea.

She spoke sincerely, "I'm really pleased that you've recovered so well, Pablo."

"Yeah, me too."

"I don't think God likes you."

He looked at her quizzically as he poured a little milk into her tea. "Why?"

"I mean, you keep going to meet your maker, but he doesn't want you, and he sends you back again."

He chuckled. "That's one way of looking at it I suppose."

She became pensive. "You've put me in an invidious position."

"Sounds kinky."

"No, not kinky. Awkward, messy, dodgy. I don't want to have to start compromising my principles for you."

"And how am I supposed to be making you do that?"

"I should have reported what I found out from Sorrentino's solicitor friend, but I didn't."

"Why not?"

"First of all, I wanted to see if it led anywhere, and if it might lead to saving your ass."

Pablo slapped his rump playfully, and he asked cheekily, "Wasn't that a good thing?"

"Maybe." She tried to sound disappointed. "But now that you're safe and well, I still haven't mentioned it to anyone."

"Why not?"

Her visage became deadly serious.

"It looks like that letter was sent because Sorrentino was about to meet someone potentially dangerous, and that someone must have been you."

"All horses have four legs. Horses are animals. That doesn't mean that all animals have four legs."

She ignored his feeble attempt to obfuscate. She answered certainly.

"You must have been involved in his abduction. I think you were the man in the department store."

198

She gave him a hard stare, but he said nothing. He sat at the table opposite her, expectantly. She continued.

"And how the hell did Lenny trace you?"

"He's a very clever guy."

"We always knew that you two were somehow connected, and now it's beyond dispute."

"So, what do you intend to do?"

Strangely, Pablo was feeling curious rather than worried. He didn't know why, but he kind of trusted her.

"It feels wrong that I haven't shared what I know, but at the same time, I feel that it would be a waste of time."

"Go on."

"I'm sure you know already that the DCI had Lenny arrested for suspected kidnapping of you."

Pablo laughed. He really thought that was comical. "I know. He's told me about that. He got nicked at the hospital a few hours after he'd taken me in, unconscious, half-dead. Of course he went 'no comment' throughout and they had nothing. I understand his solicitor intends to sue for wrongful arrest."

"Yes, and you've been interviewed and you conveniently can't remember anything."

He lent his head forward and gently rubbed the scarry patch on the top of his head.

"Yeah, funny that, how I have complete memory loss every now and then. So, what *do* you have?"

"Knowledge but no proof."

"Suspicion, not knowledge," he corrected her. "And the letter?"

She grimaced a little. "The old solicitor was reluctant to admit anything about the letter, but when he did finally tell me what he knew, he also made it quite clear that he was only trying to help with this emergency I was telling him about."

"What emergency?"

"You of course. I didn't name you, obviously, I just said that an innocent man's life was at stake. Clearly I lied about the 'innocent' bit."

"Of course!" he mused with a smile.

"He said that he would refuse to corroborate anything in a formal interview or at court. He still wanted to stand by his word to Sorrentino."

"So, Officer, you have your suspicions but absolutely no evidence. No testimony from anyone. No body and no letter."

She looked defeated. "Yes, exactly that."

"Cheers!" he said cheerfully, and raised his mug. She just frowned at him. He wasn't mocking her. He was just feeling happily safe.

"Well, as you're here, you might as well help me with something I'm curious about."

"Pablo, I'm not here to help you, just to vent my frustrations on you and moan about how annoying the situation is."

"I get that you have every reason to feel sour, Becky, but hear me out. This just might be of interest to you."

He wasn't going to explain anything to her, that would be too risky, but his mind had been playing with some of the details Eammon had given him along with something Lenny had mentioned that was in the letter.

"You know how sometimes you just have a weird hunch about something. It doesn't make any sense, but you can't shake off that faint, vague suspicion about it?"

"Pablo, you're boring me. What are you trying to say?"

"When you guys started investigating Sorrentino's disappearance, presumably you searched his house for clues?"

"Of course, with a fine toothpick."

"Was there a small silver necklace there, with a pendant on it?"

"How should I know? I didn't do it personally, you know."

"Yes, but was an inventory taken for careful examination for clues?"

"I'm not sure to be honest."

"Can you find out?"

Becky looked at her watch wearily. She really didn't know what game he was playing now, and she wasn't sure that she was that interested.

"Maybe, if I gave a toss. Why?"

"If my hunch is right, it would be of great interest to you in another case."

"What case?"

"I can't say."

"Okay, so here we go again, me running around in rings for you, and you being evasive and unhelpful as always."

"It's up to you, Becky. It might be of great interest, and it might not. That's all I am saying. I think it might be worth checking out."

He looked at her very brightly but she put on her best weary, tired look, but really, he had started to pique her interest. She got out her mobile phone and contacted one of her colleagues in the office.

"Hi Sammy, can you do me a favour? It's me, Becky. I'm out on an inquiry at the moment, and I just need to check quickly for something on the database. Could you help me?"

"Sure, hun. What do you need?"

"Can you go into the Sorrentino case, check if there's an inventory for his house contents, and if there is, check under jewellery?"

"Okay. What are we looking for?"

"A small silver necklace with a pendant."

As she spoke, Pablo jumped up and found a pen and notepad. He didn't let Becky see what he was writing, but on one half of the page, he wrote down 'small silver necklace with a silver butterfly pendant with a red ruby for a body', and he folded up the paper so she couldn't see what it concealed, and he theatrically placed it down on the table between them. He used hand signals to let her know not to touch it. She screwed her face up. Sammy was quiet for a minute or so as she scrolled down the inventory.

"Yes, there are a few necklaces here. Hang on." She read the details carefully, looking for a silver one. "Yes, here's one matching your description."

"Can you say how it's described please?"

"Yes, 'a delicate small-gauge silver necklace, fifteen inches in length, suitable for a small lady or child, with a silver butterfly pendant on it, with a dark red ruby for a body'."

Pablo was nodding and smiling broadly.

"Anything else, Becky?"

"No. I think that will do for now. Thanks, Sammy."

She was rather mesmerised by Pablo's reaction. He was clearly very excited. After terminating the call, she silently picked up the piece of paper and unwrapped it and read the words. It was a clear match, but she was mystified as to how he would have known about it.

"Okay. Very impressive. But what does it mean?"

"It means that you have to do a search on your system for that exact item in another investigation. It will be there. You will find it, and it will open up a whole new avenue of investigation for you in a cold case which you and a lot of other people would dearly love to solve."

She looked at him wondering what kind of chicanery he was up to now. She stood up to leave. He took the paper from her, smiling.

"Well Mr Pinkerton, Thank you for the tea. I'd better go now. I think I've got a little bit of digging to do."

"Yes, you have, but don't forget, I didn't say anything."

"No, you never do, do you?" she said as she smiled back.

CPSIA information can be obtained
at www.ICGtesting.com
Printed in the USA
LVHW081822140323
741614LV00031B/675